The Innocent Trap

THE INNOCENT TRAP

A Novel

Fay Foley Clark

iUniverse, Inc.
New York Lincoln Shanghai

The Innocent Trap

Copyright © 2007 by Fay Foley Clark

All rights reserved. No part of this book may be used or reproduced by any means, graphic, electronic, or mechanical, including photocopying, recording, taping or by any information storage retrieval system without the written permission of the publisher except in the case of brief quotations embodied in critical articles and reviews.

iUniverse books may be ordered through booksellers or by contacting:

iUniverse
2021 Pine Lake Road, Suite 100
Lincoln, NE 68512
www.iuniverse.com
1-800-Authors (1-800-288-4677)

This is a work of fiction. All of the characters, names, incidents, organizations and dialogue in this novel are either the products of the author's imagination or are used fictitiously.

ISBN-13: 978-0-595-41912-8 (pbk)
ISBN-13: 978-0-595-86259-7 (ebk)
ISBN-10: 0-595-41912-7 (pbk)
ISBN-10: 0-595-86259-4 (ebk)

Printed in the United States of America

The Innocent Trap is dedicated to my first born son, Max Ray Clark. He lived on this earth for far too short a time; just three and one half years.

Acknowledgments

❈

I would like to thank my many talented friends. Among these are the members of the Mid-Columbia Writers Group who have provided unwavering support for fifty years. My friend, librarian Linda Lunde, I thank for her critique and editing. Jean Mills provided many suggestions. Mickee Madden helped me a lot from beginning to end of this process. She was always ready to unselfishly help. My son, Gary Clark, I can't thank enough. He was determined to help me see my book in print. I would also like to thank all of those who showed their confidence in my writing abilities through the years. Without their encouragement I might have never seen this book published.

CHAPTER 1

❀

But for her long black braids, no one would ever suspect Shae Upshaw was a girl, much less thirteen, as she sat flat on the gumbo earth, sifting sand. Scar, her five-foot king snake, was coiled playfully around her neck. One gallus of her chopped-off overalls swung down her back, and she was as skinny as the angle worms dangling from her papa's trotlines, as healthy as a tadpole.

The dead water oak hanging half-rooted from the Cache River in northeast Arkansas, offered little protection for her on that hot, humid day in mid-July of 1931. Except for a few boughs of mistletoe, the weather-beaten tree stood stark naked.

"Scar," Shae shook the sifter back and forth. "Ease up. You're chokin' me. These skeeters are chewin' me to bits and I'm roastin' alive in this blasted old shirt."

Scar only clung tighter and the sweltering sun beat down on Shae's water-chapped body. It was ninety-five degrees at seven o'clock in the morning. She ripped at the buttons on her shirt and let it fall open all the way down. Dropping the other gallus, she bounced to her feet.

"Scar!"

She grabbed the big-muscled snake by the neck, used her papa's choke hold to pull him down, twirled him two or three times around her head, and dunked him into the murky river. Then she stood for a moment, watching the snake glide down stream. On impulse, she shucked her shirt, slung it over a buckeye bush, and dove in after him.

"I'll race you, Scar!" she yelled after him. She paddled as fast as she could through the water lilies clogging the sluggish river. But the snake was fifty yards ahead of her and gaining when she finally gave up on catching him.

Finding her footing, Shae stood waist-deep in the muddy water. Blowing muddy bubbles from her nostrils, she chided, "It's not fair, Scar! You had a head start. Besides, these old overalls slow me down awful."

Turning back toward the boat dock, she yelled over her shoulder, "You better watch out for that big water moccasin! Remember…he won't give up a fight!"

Shae's feet bogged to the bottom in the gumbo mud, causing her to flounder around in the patches of water lilies. Splashing to the bank, she crawled out onto the path and ran toward the boat dock, telling herself, "If Papa finds out I've been in that filthy water…I might get my sateen bloomers busted."

When the rains came, the Cache spilled over the swamp like hot molasses. The river lay underfed, moody and listless and with a yellowish-green color of typhoid. But it was the only means Shae's papa, Clay Upshaw, had of making a living. Each day he grabbed mussel shells from the belly of the Cache to sell to the button factory.

"If one day I ever find a pearl," Papa would assure Shae, "we won't be living on cornbread and sowbelly everyday."

The rigors of two buckegger chills and a boat too big for the low water, had kept Upshaw out of the river most of the week. Half the time he had to haul his big, skeletal body from the boat and pull it from one mussel shell bed to another. July and August was the time the Cache gave birth to the best pearls. Upshaw had only been able to harvest a mere half ton all week, and the bottom had dropped in the market. He had to get them to the dinky-train on Friday. It only made one run a week to the button factory.

School had started the week before and he badly needed the money to buy Shae's school clothes. She had missed the first week and Jake Crawford, the school director, would be out to lecture him if she wasn't in school by Monday.

Upshaw was at the dock, where he loaded the mussel shells into the cart, and then scooped up the surplus sand and piled it out into the sun to dry, making it easier for Shae to sift.

"Just in case," he always said, "we should let the real one slip through our fingers. It's best to double check."

When Shae ran up to the dock, Upshaw was too distracted to notice her wet clothes. He had more to do than his aching body wanted, and he hated to have to rely on his daughter.

"Girly-Shae," he began as he hitched the filly, Sandy, to the cart and made ready to leave for the dinky, "Be sure to run the trotlines. The minister will be out for catfish for the church fish-fry. We need twenty-five more pounds to fill his order. I don't want to disappoint him. He's the only cash customer we have."

"I will, Papa," Shae promised faithfully. She untied her boat from the root of the water oak, climbed into it and paddled slowly up the river.

Shae checked the bait in the box and found the grub worms she'd caught the night before. More than plenty to re-bait the lines and she hoped the turtles had not stripped the catfish hooks. The minister was such a fuss-buddy; he wouldn't buy any other kind of fish.

To Shae's surprise, she not only found a fifteen-pounder on the second line, but two smaller ones on another line. With the two Papa already had in the box, she was sure there would be enough to fill the order. Stashing them in the fish box, she rowed lazily back to the dock.

A flock of crows swooshed up from the sand pile as Shae stayed her boat. Unwilling to leave, several of the birds sat on the dead limbs of the water oak and scolded her. Probably, she thought to herself, one of them had guzzled the pearl her papa was looking for. She had never seen a pearl such as the one her papa was searching for, except the one in her mama's wedding ring. But money couldn't buy that. He'd kept it nested on a bed of cotton in a Garret snuff box, or around his neck on a buckskin shoestring, ever since her mama had died, except when he'd had to hock it for groceries at Murphy's store.

Lazily, Shae sat down by the sand pile and knocked the sifter of sand against her hand for a time before she heard a rattle.

"Could it be?" She asked herself aloud.

She plucked the lump from the sifter and polished it on her overall bib a few times. "Na," she tossed it aside and watched it roll into one of the tiny fissures where the hot sun had cracked the ground. "Nothin' but a buckshot."

From the corner of her eye, she noticed Scar inching up the river bank. He made his way to her feet and stretched out to sun. Feeling guilty for dunking him into the river, she dropped the sifter and pulled the snake into her arms.

"I know, Scar." She stroked his big, muscled body. "I'm sorry I dunked you, but how would you like to be a girl and have to go to school to old Miss Trisha, in a prissy dress and hair bows? You'd hate it, just like I do."

Tears welled up in her eyes. She propped her knees under her chin and sat thinking about school, until Scar meandered up her arm.

"No, Scar! It's too hot! Stay down."

She picked up a handful of sand and threw it asunder. "I will not wear hair bows to school. I won't, I won't, I won't!"

Insulted, Scar slithered toward the water oak and disappeared into his den. Shae followed him and then she noticed the can of worms in the boat. She'd forgotten to bait the hooks, which meant another trip up the river. When she got to the lines, she found a terrible jerking on one. She raised the line and found a big mud turtle.

"Old boy," she said to the turtle as she dropped the line, "you will have to stay there 'till Papa gets home."

Shae's papa had said that if a turtle bit you, it would not turn loose until it thundered. And, she thought, that could be a long time.

After screwing a fat grub worm on each hook, Shae sat watching baby turtles dive, one after the other, from a log at the edge of the water. She wondered what her papa would bring her for a surprise and hoped the price of shells had not dropped any lower.

There had been times when Clay Upshaw didn't have to count every penny. He'd built a fur trade as far away as Memphis, Tennessee. But with the bottom dropping from the markets and the saw mill moving away, there were times he could hardly make ends meet. Then, too, there had been full care of Shae after Dora's death.

Upshaw knew he was going to have to battle people to keep his daughter. Anderson, the minister, had said Shae needed a mother's care. Shae was all Upshaw had of Dora, and he was not giving her up.

A kind, gentle man, Clay Upshaw stood six-foot-two in his sock feet, and had always enjoyed good health. He was only half Chickasaw Indian, but with his jet black hair and obsidian eyes, he could have passed for full blood. He tried to befriend everyone, but was never known to run from a fight. He knew there were folks who wanted him gone from the Cache River, but it would be over his dead body!

Upshaw's family had crossed the Mississippi in the early part of the century. After reluctantly finishing grammar school, Clay had walked away from home, giving as reasons a pushy father, who frowned on a wanderer. After rambling from one job to another for a year, he'd stumbled into the Cache River swamp and found it to be the hunting grounds of his dreams. He nailed an abandoned shack together and lived alone until the age of twenty-nine. Furs were a good price and he was doing what he wanted to do.

The timber had never been cut away in Cache River. One day, a man by the name of Channing came to the swamp to set up a saw mill, and he had this beautiful daughter. Dora was only sixteen, but Clay was badly smitten the first time he'd laid eyes on her, and her feelings were mutual.

It had taken a year for Clay to win her father's favor, but Clay was a persistent man. When Dora was seventeen, her father gave permission for them to marry. Together, they'd spent every spare minute of their happy married life, building a log cabin. Being a meticulous man, Clay had cut each log to precision, and chinked them with blue gumbo mud, making it far above the average saw mill housing. Dora was little more than half Clay's age, but she had made their house a happy home. And to bless it twice, a baby girl arrived the second year. After much discussion, they decided on Shae for her name. Dora thought it complimented Clay's Indian blood, and they were happy in their little love nest in the Cache River swamp. Cache River was never a town, but in its heyday, it boasted a combination grocery store and post office, a rowdy house called a boarding house, and a row of shotgun houses lined up like wrens on a fence where the mill workers lived rent free. You could buy anything from a penny sucker to a pair of Oskosh overalls at the company store, as long as your coupons lasted. There was no green-back money, but those who worked there lived well.

Even in the days of the deepest depression, Upshaw managed to make a living for his family, fishing, trapping, and working at the mill until typhoid fever claimed Dora, leaving Clay Upshaw with a four-year-old daughter to bring up alone. With Shae being a healthy child and her father an efficient man, they had managed well. Shae was happy following her papa up and down the river until she was six. It was then Jake Crawford, the hard-nosed school director, started hounding her papa to send her to school, regular.

Shae missed a lot of school. When the Cache went on a rampage, her papa had to take her to high ground in a boat, and it was another mile in gum boots. The kids taunted her. Each night she snuggled Shadow, her favorite cat, to her, and cried under the bed cover. By the time she was in fifth grade, Shae had dropped behind a grade and she couldn't manage fractions at all. And her father was not much help, but he tried. To calm her down after her frustration, he would tell her stories about his childhood.

When the timber was cut away from the swamp, most everyone was forced to move with it, but Upshaw was able to live on in his cabin with Shae. He could still make a living fishing, hunting, and digging mussel shells, but times were hard for everyone. The banks had crashed in 1929. There had been a drought three years running. The corn had dried in tassel and the cotton bolls had fallen from the stalks in August. The soup lines were long everywhere.

Frank Murphy, the store keeper, was having a tug-of-war keeping his door open since so many people had moved away. The place soon became a hangout for hunters, tie-hackers and bootleggers, who sat around playing poker, spitting tobacco juice toward the wash pan of ashes in front of the potbelly stove, and spinning out-house jokes.

Looking up at the sun, Shae decided she had best get back to the sand sifting. Her papa would be cross if she played the morning away. She had hardly gotten comfortable on the ground before Scar came inching toward her. He crawled up her back and hung his head over her shoulder.

"Scar...." She caught the snake as he coiled around her neck. "You better keep your good eye out for Jock. Remember what he did the last time he caught you 'round my neck?"

The wolf dog had surprised Scar back in the spring, nailing a tush into the snake's eye. He had all but torn the eyeball from its socket. The gash had healed ugly. That was where Scar had acquired his name.

Scar bobbed his head in all directions, as much to say, "How could I forget? Once was enough to tangle with a hundred-pound wolf dog."

"C'mon, Scar. I can't sift sand with you on my back." She wrestled the snake down and dunked him back into the river.

It seemed that the sand pile was still mounting as Shae shook the sifter every way without a rattle. The sun beat down and the mosquitoes bored through her shirt. When she could stand it no longer, she went to her boat, pushed it into mid-stream and paddled slowly down the river to a grove of low-hanging willows where the sand was damp and cool. She heard no buzzing mosquitoes. All was quiet.

Shae pushed her boat to the bank with her paddle, crawled out on the sand, and dabbled her feet in the water. Then she peeled out of her shirt and stretched out in the shade of the willows, letting her thoughts meander with the river. She remembered how she used to build toad houses in this sand when she was five or six, while her papa gathered shells. But now she was thirteen, and this time Monday, she would be at school with her head stuck in that old 'rithmetic'. She could just hear Miss Trisha say, "Shae, you are dropping your G's again."

Miss Trisha never said things like that to the other kids, especially Mary Crawford, because she was the director's kid.

As usual, Shae's thoughts turned to her mother and she wondered if she was as beautiful as her papa said she was.

A drunken rooster blue jay wobbled to the edge of the water to drink. He had gorged himself on wild cherries, and his feet would not track.

Somehow, Shae knew her thirteenth summer was different. She had all these feelings which she couldn't sort out. And so many things stabbed at her. She could not understand why her papa insisted she wear a shirt in summertime. She never had before.

Time had slipped away again. The sun was almost straight overhead, and she still had a pile of sand to sift. Except for the blue jay bathing in the water, the woods were quiet. The bird finished its bath and flitted to another hollow log, scratched up a big grub worm, beaked it, and took flight, leaving Shae to her dreams.

As Shae lay quietly thinking, the sound of an engine caught her ear. She jumped to her feet. Sure enough, she could see the top of a car over the bushes. She pushed the boat into the water and paddled as fast as she could, but she knew she could never make it to the cabin, and her papa had told her not to talk to strangers.

Shae was almost to the dock, but she would never get across the road without being seen. She pushed her boat to the bank and ran for a big, hollow cypress snag. Victim of a lightning strike, the tree had almost burned to the ground before drenching rain had quenched the blaze, leaving an old, black snag of wood-pecker holes.

Just as Shae got to the snag, a scrawny, sore-eyed kitten wobbled weakly toward her, meowing hungrily.

"Oh, you poor kitty," Shae said, and grabbed the kitten up and skinned into the hole at the bottom of the snag, scraping her shoulder in the process. Then she thought of her shirt. She'd left it in the boat. But nobody could see her there.

Was it the minister coming out early for his fish?

"Kitty," she soothed its mangy fur, "who dropped you out here to starve? Or did your mama die like mine?" As she held the kitten closer, she could count every rib in the tiny body. "Maybe," she offered, "you can eat mussels with my cats. Shadow's a good mama cat. I bet she'll take you in."

Happy to be protected, the kitten lay purring in Shae's arms.

The engine chugged closer. When she dared to peep out again, the engine idled and stopped at the boat dock. It was a big car, but an old one. She had never seen it before. A man sat in the car puffing on a cigar. He wore a big hat, and made no move to get out of the car. Everything was so quiet; Shae knew she didn't dare move.

"Quiet, kitty," she said as she wrapped her fingers around its mouth. "Don't meow, don't purr. Don't even breathe. It might be the minister. If he catches me without my shirt again, he'll be beggin' Papa to let him take me home with him, so his wife can dress me up like a princess. Whatever that is...."

The kitten was clawing with all four feet as Shae squeezed tighter and wondered who in the world the man could be.

CHAPTER 2

❈

Trembling with fear, Shae tucked all four of the kitten's feet in one hand and tiptoed to peep out a smaller hole.

No, she reasoned, it's not the minister. He never wore a straw hat. She would know his citified clothes anywhere. He always wore a white shirt and tie, and drove a swanky car. Who can this be?

The turnip-shaped man finally wrestled himself from under the steering wheel. When he stepped out and took off his hat to fan himself with it, Shae recognized his bald head and big, carrot nose as belonging to Jake Crawford, the nosey old school director.

Now Shae turned to one big goose bump.

I'm in bad trouble.

Shae squatted down in the snag as the man sauntered past and walked down the river bank. She nearly jumped out of her skin when he gave a loud wolf-whistle, then called, "Upshaw! Upshaw, are you there?"

Oh my gosh! Shae sucked in a breath when he headed toward where she'd banked her boat. His pig eyes will never miss my shirt in the boat, and he'll have Sheriff Brody out after Papa.

Crawford stood for a moment taking in the surroundings, then again, he yelled at the top of his voice. "*Upshaw! Upshaw!*"

Then Shae heard him muttering to himself, but she couldn't hear what he was saying. He cupped a hand around one of his ears, and she, too, listened closer. It might be her papa. She guessed it was near noon. But then she heard another motor puffing toward the dock, and she knew it was not her papa. Then, too, the filly always nickered when she came home.

When the vehicle rattled closer, it looked to be a truck. Crawford stood watching as it struggled toward the dock.

"Stop it, kitty," she whispered to the unhappy kitten. "You can't go out there. That old grouch would drown you. Papa said he was probably the one that put the horseshoe in the gunnysack with the kittens that washed out on the river bank last week. Only a devil would do a thing like that."

Shae watched as the dilapidated truck coughed and wheezed toward the dock. It barely made it. And it was only a hundred yards from where she sat petrified, spying.

Blue smoke trailed the truck and, when it stopped, the radiator cap blew off. The driver stayed inside the cab. Once the smoke and steam cleared, a tall, clean-cut man stepped lightly to the ground. He looked the truck over as if he wondered which end to attend to first. Before he picked up the radiator cap, he gave the swamp one clean sweep with his alert eyes. His jet black hair and brown skin made Shae think he was an Indian. She had not seen many men with a clean shave, and she wondered what a handsome man like him was doing in the Cache River swamp.

Seemingly satisfied with what he saw, the stranger raised the hood of the truck and tinkered with the engine. He took a beat-up bucket from the bed of the truck. Carrying first one, then another bucket of water from the river, he poured them into the radiator until it ran over. He pulled a red bandanna handkerchief from his pocket and mopped the sweat from his brow. Then he screwed the cap on and stood looking the contraption over more seriously.

The truck had seen its best days, yet it sported a brand new tarpaulin.

What could he be lookin' for? She wondered.

"Lo', stranger," Crawford greeted.

The second stranger went on about his business. Without looking up he as much as told Crawford he had no time for him.

Unable to stand the suspense any longer, Crawford walked to the truck. "If you're lookin' for mushrooms…?" Crawford inched closer, spat out yonder, and swiped his hairy hand across his mouth. "They've been gone since April. And hickory nuts won't fall before October."

Raising sharp, black eyes, the second man raked long, nimble fingers through his mop of curly hair, and said, "Thanks, mister."

"Mister Crawford." Shoving a big hand toward the man, Crawford babbled on. "I'm the school director of this district. Come out to lecture Clay Upshaw for not sendin' his girl to school. It started a week ago, and she's missed all of it."

After giving Crawford's hand a short shake, the stranger dropped it and went about inserting a hoop into the mouth of a gunnysack. "Do you mean to tell me there's a girl-child living in this swamp?"

"That's right. She goes around here half-naked. Her papa keeps her around to tend the trotlines and sell the fish. Then, too, he keeps her siftin' sand, hoping to find a pearl one day."

Crawford shifted on his feet when the other man pulled gum boots, a leather jacket, and kid gloves from the back of the truck. The second stranger started to dress for a hunt, acting as if he were enjoying Crawford's curiosity.

"Don't believe I've seen you around here before. You live close?" Without waiting for an answer, Crawford went on, "If you're lookin' for catfish, you're out of luck. The old Indian's diggin' mussel shells. The catfish are muddy."

"No, I don't live here." The second man pulled on a hip boot. "My name is Jeff Locati."

Crawford waited for Locati to put on his other boot. "Trapping animals, I suppose."

"No."

Jeff Locati thought a fib would serve the busybody right. He said he was working on a degree in zoology, which was what he'd wanted to do. He pulled on gloves and threw the gunnysack over his shoulder, letting Crawford know he wasn't interested in any more chatting.

"Well," Crawford sighed, "guess I'm not going to see the old man today. But he'll catch it when I do see him. He's going to send that girl to school." Weighing his words for a moment, he added, "We need to get rid of that old coot."

"What do you mean, get rid of him?" Locati's Italian blood ran hot, and his eyes blazed through Crawford. "Does he bother anyone?"

"Well," Crawford hum-hawed, "can't say as he does. But that papoose will grow into a squaw one day." He cut his pig eyes in an insulting manner and tucked his mouth to one corner in a sneering grin. "Then one of our nice, upstanding white boys will marry her. First thing we know we'd have papooses all over the place." He crossed his beefy arms over his chest. "We can't have that. Us white folks are proud of our blood."

Locati slipped off a glove and felt in his pocket to make sure he had his snake bite kit. He turned toward the river, then whirled around and spat out, "What is your opinion of Italians, Mr. Crawford?"

Suspecting that his foot was in his mouth, Crawford shrugged. Stammering, the wrong words fell out of his mouth. "I don't know as I know. If you mean wops, I guess they're all right as long as they don't try to mix with us white folks."

"I see, Mr. Crawford." Locati's eyes spat fire, but he held his temper in check as he walked to the river and waded into the boggy water.

"Hey, buddy!" Crawford called as Locati crawled up the river bank on the opposite side. "You never did tell me what you're lookin' for. I might help."

Just to tantalize his nosey neighbor, Locati sauntered along a path next to the river. Finally, he grinned over his shoulder and said, "Butterflies."

What is his name again? Crawford stood motionless after Locati had disappeared into the cypress woods. For some reason, the man had left madder than a scalded dog. Maybe he was a wop.... One thing for sure, he wasn't white.

Shae watched Crawford return to his car and crank himself into a lather before the sluggish engine hit a lick. When it did turn over, he pushed his big, fat body as fast as he could to get under the steering wheel, to give the motor more gas before it died.

"Child? Child!" Shae fumed under her breath. "If I had my shirt on, I'd go right up to him and tell him that I'm thirteen!"

Meanwhile, Locati was doing some fuming of his own. Wop! He'd heard that word at school, and he'd taken care of it. But to hit a fifty-year-old man, unthinkable. Why, his papa would disown him. Jeff Locati felt guilty about the fib he'd told the nosey old buzzard. He had wanted to be a zoologist all his life, but being born on the wrong side of town, he thought he was about as close as he'd ever get to a degree.

Raised up in a poor family in South St. Louis, and with an ailing father, Jeff had quit school after junior high to work at Forest Park. The wages were almost nil, but it helped to keep the wolf away from the door. He had fed the animals, cleaned the cages, and done whatever grunt work there was to do.

Since there were no child labor laws, he'd worked hard, long hours for his pay. After he had proved himself, his boss had offered him the scouting job in the Cache River. And he had come with great expectations.

Jeff had been told there were stinging snakes in the swamp, and his boss had offered him a substantial price for a pair. He'd also heard there were birds and animals of all species.

"If the rumors are true…" He had grinned up at his papa while they were securing the jalopy together with bailing wire. "…I can make more money in one month there, than I can in six months cleaning cages.

"Let the kids do the dirty work," he had laughed boastfully. "I have paid my dues."

"Be sure to keep your snake bite kit with you at all times, son," his mother had warned as they made the last inspection of his camping gear. Then she'd taken a feather pillow from her spare bed clothes and tucked it in with his comforter.

"Don't worry, Mama. Remember, I'm twenty-three years old. Thanks to you and Papa for everything, but it's time I get out on my own."

With a peck on her wrinkled cheek and a hearty handshake for his father, Jeff cranked the truck and headed south.

He was prepared for the harsh river life, but the idea of a girl-child living in the swamps, didn't sit right with him.

By the time Crawford's car was out of hearing, the restless kitten lay purring in Shae's arms. "Now," she rubbed noses with the kitten, do you want to tell me about it? Where's your mama? Papa says my mama's up in heaven, wherever that is. And he says she's happy there. I wish I was happy. I would be if Papa wouldn't make me go to school in a dress and hair bows."

The kitten lay quiet with one eye closed as Shae stroked its mangy body. She was also getting drowsy, until Scar came whipping into the snag with Jock hot on his trail. The deep growl, low in Jock's throat, told her he meant business.

"No! No, Jock! Go 'way!"

Shae dropped the frightened kitten and moved her scrawny body in front of the hole in the snag. Jock clawed like a lion to get in. Scared within an inch of its life, the kitten made a feeble try to climb out of reach of the thrashing snake.

"Go away, Jock! You're a mean, *mean* dog!"

Jock tucked his tail between his legs and snuck out into the bushes.

As Shae sat calming Scar, she thought of the stranger saying that he was hunting butterflies. With a forked stick? She did not believe a word of it. She'd always used a broom to catch them.

"Zoo...zoo...What did he say he was workin' on?"

She wallowed the word around on her tongue for a time and then decided it didn't mean a thing to her fifth grade vocabulary. Scar was looking for a hole to crawl in to. She knew Jock would be waiting for the snake. He was a jealous sort of dog, wanting all Shae's attention.

While Shae sat wondering how she could protect Scar from the scout when she started school, she fell fast asleep and heard nothing until Sandy snorted at the dock.

"Oh my gosh!" Shae gasped, and stretched Scar out on the ground and jumped to her feet. "Papa's home!" She peeped from the snag and saw her papa tying Sandy to a sapling. Anxious to wallow in the river, the filly pawed the ground.

"No, Sandy, you can't drink the filthy water." Clay patted the horse's rump. "We will get a fresh drink when we get to the pump."

Noticing that the sand had not changed places, he looked around for his daughter. Thinking that she was running the trotlines, he picked up a lump from the sand pile, took his frog sticker from his pocket and whittled the niches away. But it was only gristle. Tossing it away, he moseyed down the river. There sat Shae's boat with her checkered shirt sprawled in the bottom of it.

"Girly-Shae, where are you? It's lunchtime. I brought a surprise. And Sandy is starved for water."

When there was no answer, he wondered what he was going to do with that girl. She'd never defied him before. It must be growing pains, he thought. He gave a wolf-whistle and waited. When there was still no response, he sauntered over to the strange truck. The out of state license plate and tarpaulin told him it belonged to a scout.

Funny, he hadn't seen one in the swamp for two or three years. It must be a park ranger.

As he looked the truck over, a horse nickered across the river. Sandy champed at the bits and answered the call. Clay ran to calm the filly. He certainly didn't want her running around with that black stallion. And that was another subject he had to take up with Shae. He suspected the filly might be carrying a foal. There's another case of too late to shut the barn door after the filly was out. How could he tell Shae that Sandy was going to have a baby?

He eased his weary body down on a stump and swiped his face with his flour sack sweat rag. While compiling several speeches in his mind, he prodded buck shots around with the toe of his worn shoes, but he concluded that she wouldn't understand such things like birthing.

If Dora had only lived, she would have known the right words. Why couldn't he do it? He'd bathed Shae, braided her hair and kissed every ouch since she was four years old. Frustrated, he wrestled his worn-out body up from the stump and bellowed, "*Shae!*"

When there was no response, he walked to her boat, picked up her shirt, and warned, "Shae, you're in for a bottom-bustin'!"

CHAPTER 3

❁

Weary and upset with Shae for playing the morning away, Clay compiled another speech, but it sounded worse than the first ones. Maybe he wasn't capable of bringing her up alone? He was near to agreeing with preacher Anderson that Shae needed a mother. Right now, he just wanted to find his daughter, so he called again, "Girly Shae, I brought some lunch!"

When her papa called her 'Girly', Shae knew she was back in his good graces. Glancing around, she saw Scar slithering toward the water oak. When he eased into his den, she ran to Sandy and mopped the sweat from her rump, then worked at the matted cockleburs in her tail.

"What took so long, Papa? You've been gone for hours and I'm starving."

"I had to wait for an empty boxcar, Girly. Then I stopped in town to buy you a surprise. I couldn't shop here cuz if I let Frank Murphy get his fingers on my cash money; he'd keep it all against our bill. I need the money to buy your school clothes and he doesn't handle pretty girl dresses."

"Not frilly ones, Papa. I don't like prissy dresses. What did you bring for lunch?"

"You'll see."

Clay climbed over the cart wheel, picked up the check-lines and turned Sandy toward the cabin.

"Jump into the cart, Shae. Sandy's starved for a fresh drink."

"But, Papa...." Shae hesitated. "Sandy needs a good wallow in the river. She loves it."

"No. No, I don't want her in the filthy water. Crawl into the cart and let's go. You said you were starved."

Giving in, Shae stepped up on the coupling pole and tumbled into the cart. Spying the brown bag in the corner of the cart, she peeped inside.

"Oh, Papa!" she cried, "bologna, light bread and red soda pop! It's the best treat I've had all summer!"

When they got to the house, in spite of her hunger Shae climbed from the cart and worked at the matted cockleburs in Sandy's tail, while her papa primed the pump.

Sandy pawed at the ground, anxious for water. She sucked the trough dry as fast as Clay could squeeze the water from the pump. The stray cattle kept the trough sipped dry most of the time.

Next to Scar, Sandy was Shae's best friend. Clay had pulled the tiny foal from a bed of quicksand after her mother had given up and left her to die. They had named her Quicksand, but had shortened it to Sandy, thinking it had complimented her beautiful palomino coloring.

Together, Shae and her papa had nursed the frail weakling to a beautiful, healthy filly. Many times, Shae waited up long after dark for a fresh range cow to come for water, so she could steal milk for Sandy. Now she was paying them back by pulling a ton of muscle shells to the dinky-train every week. She was only a wood colt, but to Shae, she was a thoroughbred.

Shae gave up on the cockleburs in Sandy's tail and worked on the mare's mane. She would have to use the curry-comb on Sandy's tail after lunch.

"Papa, where did Sandy get all these cockleburs? I'll never get them all out."

For an answer, Clay kept pulling the pump handle up and down. He wasn't feeling well, and he was sure he was coming down with one of those buckegger chills.

Deciding that removing the cockleburs was a hopeless job, Shae ran for the brown bag in the cart.

"Yummy, yummy!"

She took the bottle of soda pop from the bag and made a guzzling sound in her throat as she dropped the bottle under the stream of water into the trough.

"You cool the soda pop, Papa, and I'll make the sandwiches. I can't wait. Remember, we only had soakie (bread and coffee) for breakfast."

Butchering the bread and bologna out with the sharpest knife they owned, Shae pasted the sandwiches together with mustard. Fidgety while waiting for her papa, she gorged down on a hunk of bologna without any bread, and impatiently waited for the soda pop. When her papa uncapped the bottle, Shae slapped her hand over the mouth, saving most of it from fizzing out, and then picked up the sandwich. She sat with the sandwich halfway to her mouth and took a long swig of the soda.

Clay slowly eased himself down on the wooden bench by the table. Food smelled awful to him. All he wanted was cold water.

"I thought you'd enjoy a strawberry soda." Clay picked up a sandwich and nibbled at it, then dropped his head into his hands. "I sure hope this headache's not the forerunner of another buckegger chill." He had that awful bitter taste in his mouth like he'd heard Dora complain of before she had come down with typhoid fever, and he prayed it wouldn't happen to him.

How would Girly manage?

After a minute, he raised his head and drank the tall glass of water, and asked for another. When Shae brought it, he drank it down without taking it from his lips. Then he wrestled himself from the bench and made his way to his old willow-cane rocker.

"Don't you feel well, Papa? You hardly touched your sandwich." Shae put her hand to his forehead. "And you're scorchin' with fever."

"I'm not hungry, Girly. Just get me another cold drink, please."

Shae had to go to the pump for water. When she got back, she found her papa's eyes closed. He was mumbling that he would rest a spell before going to dig shells.

"Maybe it will cool off, later on," he murmured.

Shae sat the glass on the table and rushed outside to where Sandy stood munching on corn fodder.

"You are a pretty thing, Sandy. Where did you get all these cockleburs?" She reached for the curry-comb on the fence post, and combed at the matted burrs. "Be still. Don't switch me in the face with that sticky tail. You can rest all afternoon when I get the burrs combed out. You're lucky. I have to sift sand in the hot sun."

After an hour of combing, Shae had Sandy slick and shiny, so she decided she would make amends for playing the morning away by letting her papa sleep and going and getting the sand sifted. Then, too, she was worried about Scar. She was sure the stranger wasn't in the swamp to catch butterflies.

Just as she expected, when Shae got to the dock, she found boot tracks around the water oak. The hunter's truck was gone. She went to Scar's den and threw out all the usual signals, but the snake did not show. Maybe he was napping longer. The sun was at its hottest, at least one hundred degrees. She sat for a while thinking how she could protect Scar from the hunter. He didn't know the snake was her pet.

Climbing into her boat, Shae scooped the water from it and rowed lazily down stream, hoping she would catch sight of the hunter. When she got to the grove of willows, she docked the boat and crawled out on the cool, damp sand. It was her best thinking place, and there were a lot of things she needed to work out. For instance, if it wasn't for that nosey old school director, she wouldn't have to wear this old shirt all the time.

With her hands tucked under her head, Shae laid thinking of how the hunter had grinned when he'd told Crawford he was hunting butterflies. She'd known he was pulling the old busy-body's leg.

Birds of every color twitted and bathed in the edge of the river. A baby flying squirrel tried its wings in a persimmon sapling.

The afternoon was slipping away and Shae had not sifted a grain of sand. Maybe, she thought as she watched cotton clouds waltz around the sun in three-quarter time, they will cover it over and I can work for a while. She had never remembered her papa sleeping so long at noon. She hoped he wasn't sick again.

Except for the birds and squirrel, the woods were still. Then Shae thought she heard footsteps. She quickly pushed her boat to the far side of the river under the high bank and sat very quiet. Soon, she heard gum boots flopping and she knew the hunter wasn't tracking. He was on his way to his truck, which must be his home for now. It sounded as if he was headed straight toward her.

She leaned into the bank as close as she could and didn't dare look until he passed on by and kept to the path along the bank. As soon as she dared peek, she saw a gunnysack hanging from a forked stick over his shoulder, jerking on his back. It looked half full of something, and the hunter seemed to be struggling with it.

Knowing the hunter would have to cross the river to get to his truck, Shae watched until he disappeared around the curve. She then pushed her boat back to the sandbar under the willows and eased her way along the bank, tangling with berry briers and cockleburs as she tried to stay undercover.

She struggled for a half mile before she caught sight of the hunter's black jacket. She darted behind a scrub oak and watched as he waded across the river and headed toward his truck, which was not more than a hundred yards from the river bank.

The truck faced Murphy's store, giving her full view. After dumping the gunnysack on the ground, he peeled off his gloves, jacket and boots, and stood wiping his face on a red bandanna. He then took a long swig of water from his canteen. When he untied the tarpaulin, Shae could see wire cages stacked back against the cab. The one he took out looked as if it was made of screen wire, telling her it was a snake cage. Animal cages were made of bigger wire.

After opening the cage door, he stood for a minute looking the situation over then stashed the gunnysack inside the cage before untying it. He quickly emptied the contents into the cage and slammed the door shut, then rested himself on a stump. After a time, he put the cage into the truck and pulled out what looked to be a tent.

He's going to camp here, Shae thought. How can I keep watch on Scar when I have to go to school eight hours a day?

Knowing her papa would be cross if he came to the dock and found her gone again, Shae gave up the watch and crawled along the river bank until she knew she was well out of sight. She then ran back to her boat and paddled to the dock. Her papa's boat was still tied to the root of the tree. Shae wondered why he had not come for it yet. Again she hoped he hadn't come down with another river chill. Pushing the thought from her mind, she tied her boat next to his and sat quietly by for a while. Scar was still nowhere to be seen. She paddled her feet near his den, trying for his attention. When he made no show, she pulled her knees up under her chin and let the tears flow. She was sure the hunter had her snake in that gunnysack. Whatever it was, it was big and unhappy to have been captured. What if it was Scar? What would she do without him? She couldn't remember when she didn't have him!

Swiping her tears away on her shirtsleeve, Shae tried to get her straggly hair back into the braids. She had lost the fish cord they'd been tied with, and she worked at two or three cockleburs low on the back of her neck. They were buried like Sandy's, and it pulled awful. Once she had worked them out and rebraided her hair, she wet her hands and slicked the stray strands back from her face. She felt somewhat cooler now. Maybe she could get some sand sifted.

The sweltering sun still beat down. It was too hot for bird or beast. Not even a fish flopped. The sifter handle had not cooled at all but the sand had to be sifted if her papa expected to find a pearl. Someday their luck would change. That's what her papa would say, and he knew all the signs and sayings.

After an hour of cooking under the punishing sun, Shae took the sifter and tapped it against the root of the tree over Scar's den. Cautiously, Scar surfaced and scanned the surroundings for Jock. When he saw Shae, he swam toward her.

"There you are, Scar! You sure scared me half to death!"

Shae scooped up the monstrous snake into her arms. Forgetting everything else, she hot-footed it toward the cabin. Scar didn't stop squirming until he was wrapped snugly around Shae's neck. They were a happy twosome. All was again well with the world. Shae had slowed to a saunter, letting Scar enjoy the ride, when suddenly she thought of her papa.

What if he's sick and needin' me?

She quickened her step and was almost to the cabin when she heard an awful, savage growl. Within a split second, Jock was upon them. Scar made a leap for safety, but it was too late. Jock caught the snake with two long jumps, grabbed him in the middle, whipped him up and down the sun-baked earth, then turned him loose and slashed a gash down his back.

For what seemed forever, Shae stood petrified. But when Jock picked Scar up, tossed him into the air, caught him and shook the life out of him, Shae came out of her shock. She looked for a weapon, but there was nothing to battle the hundred pound wolf dog with. Breaking off a green limb, she closed in on Jock, but he didn't even look her way, just kept shaking and beating Scar against the ground.

"No, Jock! *No!*"

Jock slung Scar into the air the third time. Shae threw the limb down and screamed at the top of her voice. "Help! Help me, Papa!"

CHAPTER 4

❁

Clay Upshaw half-opened his weary eyes and looked around the room. What's all the commotion, he wondered? Guess I must have dropped off to sleep. He was so tired he didn't stir until he heard another scream. Finally, he pulled his head from the back of the chair and listened.

"Girly, did you hear something?" When there was no response, he gazed around and noticed the glass of water on the stand table. He remembered how thirsty he'd been when he'd sat down. He anxiously lifted the glass to his parched lips and found the liquid to be like slush-water. He tried to bring his mind back into focus.

What in tarnation is going on around here, anyhow?

When the next scream jarred his senses, he tried to detect where it was coming from. He sat up wide awake and looked for Shae. Where could that girl be? She was right there a minute ago.

Pulling his weakened body from the chair, he wobbled outside, looked in all three directions, then cupped a hand around his good ear and listened. It was then he heard Jock's savage growl. Shae's next scream started his adrenaline flowing. He hit the path in a long lope and ran as fast as his legs would carry him. He could see Shae wringing her hands and he knew there was something terrible going on, but the action was behind bushes.

Then he saw Jock fling the king snake into the air, catch him as he came down, whip him against the sun-baked earth, then toss him up again.

By the time Clay got there, Jock had Scar under his paws and was tearing into him with his long, sharp claws. The snake was a put-it-out-of-its-misery-case if he'd ever seen one.

"Jock!" he yelled, but the wolf dog never looked up until Clay straddled its neck. He twice whacked Jock across the nose with his open hand before the snake was dropped.

Jock had been going for the kill. Although this was the chance he'd been waiting for, the last whack sent him howling to the cabin, and he didn't stop until he was well under cover.

Out of breath, Clay stood panting. Shae rushed to where Scar lay writhing in agony. She fell to her knees beside the snake, trying to calm him, but he flopped around until she couldn't hold onto him. When Scar stretched out on the ground and lay in shock, she gathered him into her arms and soothed his mangled body.

"Oh, Papa," she begged. "Do somethin'! He's dyin'!"

"Calm down, Girly. Maybe it's not as bad as I thought. The gash on his back will heal in a hurry. We'll take him to the cabin and doctor the puncture wounds with coal oil."

"No! No, Papa, coal oil hurts so bad! Can't we smoke him with hickory chips, like we did when Jock tore his eye from the socket?"

"Coal oil will heal faster, Girly."

Her papa headed toward the cabin. Shae reluctantly followed. When they reached their home, he got the coil oil can and gave it a shake, wondering if there was enough in the can to doctor the snake.

"I'll hold, you pour," he said, handing the can to Shae. "Let me get a choke-hold on him before you pour, though."

Clay had not realized how weak he was until he clamped both hands around Scar's neck and squeezed tight. But when the coil oil hit the punctures in the snake, Scar coiled up into a tight ring, then broke Clay's grip and raced back toward the river.

Shae ran after him and twice had her hands on him, but he slipped away and she couldn't catch him again. She followed him to the river and waded into the dirty water, then lost sight of him.

"Let him go, Girly. He'll go into his den. That'll be the best place for him until he heals. He'll come out when he's well."

Shae walked back toward her papa, her chocolate brown eyes flooded with tears. Clay worked at holding his own back as he wondered if he should have put the snake out of its misery. But could he do that? Scar had been Shae's playmate ever since her mother had died.

"Papa...." Shae stood measuring her words for a moment, then blurted out, "I hate Jock!" She dropped her head into her hands and sobbed.

"Now, now, Girly-Shae, Jock was only tryin' to protect you. He thought Scar was attackin' you."

"Anyhow, I hate him!" Shae ripped at the buttons on her shirt. "And this old shirt, school, and everybody..." When she saw the look on her papa's face, she said, "Except you, Papa."

"Girly, girly, calm down." "You can't hate people. And what would you want Jock to do? Let's go inside and talk about it. The sun is too hot for man or beast."

"I'm sorry, Papa. I guess I felt like you do when you get mad at Jake Crawford." Her papa smiled, and Shae picked up the stray cat meowing behind her.

"Looks as if we have another mouth to feed around here," Clay said as he looked the skinny Kitten over. "I see its problem. We'll have to get rid of that wolf worm in its neck."

When Shae looked puzzled, he explained that a fly had stung the kitten and a worm had hatched from the egg. Then he reached for the coal oil can, turned it up and let a drop fall into the face of the fuzzy worm. He watched it squirm, knowing the kitten would soon be fat like Shae's other cats. When her papa screwed the cap on the can, he reminded Shae that she would have to go to the store before night for more oil. The lamp and lantern were both empty.

"And," he added, "I'm out of chill tonic."

"Do I have to go, Papa?"

Clay wished he could go himself, but he knew he would never make it there, much less back.

Shae's gaze dropped to her water-chapped feet. She looked up into her papa's faded, obsidian eyes and said, "I'll go, Papa, but..."

"But what, Girly, why don't you want to go?"

"There is always a bunch of men, there. And Mr. Murphy pulls his specs down on his nose and looks funny at me before he asks me if I have the money."

"I think I have enough money, Girly." Her papa reached into his overall pocket and fished out some change. He added aloud, "Ten cents for coal oil, and forty-five for chill tonic. Yep. I have it, with a nickel left over." He handed the change to Shae. "And the nickel is for a Baby Ruth."

Shae noticed her papa's hand tremble when he handed her the money, and she knew he was coming down with another chill.

"Papa, let's get you to bed." She felt his forehead and found it scorching hot. "I'll pump the water off cold, and we will put cold packs on your forehead. We will get the fever down."

Shae took her papa's arm and guided him toward the porch, where he stopped and leaned against the porch post for a while.

"My head aches so bad," he dropped it into his hands and lowered his long, lean body to the floor, where he lay shaking in the ninety degree sun. Only a few minutes ago he'd wanted to get in out of it. But now it felt so good.

Try as she might, Shae could not persuade him to go to bed. She needed to go to the store before dark, but she couldn't leave him there for the flies and mosquitoes to swarm.

It was an hour before the minister came by for his catfish. Between the two of them, they helped Upshaw into the house. By the time he was in bed, it took two heavy quilts to warm him. When he quit shaking, he finally dozed off to sleep.

Assuring Shae he would be back by to check on her papa before bedtime, the minister paid her for fifty pounds of catfish. Although he knew there wasn't more than thirty-five, Clay and the girl needed the money. Anderson knew there wouldn't be enough catfish to go around, but some of the folks who only came for the food would have to tighten their belts a notch.

"Papa," Shae touched him on the forehead and found his fever had cooled down. "I'm going to the store. I will hurry right back."

Hoping that her papa would sleep until she got back, Shae thanked the minister, picked up the coal oil can, and hurried toward the dock. Jock came sneaking from under the cabin. He didn't offer to go with Shae, and she didn't ask him to. He had done enough dirt for one day.

When she got to the boat dock, she looked for snake tracks, but there was none. Nor boot tracks.

It was so nice rowing down stream in the cool of the evening. Baby turtles jumped from the river bank with a clump, and birds were going to their nests. Before she realized it, she was at the back door of Murphy's store. As she stayed her boat to a willow sapling, she could hear the boisterous voices of a crowd of men inside the store. She noticed a well-worn tent near the stranger's truck.

What if he was there?

For the first time in her life, Shae was self-conscious of her water-chapped feet and dirty overalls.

Shae recognized Jake Crawford's voice as the men talked simultaneously. Without meaning to eavesdrop, she stopped outside the back door and waited, hoping the crowd would thin out before she had to go inside. When no one left, she sat down behind a scrub oak tree and leaned against the rough bark. Somehow, she felt the tree was protecting her from the stares of the crude crowd inside the store. She waited for as long as she could. The sun was sliding behind the tree tops, and the bark kept biting into her backbone. She knew she had to go inside.

When she got to the bottom of the rickety steps, she heard Jake Crawford blab out, "Preacher, when have you seen the old Indian? I understand you buy catfish from him. Ain't they gettin' purty muddy?"

The minister said nothing, which should have told Crawford he wasn't interested in gossip, but Crawford caught his breath and started over.

"I've been out to the swamp three days runnin' to lecture him about sending that girl to school, but he keeps dodgin' me."

"Mr. Crawford, if you are speaking of Mr. Upshaw…" The minister gave Crawford an unpleasant look. "I was there this afternoon. He was in bed with a buckegger chill."

"Yeah, that's one of his old tricks. He's afraid you are there to inquire into the welfare of that young squaw. I hear that you have offered to take her off his hands…. Is that right?"

"Mr. Crawford!" The minister began to dress Crawford down to size. "Mr. Upshaw has every right to privacy. I refuse to discuss his affairs in public. The man is having a stroke of bad luck. He needs sympathy, not criticism. Mr. Upshaw is a fine man."

Not to be stopped, Crawford rushed on, "I doubt that you or anybody else could handle that girl. She's wilder than a didapper duck." Crawford took time out to spit toward the ash pan in front of the heater. "But he's going to send her to school if I have to sic Sheriff Brody onto him."

Being too much of a gentleman to argue with a blowhard, the minister excused himself and left.

When Shae saw the sun drop behind the tree tops, she knew she had to go inside. Her papa would be worried if she wasn't back home before dark. With all the courage she could muster, she picked up the coal oil can and climbed the steps, and walked quietly into the store, among the roughnecks. All the men clammed up and sat gawking at her as she eased up to the counter where Frank Murphy stood writing in his ledger.

The scout stood near the counter, waiting to pay for a purchase. Nodding his head as any gentleman would do to a lady, he stepped back with a polite, "Ladies first. I'm in no hurry."

Knowing that the stranger had taken full measure of her, Shae felt a flush creep to her cheeks as she waited for Frank Murphy to acknowledge her.

Murphy kept jotting figures in the account book. When he did look up, he pulled his wire-rimmed specs down to the end of his Roman nose and quipped, "What's for you, kid?" Noticing the coal oil can, he added, "Besides coal oil?"

"A bottle of chill tonic," Shae said her voice barely audible.

"What kind?" Murphy stared from under hooded eyelids at her. "I'm out of Groves. Do you want 666?"

Shae shifted her weight from one foot to the other, in indecision. Remembering that her papa was so awful sick, she opened her mouth to speak then closed it.

Agitated, Murphy barked, "Make up your mind! I've got other folks to wait on. Do you want it, or not?"

"I'll take it." Shae fumbled the change in her hand, so he wouldn't ask her if she had the money in front of everyone.

Murphy shuffled from behind the counter, snatched the coal oil can from her hand, and limped toward the storeroom to fill it.

"Well, fellers…." Jake Crawford wrestled his big, round body from a cane-bottomed chair, where he'd spent the afternoon playing poker. He sauntered over to the counter, allowing that he had to get home as he had a meeting to attend. He waited for someone to ask the nature of the meeting. When no one did, he said, "I've got to go to the school board meetin'. I gotta straighten out the board of education."

Standing as close to Shae as he could, he stared down on her. His tobacco breath was so offensive, Shae stepped away from him. Crawford then moved in front of Jeff Locati and stood tapping his fingers on the counter.

Locati held his peace when Crawford took change from his pocket and rubbed it together. He leaned against the counter and mumbled under his breath, "C'mon, Murphy. I'd like to get a sack of Bull Durham…if you ever get the darkies waited on!"

Crawford had not intended for the statement to be heard, but a hunter's ears are keen. The words had hardly dropped from Crawford's malicious tongue before Locati's left fist shot out with the speed of sound, striking Crawford in the mouth. The lick was not hard enough to floor the two-hundred-and-fifty-pounds of blubber. It staggered him over a chair, reducing it to splinters as he tumbled over onto the hard, wooden floor.

For a moment, Crawford lay stunned, while his buddies sat open-mouthed, wondering what had happened. When he finally wiped his big hairy hand across his mouth and saw blood, he rose up on one elbow and spat out, "You dirty, black wop, If I didn't hate to hit a kid, I'd mop this floor with you! You'll pay dear for this!"

"Now, now, Jake," one of the poker players went over to help Crawford up. "You asked for it. The minister wanted to do it, but his reputation was at stake."

"All right, fellers." Frank Murphy came hobbling from the storeroom as fast as his rheumatic leg would allow. "What's going on here?" He noticed the splintered chair, and roared, "Somebody's going to pay for that chair!"

Stashing the coal oil can at Shae's feet, Murphy went behind the counter, took the receiver from the wall telephone and rung two longs and a short.

Everyone knew that number belonged to Sheriff Brody.

"Sheriff Brody?" Murphy lost no time when the sheriff's voice came over the wire. "Could you come out to Murphy's store right away? I have a couple of knot heads into a knockdown, and they're wrecking my furniture."

"Guns involved?" asked the sheriff.

"No. No guns, but I want you out here now!"

When Murphy hung up the receiver, he noticed Crawford making his way to the door, and he was making every toe push a little.

"Crawford!" Murphy bellowed. "You had better stick around here until Brody comes. He'll want your side of the story."

Jake Crawford wanted no part of the sheriff. He'd seen Brody work before. Paying Murphy no never-mind, he rushed on out to his car, cranked it up and drove away.

"I'm so sorry this happened, young lady," Jeff Locati apologized. "I should have walked away."

Shae was scared speechless. She wanted to run away, but her papa was so sick. She knew she had to wait until she got the medicine, which he needed to keep his chill off the next day. Fumbling the change in her hand, she counted in her head. She knew the 666 cost more than the Groves chill tonic. Hopefully she had enough money. Her mouth was still watering for a Baby Ruth, but she would have to forget about it.

"Let's see." Murphy turned to the counter, tapping his fingers to his temple. "Where was I, Oh, yes, the chill tonic?" He lifted the bottle of 666 from the shelf and sat it on the counter. "That will be seventy cents."

Again Shae counted the change. "I don't have but sixty-five cents." Shae's voice quivered as she offered him the money. "I only brought enough money for the Groves Tonic. Could I bring the other nickel over, later?"

Murphy stared down at Shae from beneath his hooded eyelids.

When he didn't say yes or no to her question, Jeff Locati fished a nickel from his pocket and slapped it on the counter. "I happen to have an extra nickel."

Embarrassed, Shae laid her sixty-five cents on the counter, picked up the bottle and rushed toward the back door. The sun was down, and she told herself she had to hurry home.

"Just a minute, young lady," Jeff called after her. "You forgot the coal oil." Picking up the can, he met Shae halfway as she walked back into the store to get it. She thanked him, and then hurried out the door.

CHAPTER 5

❀

It was suppertime for all the loafers, but they stuck around to see what the sheriff would do with the wop, if he was a wop…? Nobody knew for sure what one looked like.

The sheriff made it out to Murphy's in record time. Every eye locked onto the six-foot-three, two-hundred and fifty pounds of bone and muscle as he stooped to enter the store. His arms were a yard long, his hands as broad as a broom, and he swung a billy club that would fall an oak tree.

"What's the problem, Mr. Murphy?" Brody brushed his tousled red hair back, and looked the crowd over. "Everything's peaceful enough here now. Did anyone get hurt?"

"Ah…this feller," "Murphy pointed to Jeff Locati, "and Jake Crawford got into a fistfight about something, and Crawford wound up on the floor with a busted lip. You can see what they did to my chair." Murphy's voice rose to a shouting pitch. "Somebody's going to pay for it! I'm not putting up with that around here!"

Brody searched the room. "Where's Crawford now?"

"Jake had to go home," one of the man's poker buddies spoke up. "He had to go to a meeting. He said he had to straighten out the board of education."

Brody looked at Jeff. "Why did you strike the man, mister…?"

"Locati, Jeffrey Locati," the scout furnished. "I'm here in Cache River working for Forest Park of St. Louis. It strikes me that Mr. Crawford doesn't like my nationality in these parts. I'm sorry this happened. I'm used to racial slurs, but Crawford also kept antagonizing a girl who was standing nearby, and I forgot my manners."

""But..." Brody half-grinned down his nose, "...did it call for a busted lip? I'm here to enforce the law, you know."

"Well, I suppose I thought it did at the time, my father will disown me."

"Crawford had it comin', Sheriff." A crusty lumberjack got up from a bench, knocked the dead ashes from his corn-cob pipe, and threw them into the pan of ashes in front of the King heater. "Jake thinks because he's the school director here, he's some kind of god. He wants everybody to dance to his music. Well, I ain't got nuthin' fer 'em. He ain't nobody in my book but a low-down dirty hog thief!"

"Watch your mouth, Sam. That's no way to settle an argument. If something should happen to Jake, the law would be hot on your tail."

"Well, the truth never hurt nobody!" Sam spat over his shoulder as he turned and left.

Brody let him go, and went back to lecturing Jeff Locati, cautioning him to watch his temper and keep his fists to himself.

"What about my chair?" Murphy picked up the pieces, carried them to the stove and dumped them inside. "It will make good kindling come cold weather, but somebody's got to pay for it."

"I'll pay for the chair." Locati pulled a dollar bill from his pocket and shoved it toward Murphy. "Will this take care of the damage?"

Murphy took the dollar and sullenly acknowledged that was about what a new one would cost.

"May I be excused, Mr. Brody?" Locati turned to the sheriff, half expecting to be arrested. "I have some work I need to do."

"I suppose you may, since the victim's not around. But if I hear of anymore trouble from you, I will have to take you in. I'm sure you understand the law."

"I certainly do, Mr. Brody." With a nod of thanks, Jeff turned toward the door then added, "It wasn't my intent to break it."

Locati had never had reason to make an account to a sheriff. He walked out the door, went straight to his tent, stretched out on his cot and wondered if coming to Cache River had been a good idea.

What had he gone to the store for? He'd been so hungry when he'd gone, but now he felt that food would choke him. Lacing his fingers under his head, he lay on his cot thinking.

On the river, Shae paddled as fast as she could, but it was dusky-dark by the time she tied her boat to a willow behind the cabin. She heard her papa calling for water, but he was calling for Dora to bring it.

Why would he do that?

Shae realized he was talking out of his head. She grabbed the can of coal oil from the boat and dashed to the cabin. When she got to her papa, he was propped up on one elbow, calling, "Dora, please bring me cold water!"

"What hurts, Papa?" Shae cradled his head in her arms and brushed his matted hair from his feverish brow. "What can I do, Papa? It's me, Shae."

"Where did Dora go?" Clay asked thickly. "She was here a minute ago."

Shae had never seen her papa so sick. When he quieted down, she filled the lamp and lit it. Then she hurried to the pump and pumped the water off real cold. He drank the gourd dipper empty twice. She then placed cold cloths on his forehead until his fever cooled, and he was talking rationally.

"What would I do without my little girl?" He patted her hand as she laid another cold cloth on his brow.

"I got the chill tonic, Papa. Mr. Murphy was out of Groves. I got 666. We will start it now." She went for the spoon. "So you will miss your chill day after tomorrow."

Shae kept the 666 going every two hours until midnight and then her papa was able to take it from then on while she got some sleep. But it was two o'clock before she shut her eyes. She laid thinking of what she'd heard Jake Crawford say to the minister, and about the fight. She felt fit to burst her britches when she thought of the stranger calling her a 'young lady'. Then she wondered if her papa would give her away. She would ask him tomorrow.

When Shae woke up hours later, the stray kitten was curled up beside her, sound asleep. She heard her papa in the kitchen rattling pots and pans.

"Are you feeling better, Papa?"

"Yes, thanks to you, Girly. I feel good, and I'm starved."

"What are we going to do today, Papa?"

"Well, first thing we're going to town and buy you some school dresses. Wash your face. The flapjacks will get cold."

For the first time in a week, Clay was anxious to get to the table. It had been twenty-four hours since he'd eaten. He flipped the last flapjack on the stack and poured sugar-syrup over them.

"Get a move on, Girly Shae! It's going to be another scorcher. It must be eighty degrees already."

Clay poured himself a cup of boiling coffee and sat down on the bench. With a long face, Shae sat on the other side of the table and watched her papa dig into the flapjacks.

"What's the matter, Girly? Aren't you hungry? Breakfast is getting cold."

Shae cut off a bite of the flapjack and handed it to the yellow kitten, then patted it when it jumped up on the bench beside her. "Do we have to go to town today, Papa?" Before he could get his mouth empty, Shae wiped at her tearful eyes and asked, "Papa, would you give me away?"

"Why, of course not?" he swallowed hard, almost choking on the flapjack. "Why do you ask that?"

When Shae told him what she'd heard at Murphy's store, he sat for a moment, laid his fork down, and then slapped his hand on the table. "That low-down, lyin'…!" He stopped before he let out the swear word going through his mind, for he had never used bad language around her.

Shae had nearly jumped out of her skin when he'd shouted. The kitten gave a screeching howl and skidded under the bed. In spite of the tears creeping down Shae's cheeks, she laughed and her papa laughed with her.

"Pa…Pa! You scared the poor kitty to death!"

"I'm sorry I lost control, Girly Shae, but Jake Crawford really gets under my craw. I don't know where he got his name, but they got it right that time. That nosey old son of a so-and-so…. Don't you ever worry about the hear-say around here. Nobody will ever take you away from me. I may not be as big as Crawford, but I'm strong." He made a muscle on his skinny arm and laughed. "I can take care of my daughter."

Shae couldn't stop the tears from welling up in her big brown eyes.

"Now…now." Clay got up from the table, went to her, and patted her shoulder. "Dry the tears." He combed her hair back from her face with his fingers, and tucked it behind her ear. "You mess up your pretty face when you cry."

Shae broke into sobs. "The kids at school say I'm ugly."

"The kids at school don't know what they're talking about. You're the prettiest little Indian princess I have ever seen, or ever will see."

"Do we have to go to town today, Papa? I want to look about for Scar, and it will take Miss Bickles half the day to fit me. She always tries two or three of the prissy dresses on me first. I hate ruffles and lace."

"We will see. I'm sure we can find some you will like. And let's don't forget to buy some hair ribbon. Your mama always kept your pigtails tied with ribbon."

"But, Papa, twine holds better."

"All right, we'll talk about it later. Eat your breakfast, now. Time's wasting."

Thinking the worst was over Clay walked back around the table, plopped down on the bench, and dug into the flapjacks. He'd never tasted food so good! He forked down one mouthful after another, and finished his coffee. When he got up for a refill, he noticed a car pulling up out front. He answered the knock at the door. Preacher Anderson was standing there.

"Morning, Clay." Anderson's face lit up. "This is a pleasant surprise. I didn't expect to see you out of bed." He rushed on, "I'm sorry that I didn't get back out as I promised, but I got tied up. I just couldn't get away until it was too late."

"No problem." Clay further opened the door. "Come in. I'm fine. I took a half bottle of 666 last night. It will knock a chill," but—He laughed "—what a fall."

"I know what you mean, Clay. I have taken a few bottles of it, myself."

Anderson straddled the chair Clay offered, making himself at home. He glanced at Shae and noticed she'd been crying. "Morning, Shae."

"Cup of coffee Preacher," Clay asked. "It's still hot."

"No thanks. I finished breakfast, earlier."

Feeling ill-at-ease, Anderson straightened his tie and cleared his throat.

Clay knew he was wondering what Shae was so unhappy about, so he went right to the point. "Preacher…" He weighed his words. "…if you're here to talk about the girl, you're wasting your time."

Taken aback, Anderson's face turned a deep pink. For a moment, he was at a loss for words. Finally, he said, "Clay, I don't think I know what you are talking about. I came by for one reason only, and that was to see if I could help."

"I'm sorry to offend, Preacher, but some folks around here think that I'm not capable of caring for my daughter and would like to take her away from me. But I can tell anyone, it would be over my dead body."

Anderson asked, "Who's saying this?"

"Jake Crawford for one."

"Clay," Anderson assured, "I have no doubt of your capability. You have done a fine job with Shae. But when one gets down sick, he needs help. I would never think of asking you to give up your daughter, but if there is any way my wife and I can help, we're here."

"Thanks, Preacher, but we're doing fine. We made it when she was four, and we can make it now."

Changing the subject, Clay asked, "Say, did you have enough fish for the fish fry?"

"Sure did."

"I'm sure you paid the girl too much. There couldn't have been over thirty-five pounds."

"Skip it." Anderson got up from the chair and held out his hand. "I pray the Lord will keep you in good health, Clay, but if you need me...."

"Thanks again, Preacher, for stopping by."

After the minister left, Shae sauntered outside, and her papa thought she was going to the privy. "Hurry back, Girly," he cautioned.

Shae made no promises. After he waited more than long enough, he went to the door to rush her up some, but he got there in time to see her mount the filly. She flanked the mare in the side and then was gone with the wind.

"Shae!" he called. "Come back here!"

CHAPTER 6

❀

"Wild, wild, wild!" Clay stood shaking his head as he watched Shae disappear around the curve in the path. Sandy's hoof beats went out of hearing range. "Whatever am I going to do with that girl?" All that he could do was wait until she took a notion to come back.

Going into the cabin, he first cleared the dishes from the table and put them in a dish pan of water on the stove. Then he reached for his corncob pipe on the shelf, filled it from a twist of cotton-boll tobacco, struck a match to it, and sat down in his willow rocker. It had been months since he'd smoked, but he hoped it would maybe settle his nerves. For an hour, he sat blowing smoke-rings toward the ceiling, thinking, *I must have a talk with that girl. She's getting so…so…unruly.*

Shae slipped over Sandy's rump to the ground, tied her to a persimmon sapling, and ran for the water oak, where she hoped she could coax Scar from his den. She found no sign of boot or snake tracks, which told her that no one else had been around and that the king snake had not stirred from the hole under the tree. She waited as long as she dared. When Scar made no show, she went back to where Sandy stood pawing the ground, begging to take a wallow.

"No, Sandy. We can't go in the water. If I get my hair wet, I'll be in bad trouble. Papa's takin' me to town to buy school dresses. I can just hear Miss Bickles say, 'Honey, you would look pretty in this dress with the red ruffles'. Blah, blah, blah...."

Shae combed at the filly's mane with her long, thin fingers. "I'll probably come home with Mary Jane slippers and hair bows. I won't wear 'em! I hate ribbons and prissy dresses."

Clay had almost dozed off to sleep when he heard the stray cows come bawling to the watering trough. Dolly, the cow they had been milking since the wolves had slaughtered her calf, looked as if her bag was about to burst.

Taking a bucket from a nail on the sweet gum tree, he rinsed it out and milked it full. "Good girl, Dolly," he said, patting her rump. "We have been out of milk for two days." He strained the milk through a flour sack and placed it into a bucket of cold water to cool.

Shae would like a glass when she came back....

Clay looked up at the sun, which was getting higher and hotter every minute. That girl needed her bottom busted, if anyone did. If she wasn't thirteen, he'd do it. He wiped a tear trickling down his cheek. What would Dora think if he laid a hand on her little girl?

It was another fifteen minutes before he heard the clip-clop of Sandy's hooves, and he knew Shae was racing the filly again. He just had to tell her of Sandy's condition, for she could lose her foal.

"Shae," Papa met her as she rode Sandy up to her favorite stump, and piled off the animal's back. "Haven't I told you not to race the filly? Get into the cabin and get scrubbed up. We should have been to town by now."

"I'm sorry, Papa." Shae's big, innocent eyes gazed into her papa's angry ones. "I had to look for Scar before we went, Papa. He's gone. Jock has killed him. I know I'll never see him again!"

"No, he's not. It might be a week before Scar ventures out of his den. He had quite a scare. Now get into the cabin and scrub your neck and ears. Miss Bickles won't like trying dresses on a girl with a dirty neck."

When Shae's papa came in after harnessing Sandy to the cart, she'd wrestled herself into her best dress, which was a little too snug, and had put on her tennis shoes.

"I will help you with the tangles." Clay brought the hair-brush to where she stood in front of a cracked mirror on the wall. "Then you can braid one side while I braid the other. Two hands are faster than one."

When the braids were neatly done, he reminded Shae, "Let's not forget those ribbons."

He shooed Shae out the door. Boosting her into the cart, he climbed over the wheel behind her, and soon they were eating dust from Sandy's heels.

The sun beat down at ninety degrees and the filly was in a lather before they got halfway to town.

"Why do you keep holdin' Sandy back Papa? She loves to race, and I'm roastin' alive in this sun."

Her papa didn't say anything. He knew this was a good opening to tell her why Sandy shouldn't run, but he couldn't blurt out that the filly was going to have a foal. Girly Shae didn't know the first word about the facts of life, and it would bring on questions. Maybe there would be a better time.

When they arrived at the store, Miss Bickles, the clerk, greeted them with a furrowed brow, as much to say 'Not again'. She finally asked if she could help.

"Yes." Clay pointed to Shae. "I would like some suitable clothes for my daughter to wear to school."

Mumbling to herself as to what size the girl would need, she allowed that maybe she had best measure Shae. She got out a tape measure, walked over to Shae and lifted the inside tag of the dress she had on. "This is a size ten, and I'd say a little small. She might be able to get two seasons from a size larger." She waited for Upshaw's nod of agreement.

"We will wait and see how it fits," he said. "I don't want her to look different. She will also need some under things and shoes."

"These are what I want, Papa." Shae handed him a pair of overalls and a Mexican hat with balls around the brim. He laid them on the counter.

After measuring Shae for her chest size, Miss Bickles threw the tape over her shoulder and took a size-twelve blue gingham dress from the rack. But it swallowed Shae up in the bodice.

"Let's try this one with the red ruffles in a size ten. With your brown eyes and black hair, you'll look beautiful in it." She slipped the dress over Shae's head, tied the sash, and stood back. "Perfect."

Clay nodded in approval, and said she would need another one in the same size. "She really needs three, but we will have to wait for another payday."

Miss Bickles rummaged through the rack and found a solid blue one in the same size. Shae liked it. The clerk led her to the counter of panties and slips. Sighing, Miss Bickles folded her arms against her chest while Shae tumbled the undergarments around.

"Don't you have any black sateen bloomers?" Shae asked with disgust.

"But child…. Sateen's too hot for summer, especially black." She picked up a pair of dainty cotton ones. "These would be nice with your pretty dresses, don't you think?"

"All right," Shae added two more pairs in different colors to the ones in Miss Bickles' hand. "I don't like short bloomers."

Giving up on Shae, the clerk walked back to the counter and left Shae with her papa to pick out shoes and stockings.

Standing alongside his daughter, Upshaw watched her try on three pairs of tennis shoes. When she finally found the pair she liked, he agreed with her choice. Placing them in a box, she put her old pair back on, picked up two pairs of stockings, and went to the counter, where Miss Bickles stood with gathered eyebrows.

"You will need some garters to hold your stockings up." Miss Bickles walked to another counter.

"Wait a minute, lady." Clay carefully counted his money. "I was countin' on five dollars for the clothes. I only have seven dollars. Maybe you'd best figure it up before you add anything else."

"The garters are only ten cents, Mr. Upshaw. If you should run short, I will throw them in free."

"I wasn't looking for a handout, lady." Clay held the money in his hand. "She can make do with a string."

"No…No." The clerk worked at the figures. "Our summer sale starts next week. Since your daughter will be in school," she cracked her first smile of the day, "I'm going to give you the benefit. The bill comes to four dollars and seventy-eight cents."

"But you forgot the overalls," Shae said, pushing them toward the clerk, then glanced at her papa for approval.

"Oops." Miss Bickles look for Upshaw's nod. When he remained motionless, she asked, "Do you want her to have the overalls?"

"I'm afraid not, Girly. We will have to wait until another time. You wouldn't want to go home without a hamburger, would you?"

"No," Shae admitted. "But could we swap one of the dresses for them?"

"Not today. You will have to have two dresses to keep clean."

Blinking back tears, Shae put the Mexican hat on, tied the strings under her chin, and picked up her packages.

Sighing a long sigh, Miss Bickles stashed the overalls back on the shelf, mumbling, "Thank heaven it only happens once a year."

It was straight up twelve noon when Clay hitched Sandy to the hitching post at Powell's hamburger joint. Sandy was in a lather, and she drank thirstily at the watering trough.

The minute Shea and her papa entered the restaurant; she boosted her thin body upon a high stool at the counter and made herself more comfortable. Being upset, she'd missed breakfast. Now she was famished.

Sally Ward, a short, dumpy waitress who tried to hide her two-hundred pounds inside a stave corset, came puffing from the kitchen. When she saw Clay Upshaw standing at the counter, she stopped with a skid. Her face turned a pinkish-purple, and she opened her mouth to speak just as he seated himself next to his daughter. Little did he know that she had been forbidden to serve anyone but white folks, and was asking herself what she should do now?

As she stood with her mouth agape, Clay ordered two hamburgers and two strawberry sodas.

Sally walked to the icebox, lifted the sodas from the box, uncapped them, and set them on the counter. "Two hamburgers coming up," she said. She went to the stove, her eyes shifting around like a skittish kitten's. If Jack Powell caught her serving the Indians, she knew she'd get fired. Powell, like everyone else, thought if they made it hard enough on Upshaw, he'd leave the area. But that was the last thing on Clay Upshaw's mind. Cache River was his home, and Sally was sure he planned to stay here.

Clay pulled a red bandanna from his overall pocket and mopped the sweat from his face. Shae guzzled the red pop, and he smiled.

"How is school going, young lady?" Sally asked Shae as she delivered the burgers.

Shae's face lit up like foxfire at the word 'lady'. Did everyone know she was thirteen? She swallowed a mouthful of hamburger and said, "I missed last week. Papa's been sick, and we didn't have the money to buy school dresses. I got all new clothes today, and I will start on Monday."

Clay couldn't enjoy his hamburger for wondering why the waitress was so nervous. Her breaths came in short spurts, and she looked as if her corset laces should break, she would go straight through the ceiling.

When they were finished with lunch, he handed Sally fifty cents with the ticket. She put it in the cash register and handed him back a nickel, thinking they were going to get away before Jack got back. But no such luck. Shae had to have another soda pop. As she sat enjoying it, a spit-polished Irishman popped in at the front door. One look told Sally that Jack Powell was one mad Irishman.

For a split second, the small two-by-four man stopped and sized up the tall Indian before he turned on the waitress with blazing eyes. "You didn't feed these redskins at my table, did you?" He turned and looked at Upshaw. "Can't you read?"

Upshaw stood puzzled. "Read what?"

"That sign over the door says *whites only!*" The Irishman's eyes flashed fire. "And that's what it means."

Stunned, Clay stood confused for a moment, then stammered, "I'm s-sorry, Mr. Powell. I guess I don't know what you're talking about. Was the sign over the door when I was here before?"

"No." Powell looked Shae over with a critical eye. "That was different, but I have a fine young son growing up, and you never know what notions a growing boy might get." He crossed his beefy arms over his chest. "I would rather you didn't bring that young squ…"

"Why you snivelin', little skunk!" Clay hissed, squeezing his big bony hand into a fist then relaxing it. Livid, he grabbed the Irishman by the collar, lifted him up on his tiptoes.

Powell's face contorted and his eyes bulged out until he blurted, "But I meant no harm, Mr. Upshaw. What am I supposed to call her? I just didn't think!" He tried to squirm away, but Upshaw held on.

"You slimy little weasel! Don't you ever call my daughter a squaw! I should stomp you through the floor. She's an Indian princess, and be sure you call her that from now on!"

Clay shook the Irishman a good one, spat on his bald head, and then shoved him away. "Now stay out of my way before I *really* lose my temper!" He looked around for Shae, but she was gone. Glaring at Powell, he added, "I won't be back here to eat, but I will be in Cache River. That's my home and there are not enough white folks in the town of Braden to chase me away. You remember that!"

Jack Powell made his way to the kitchen, wiping the spit from his head on a soft, white handkerchief. Sally stood holding the phone receiver in her hand, but she couldn't remember if the sheriff's ring was two long and a short, or two shorts and a long.

"Don't bother to call the sheriff, lady," Clay said. "I won't be back here to eat. I was unaware of the sign over the door. If my daughter's not welcome, neither am I."

Clay walked out of the building and went to the hitching post, feeling terrible about losing control again.

CHAPTER 7

❈

Inside the burger joint, Sally held the phone receiver at half-mast until Jack Powell barked from the kitchen that he'd like to have a talk with her. She walked into the kitchen, untied her apron, and shoved it toward Powell, shouting through gritted teeth, "I quit!"

"What's this?" Powell tossed the apron aside. "You can't walk out on me in the middle of the lunch hour!"

"Why not?" Sally shrugged? "I have never ordered anyone from my house, and I'm not starting now. Not for Jack Powell or anyone! That Indian's money is just as green as yours, and he is one of the most polite men that I know."

Sally turned to the counter for her purse. "And," she added, the child "is a girl without a mother."

"Just a minute, Sally. Can't we talk this over?" He walked closer. "I know I should have handled it differently, but…."

"But you have talked too much already. To call a child a squaw, you are a disgrace."

"I know, Sally, but when it comes to your son's future, you might do the same. I spoke in haste, and I'm sorry."

Sally held her ground. Job's were hard to find in Braden, a one-horse town with only a combination grocery-post office, a filling station, two hamburger joints and a doctor. But people called it 'town'.

"Sally...." Powell followed her to the door. "I've been thinking I need to give you a raise. What do you say? Will you stay?"

"How much of a raise do you have in mind, Jack? I can always go back to King's, you know."

Antsy, Powell thought in a jiffy and offered, "How about two-fifty a day?"

"Well, since we're on the subject, and I'm doing two jobs, I don't think three dollars would be out of reason." Sally stood in the doorway, awaiting his answer.

Powell stalled, but he had no choice. He'd heard the rowdy bunch of timber men at the hitching post, and he knew if he didn't feed them, they'd go to King's. "All right," Powell wrung the words from the corner of his mouth. "We got a deal. Three bucks a day, nine-to-nine."

Sure enough, by the time Sally tied her apron, the joint was bustling with a dozen lumberjacks, tie-cutters, and sawmill workers. After taking their orders, she went into the kitchen to flip hamburgers while Powell meandered, making conversation with the glutinous crowd.

"I heard you had a little trouble with the Indian a while ago," said Sam Smith, a big-mouthed lumberjack.

"Yeah," Jack went about pouring coffee for the men. "I should have thrashed him good, but I have to think about business."

"Jack," Sam laughed. "You better take a fool's advice and leave that Indian alone. He ain't lookin' for trouble, but you get him riled, he can whup two of us with one hand tied behind him."

All the ruffians let out a big horse-laugh, and Sally laughed into the hamburgers when she remembered how scared Powell had been when the Indian had held him close and threatened to stomp him through the floor.

When Clay got out to the hitching post, Shae was nervously calming Sandy. The filly was hungry and anxious to be on her way home.

"We'll be goin' now," Shae said, patting Sandy when she saw her papa coming toward the cart. He stopped once as if he didn't know what he should do, go home, or go back and finish the Irishman off.

"Hurry, Papa." Shae climbed into the cart. "Sandy's starvin'. She wants to graze on green grass."

"I know, Girly." Clay crawled clumsily over the cart wheel and picked up the check lines. "All right, Sandy, we're on our way." He touched the filly on the rump with the willow switch he'd tied buckskin strips onto the end of. It only tickled her, and horse-sense told her that it meant 'take it easy'. But the horse was anxious to get home, and Clay had to saw on the bits to hold her back.

"Why do you hold Sandy, Papa? We'll never get home, and I'm dyin' in this heat."

What could he say? He couldn't just blurt out that Sandy was going to have a baby. Could he? After a moment, he said, "Sandy needs to take things easy. She's looking for a baby."

"Honest?" So excited she almost swallowed her tongue, Shae asked, "When will she find it? Where do you think she's lookin' for it?"

"It won't be before spring. You see, she has to plan for it, like your mama and I did for you. Then one day she will come home with it, walking on all four feet."

"Papa, will it be like Shadow findin' her kittens in the cypress stump?"

"Uh-huh."

Shae thought for a minute then asked, "Papa, where do babies come from? Where did you and Mama find me?"

Still shaken up from the trouble at the hamburger joint, and without an easy answer, he said, "The doctor brought you."

Satisfied for the moment, Shae sat thinking. She knew her papa was tired and upset. For a while, they rode with the dust fogging around the cart then she broke the silence with, "Papa, what's a squaw? Are they ugly?"

Still shaken, he said, "Girly, there's no such thing. It's a slur people use on Indian women, people who have not been taught better."

"Why did you get so mad when the man called me that? The kids at school call me squaw. Mary Crawford called me a half-breed."

"I don't know, Shae. People say things. It's just scorn."

Shae knew as much about scorn as she did fractions. She looked straight into her papa's troubled eyes and asked, "What's scorn?"

"Girly Shae, would you like to move away from the Cache River, closer to our people, across the Mississippi?"

"What do you mean, Papa? We can't leave our cabin…Scar…. We have to be there when the spring flowers bloom, so we can take them to Mama's grave. And what would Sandy think if she came walking home with her baby, and found us gone? We can't go away, Papa! Never!"

"It was just a thought, Girly, that you might be happier."

"Papa is it 'cause the man called us redskins that makes you want to go far away to our people?" Shae looked at her papa's weary-face. He wasn't mad anymore. He looked older, somehow. Beat down.

"We'll talk about it later, Girly. There are other things we need to talk about when we're not so hot and tired." Then he sat thinking of the first year of his and Dora's marriage, when love was young, when they'd built their cabin log by log, when their happy expectations of Shae—

Shae had taken her first steps, and learned to say 'Papa' first, which Dora said was a sign that the next baby would be a boy. His memories ran on and on until Shae broke his train of thought.

"Papa, tell me you won't take me away from Cache River!"

"Getup, Sandy." He left Shae's demand unanswered, and tapped Sandy on the rump with the switch. They rode along without a word the rest of the way home.

When Sandy stopped at the horse-lot gate, Shae grabbed her packages and ran into the cabin. She didn't stop until she got to her room, where her mama's tin-trunk sat at the foot of her bed. Two of her mama's Sunday dresses still lay folded in the trunk. Shae had often held them up to her frail body, wondering if she would ever grow to fit them, or if her papa would want her to wear them. But right now, she had other things to think about. She needed to look about for Scar first thing. Raising the lid of the trunk, she dropped the packages, and closed the lid without looking at her new dresses.

Changing into her overalls and shirt, she was soon at her papa's side. Sandy had drunk her fill of fresh water, and stood snorting it on the ground.

"Sandy." Shae rubbed noses with the filly. "I know where there's a patch of green grass, if papa says I can take you there. Can I, Papa? She missed her breakfast, same as me."

"Only if you promise to keep her out of the river, and stay out yourself." Her papa waited for her answer.

Promising him faithfully that she would, she led Sandy to the stump nearby, straddled her, and rode slowly down the path. When she got to the water oak, she tied Sandy to a sapling, rushed to Scar's den, and tried all her little tricks to bring him out. But she found no sign of him. Discouraged, she led Sandy on down the river to the patch of grass she promised the horse, near the edge of the water. Sandy was so hungry she started munching grass before Shae could get the bridle over her neck.

"Just a minute," she scolded as she tied the reins to a branch just over her head. "This means you stay right here!"

While Sandy grazed, Shae found a cool, shady spot, and sat thinking over the events of the day. She had never seen her papa so upset. Then school crossed her mind. If she couldn't fake a chill or a bad headache, she'd be in that old hot school house this time Monday.

"And Miss Trisha will be sayin', 'Shae, you are going to have to study hard to catch up with your class'. And she'll want me to say all them proper words. She's always sayin, "Shae, don't forget your 'Gs'. And the kids will snicker."

While Shae sat thinking, she noticed two big, brown tarantulas battling it out while another sat on the sideline, seemingly enjoying the affair.

"What's the trouble?" She pulled them apart. "I don't think you will settle it that-a-way." Tossing them in opposite directions, she watched as they crawled back together and locked long feelers with each other, rolling over and over until one admitted defeat and crawled into the tall grass. The winner bounced cockily toward her, with what Shae thought was a grin on its face.

What, she wondered, could they be fighting about?

When Shae looked around at Sandy, the filly was inching down to the edge of the river. "No, Sandy!" Shae jumped up and ran to catch the horse. "I promised Papa! You can't go into the river!"

Shae led the filly back to the grazing spot, and started back to the shade when she heard the black stallion nicker out in the timber. Sandy answered his call. Before she could get back to the horse, Sandy splashed into the water and was halfway across before Shae shed her shirt and overalls. Being a good diver, she hit the water close behind the filly and caught the bridle, but Sandy jerked away, and went headlong across the river. She was halfway up the bank before Shae caught her again. The black stallion stood at the edge of the river.

Shae had quite a tussle with her horse, but she pulled hard in the bridle bit until Sandy followed her back across the boggy river.

Making sure she tied Sandy fast to a sapling, Shae hurried to her clothes and dried her hair on her shirt. Her papa would be along any minute if he didn't go to sleep. He'd said he was going down to his favorite mussel shell hole to dig shells after he rested.

Shae slipped into her shirt, and had one leg into her overalls when she looked up and saw her papa's boat gliding around the curve.

"Oh…no," she moaned. "It was all Sandy's fault, but he'll never believe me."

She got into her overalls and stood buckling the galluses as her papa banked his boat and sat staring at her. Like a lamb at slaughter, she stood waiting for the verdict. It seemed that his eyes were locked, and would never turn away from her. Then finally, he spoke. "Just as I expected, Shae. Promises mean nothing to you anymore. Why do you defy me this way? I can't trust you out of my sight anymore. What if Jake Crawford had come along before I did? He'd like nothing better than having Sheriff Brody after me. You wouldn't want that, would you?"

"No." Shae dropped her gaze to the ground. When she looked up again, she said, "I'm sorry, Papa. I didn't mean to go in the river, but the black stallion nickered across the river, and Sandy jumped in. I had to catch her. You said you didn't want her runnin' with him."

"I don't." Clay looked around. "Where is he now?"

"He went away when I caught Sandy." Shae thought for a moment. "Papa, is that why Sandy's lookin' for a baby?"

For a moment, her papa stood looking into her brown eyes. Maybe nature was telling her what he didn't know how. "Could be, now take the filly home, put her in the lot, and wash the dishes for your papa. I don't want you playing around the dock alone."

"Why, Papa? I can't sift sand and bait the trotlines if I don't go to the dock."

"Don't know. I guess your papa will have to get up earlier and work later. I want you to go to school and learn to be a lady. If something should happen to me, you would have to take care of yourself. Besides, you will grow up and marry someday. You will need to know how to keep house, and be a mother."

"A *mother*?" Shae looked at her papa as if he must be out of his head, like when he had a chill. "How could I be a mother? I never even touched a baby."

"I know. I know...Girly, but you're only thirteen. Most girls don't marry until they're eighteen, or twenty. Run along now. Get yourself washed up and put on one of your pretty dresses. I want to see how they fit."

Taking Shae's foot into his hand, Clay boosted her upon the filly's back, and she rode toward home. He got into his boat and oared to his favorite mussel shell spot. He always grabbed a boatful from that hole, only he had to wait a week or ten days between hauls.

Shae stopped at the water oak as she passed, but still didn't see Scar. There were snake tracks, and she was sure they belonged to him. Jock had hardly been back to the dock since Shae's papa had whacked him across the nose, and he was still mad at Shae. He hunted rabbits, and if her papa happened to stay out too late, the wolf dog went looking for him. The brindle cat was scared to come out of the Sweet Gum tree when Jock was around.

When Clay came home from the river, Shae had the house all spick n' span, but she was still in her chopped-off overalls and a short-sleeved shirt.

"I thought sure," Her papa complained, "I'd get to see you in one of your new dresses. I like the one with the red flounces. Is that what Miss Bickles called them?"

"Ruffles, Papa."

"Ruffles.... I guess I don't know much about girl stuff, but I know you're going to look like a princess in them."

"Why do you want me to look like a princess, Papa, whatever that is? That's what the minister said that his wife wanted with me, to dress me up like a princess. But I don't want to be a princess."

"But, Girly, Indian princesses are beautiful, and that's what your mama would want you to be."

"Papa, all we have for supper is sardines and crackers," Shae said, changing the subject. "Unless we fire up the stove. But then it will be too hot to sleep."

"That'll be fine," he agreed. He was almost too tired to eat at all. He'd grabbed a boat load of dark-purple mussel shells in three hours, and he could hardly wait to get a knife into them. Most of the pearls he'd ever found were in purple mussel shells.

After her papa dozed for an hour, Shae called him to supper. The milk he'd gotten from Dolly that morning was soured, but churned up, it was better than water.

"A good supper, Shae. Papa knew you could do it."

After eating two cans of sardines and a stack of crackers, he left the table, went to his chair, and picked up a book. He loved reading, but there wasn't much around, usually only old newspapers he picked up when he hauled off the shells. But they were new to him.

"Girly, give the sardine cans to the cat to lick. It will clean them. They make an awful stink if they're left around."

"What do you plan to name that critter, anyway? It is worth some kind of name. Looks like it might grow into another tom cat one day. How about…Hobo? That's what he was doing when you found him. Hoboing. I'd say he's perfectly happy here."

"And I love baby kittens."

Shae set the sardine can on the porch and watched the kitten dive its head into it.

Clay was so bushed he got up from the table, went back to his rocker, and fell sound asleep.

After Shae cleared the table, she went into her room and gathered her books together. She had not cracked them since school was let out last spring. She dreaded to go back, knowing that she would be a week behind her lessons.

The sun had gone down and a slight breeze stirred the curtains at her windows. She straightened the mosquito net over the head of her bed, undressed and lay down next to the yellow kitten coiled up on her pillow.

"Know what, kitten? You have a name. Papa says you're a hobo. Would you like that for a name? I think it fits you."

The kitten purred as she stroked its mangy fur, but it wasn't as skinny. She could no longer feel every rib, like when he'd followed her into the snag.

"I'll take you to the dock tomorrow. You can fill up on mussels."

Shae had hardly relaxed when her papa called, "Girly Shae, would you care to pump your papa a fresh drink? The salty fish are calling for water."

Shae's papa thanked her over and over after he'd swigged two gourd dippers of water, and she went back into her room.

It was hours before she closed her eyes for sleep. Wolves howled across the river. Hoot owls hooted. Bullfrogs croaked for rain. Then, too, all the pesky feelings kept jabbing at her, and she wondered about so many unanswered questions. She flounced around, turned over and over and then lay still in her innocent trap, thinking and thinking and thinking....

Why do I have to do this, and not do that? Why? Why? Why?

CHAPTER 8

❧

Sunday morning dawned with a cloud cover and a light breeze stirring the leaves in the trees. Clay was up early, anxious to crack the purple mussel shells. He couldn't believe the size of them. He hadn't found that many in the last week, much less in one afternoon. Every pearl he'd ever found had been in a purple mussel shell.

"Roll out of bed and get up," he called to Shae, "if you want to go to the dock with me today."

Taking the water bucket from the shelf, he went straight to the pump. He was starved for water. He told himself that he wouldn't be guilty of eating sardines for supper again, but he wouldn't mention it to Girly. He primed the pump and filled the trough half full of water, before he opened the lot gate and let Sandy out. When she drank her fill, the filly nickered for the stallion, but got no answer.

Deciding to let Sandy run free for the day, and hoping she'd come home by nightfall, he held her fodder up. Dolly had lain out, which meant they wouldn't have fresh milk today. What he'd milked yesterday had soured, but at least it would make butter for breakfast.

After pumping a bucket of water, he went into the cabin, filled the coffee pot, and kindled a fire in the cook stove. He and Shae had to have something substantial for breakfast. They couldn't work on sardines and water.

"Will you grind a half cup of coffee, Girly?" He handed her the grinder as she came toward him. "I will mix up a pan of biscuits to go with our simple syrup. Soon as we're done, Girly, we need to rush and get to the shells, before the sun decides to pop out." After a moment, he added, "Though it might come a shower. It's time for the moon to full. That's the way our forefather's predicted the weather before almanacs."

Shae waited for the water to boil, added the ground coffee, and watched it boil to the top of the pot. She put the lid on and slid the pot to the back of the stove to simmer. Then she watched her papa choke out the biscuits, and squash them into an iron skillet. He then melted meat grease and spooned it over the tops, and set them into the oven.

"Papa, why do you snuggle the biscuits so close together?" Shae asked as she went to the cupboard for coffee cups.

"So they can help each other rise. If you watch me close, you can soon be mixing the biscuits."

Since it looked like a messy job to her, Shae didn't think much of that idea.

After they'd eaten their soakie, Clay filled a jug with fresh water to take along to the dock. It wouldn't be cold, but it would be wet.

Shae pitched three biscuits out the door for Jock. He caught the first one, carried it under the cabin, and came back for the others. He gratefully eyed Shae until she said, "Stay home, Jock. We don't need your help at the dock." With his tail between his legs, he returned beneath the cabin. Shae felt a little sorry for Jock, but she knew Scar would not come from his den if he smelled the dog around.

When Shae and her papa reached the dock, she exclaimed, "Oh, Papa! How did they grow so big? You have never found mussels this size!"

"They grow fast in August, when the days are long and hot. Here." He took two pocket knives from his pocket, opened them, and handed one to Shae. "You open," he laughed, "and I will whittle the niche from the pearl."

They opened and probed until about noon. The water jug was near empty, and they were famished. Overhead, a dark cloud gathered and thunder rumbled. A few streaks of lightning flashed, but Clay thought it was dry weather lightning. He was hoping he and Shae could get all the shells cracked, so he could go to Elm Slough the next day. But when the wind began to howl through the timber, he wiped the blades of the knives, folded them up, and stuck them back into his pocket.

"I think we'd better head for the cabin, Girly. The lightning is too dangerous among these trees."

Shae grabbed the water jug and followed her papa toward the cabin. By the time they reached it, big drops of rain splattered in the dust. But the clouds went around without enough rain to settle the dirt. The storm was a complete hoax.

Knowing that she'd have to leave early Monday morning, Shae busied herself in her room, collecting her books. The thought of school still gave her a knot in the stomach. She thought of the taunts and name-calling. Maybe if she wore one of the new dresses, tennies and stockings, the other kids would treat her differently. Since she couldn't think of an excuse to stay home, she stacked her books together.

While they were home and the weather was cool, Clay made good use of the time by churning fresh butter and baking corn bread. They enjoyed a good lunch, after which he sat down to rest his weary bones, and said to Shae, "Girly, don't forget to pump a tubful of water to warm for your bath, tonight. You won't have time in the morning."

By the time Clay woke from his nap, the storm had blown over and he decided they'd best go finish the shells. It was still a lot cooler than it had been all week.

They were halfway to the dock when Shae looked back and saw Jock sneaking along through the bushes. "Jock!" She stomped a foot. If Scar got one whiff of the wolf dog, he'd never surface, although she was beginning to wonder if he ever would, anyway. "Go back home!" To her relief, Jock took off back to the cabin.

After they had worked awhile, Shae got tired and asked if she could paddle her feet in the river near Scar's den. She'd been keeping an eye out for the wolf dog, and hadn't cracked many of the shells. "I know," she said to her papa, "that he ought to be healed by now. He's afraid of Jock. I think we should tie Jock up for a few days."

Clay didn't pay much attention to Shae's suggestion. She was just still mad at Jock. When she asked him again, he simply said they needed to get the shells finished.

Preoccupied with Scar, Jock and school, Shae hadn't even thought of a pearl until she heard her father whistle. She looked up to see his eyes bug out at the gristle in his hand. He fished his knife from his pocket, exclaiming, "Wow!" She realized he must have found a mollusk gem, one of the most sought after pearls on the market. He opened the knife and whittled at the niche with extra care.

She could hardly wait while he slowly worked. "Papa, does it have a pearl in it?"

"Hope so, Girly. I'll be awful disappointed if it doesn't."

When he finally got the niche cut away enough to split the cover and work away the soft nest bed of the gristle, there it was. A beautiful, pink pearl, not as big as he had hoped, but it was a real one.

"How much is it worth, Papa?" Shae beamed at it. "Now we can buy a loaf of light bread to make sandwiches, and the smart-aleck kids won't be snickerin' at my funny biscuits."

"That we will do, and some bologna to go with it." He eased the pearl, bed and all into his pocket for safekeeping. "Now we won't have to hock Mama's ring to Murphy again. The pearl dealer should be around any day, now. Hopefully, I can get this to him before we run out of groceries."

Clay's only concern was keeping Murphy from getting his greedy fingers on the pearl before the dealer came around. Despite that, and knowing that he had a grubstake for a few weeks, he slept soundly that night.

Shae woke on Monday morning to the sound of her papa pounding nails, and she knew he was punching holes into the lid of a lard bucket for her to carry her lunch to school in. He'd told her that it kept the biscuits from sweating when he packed them warm.

"It's time to get up and get dressed, Girly," he called into her room. "You don't want to be late the first day."

Crawling drowsily from the bed, she went to the kitchen to wash her face. "Papa?" She dried her face on a flour sack towel. "Do I have to wear the ruffled dress today? The kids might let me play leapfrog with them, and I can't play with that dress on."

"I'm afraid so, Girly. The teacher will frown on a girl in boy's clothes. Besides, girls didn't play leapfrog with boys when I went to school."

Shae pulled the fish cords from her braids and asked, "What did kids play when you went to school, Papa?"

"Oh…" He flipped a flapjack. "…we played wolf-over-the-ridge, farmer-in-the-dell, hopscotch, and we danced around the Maypole. And London Bridge was a good game." He flipped another flapjack and forked the fatback onto a platter. When he noticed Shae take the comb from the box under the looking glass on the wall, he suggested, "How about we eat before you dress? Then I will help you with your hair. You know what we forgot Saturday? Ribbons."

"Fish cord holds better." Shae took her place at the table and patted Hobo as he jumped up beside her, meowing for food. When her papa set the food on the table, she cut a corner from one of the flapjacks, smeared it with butter, and poured sugar syrup over it. Then she forked a bite to Hobo.

Nibbling on her food, she asked, "Papa, did kids say mean things to you when you went to school?" Tears welled in her eyes as she forked Hobo another bite of her breakfast.

Without answering her question, he asked, "What do the kids say?"

"Nothin'." Shae left the table and went to her room to dress.

"Whee-eee!" her papa whistled when she came out in her red, ruffled dress. "You're going to be the prettiest girl in school today."

Picking up the tin-bound comb, Clay motioned her to a cane bottomed chair, and combed at the tangles in her long, black hair. He told himself there wasn't a girl in school with hair as pretty as hers. When he got the tangles combed out, he parted it in the middle and said, "You do one side and I'll do the other."

Still wondering what the children had said to her, he asked, "What do the kids say to you, Girly Shae?"

Shae's chin quivered and she looked down at the floor.

"Tell me. What do they say?"

"Awful things, Papa. They won't hold my hands. They…they all hold on tight when I try to break the ring at play. One girl said my hands smell like fish worms."

"Ah," Clay sighed, hurting as much as she was. "We know that's not true. You had a bath last night. Your clothes are clean. Ignore them, Girly. You couldn't look better. Remember, words can never hurt you. Sometimes, kids say things they don't mean."

With her papa's hard-to-follow advice, Shae gathered her books, picked up her lunch pail, and walked slowly toward the door.

"Good-bye, Girly." Clay patted her on the shoulder. "Be sure to come straight home from school. I'm going to try to see the gem buyer today. I might be late."

"I will, Papa," she said, and marched off to school.

Shae heard the kids shouting and laughing before she got in sight of the schoolhouse. It sounded like fun. She hurried on, hoping that they would hold hands with her, but first she had to put her things away. Inside the schoolhouse, she went to the old seat she'd sat in last spring. She found the desk piled with books, and the arithmetic paper had Ted Brody's name on it.

"Miss Trisha?" Shae walked toward the blackboard where the teacher was working on a math problem. "Where can I sit? Ted Brody has my seat."

"Oh, good morning, Shae, It's so good to see you. What a pretty dress you have on."

Shae's face lit up as Miss Trisha thought for a moment. "Let's see...." She walked down the aisle and stopped at the fourth seat. "I have a nice seat for you, across from our new girl. You will like her, Shae. Jenny's her name. And to make it double nice, she's in your class."

Shae didn't know about that, but she had no choice. She placed her books inside the desk and set her lunch bucket on a shelf with the others, then rushed outside to where the kids were playing ring-around-the-rosy.

"Hi!"

She stood for a minute, and when no one spoke to her, she tried to break into the ring. The kids wouldn't break away.

"Don't let her in," Mary Crawford prompted the girl next to her. Tossing a curl back over her dainty white collar, she added, "She plays with snakes."

"And her hands smell like grub worms," said David Spincer.

"Besides," added Tracy Allen, "she's a redskin."

Hurt as they knew she would be, Shae remembered her father's advice, and turned to walk away. Butch Thatcher accidentally tripped her on purpose. Picking herself up, she brushed her stockings and walked to the Catalpa tree, where she'd suffered through so many games. Another girl sat next to Shae, her dark calico dress pulled down to her shoe tops. And she was crying.

Shae looked her over. "What's the matter? Won't they let you play, either?"

"No." The girl kept her head on her knees, sobbing. "They said I looked like an alley cat."

"Of course you don't." Shae reached for the girl's hand. "Want to play with me? I'll be your friend."

"If you want to."

Clasping the girl's hand, Shae ran with her to the schoolhouse steps. Just as they sat down, Butch Thatcher yelled, "Whatta you know! The river rat's makin' friends with the alley cat!"

All the kids laughed, but clammed up when they saw Miss Trisha walk out the door. Butch had his back to her, and had no idea she was there until she touched him on the shoulder.

For what seemed like a full minute to Butch, her angry dark eyes held his without blinking. Finally, she said, "Butch, would you care to tell me what that smart remark was about?"

Butch was speechless, shifting from one foot to the other. Then he whined, "I wasn't the only one pokin' fun!"

Wheeling Butch around, she marched him into the schoolroom and pulled the five-minute bell.

Admiring the new girl's dress as they sat on the porch step, Shae asked, "is your name Jenny?"

"Yes, my name is Jenette, but everyone calls me Jenny. This is my first day here. We've only lived here a week." Jenny fingered the soft gingham of Shae's dress. "What is your name?"

"I'm Shae Upshaw. My father calls me Girly, but it's only a pet name. That's what he said."

Jenny looked askance for a moment. "What does your mama call you? Did she sew your dress?"

"No. I don't have a mama. I live with my papa, just us two."

"Oh? Everyone has a mama."

Shae hesitated. "My mama died a long time ago. My papa buys my dresses ready-made."

"Pretty. My mama sews mine, but I love ready-made ones."

The books-bell cut their visit short. Shae ran to the pump for a drink, and Jenny followed.

Butch Thatcher sat with his nose in a book when the kids came inside, and didn't look up until Miss Trisha asked everyone to stand and sing 'America'. When the song was done, they took their seats.

Miss Trisha was a mite of a girl, no more than eighteen. She stood five-foot tall with shoes on, but she carried a big stick when she was riled, and she was riled, now. When she got control of herself, her pursed lips parted and she said, "Children, I am sure each one of you has heard the word loyalty defined in this schoolroom many times." Her angry eyes cut around the room. "Who will define the word for me now?"

Everyone sat as if they were blind, deaf and dumb. Not one hand went up.

Turning her stony eyes on the guilty four, she said, "All right. We will define it now. I want the four of you who were calling names on the playground, to come forward, please."

Having been caught in the act, Butch Thatcher had no choice. He slowly pushed himself from his seat and moved toward the front of the room. The other three sat staring at a book, or out a window, until Miss Trisha said, "I know who you are. Butch made sure of that." She glanced at the willow switch in the corner. "Now, are you coming or shall I…"

Before she could finish the sentence, David Spincer bounced from his seat. Tracy Allen followed.

Defiantly, Mary Crawford sat with that 'you-wouldn't-dare-strike-a-director's-child' look in her mocking eyes.

"Mary Crawford." Miss Trisha's dark eyes flashed fire. "I'm giving you one more chance to apologize to those girls. If you do not, you're going to be sorry."

With eyes blinking, her hands laced together on her desk, Mary sat until Miss Trisha came darting down the aisle like a rapid fox.

CHAPTER 9

❦

The 'you-will-look' in Miss Trisha's eyes told Mary she had to act. "My father said for me not to mix with that trash!" she cried, then burst out bawling.

The word 'trash' was hardly out of Mary's mouth before Miss Trisha was upon her. Jerking Mary from her seat, the teacher pushed her toward the front of the room. "Now," shaking with anger, Miss Trisha turned Mary around. "I want each of you to go to those girls and apologize! I will not tolerate such conduct in this school room. Mary…you may go first."

Half a dozen snickers broke the silence as the director's daughter walked humbly toward Shae Upshaw and Jenny Stevens. Miss Trisha gave no rebuke. Although her words were hardly audible, Mary mumbled her apologies, and then turned quickly in the direction of her seat.

"Back up front, Mary, please," Miss Trisha ordered.

After Butch, David and Tracy apologized and returned to the front of the room, Miss Trisha called all four to the blackboard. She handed each a new stick of chalk, and asked them to stand closer to the board.

"Now, I want each of you to tiptoe as high as you can."

David alone was reluctant.

"Come on, David," Miss Trisha demanded. She nudged him. "You can do better than that."

Satisfied, she pressed their noses to the blackboard and drew a ring beside each. "Now you may place your nose in the ring nearest you, and write the word 'loyalty' one hundred times. I will be around to count."

"Oh, no," David Spincer sighed.

"Oh, yes," Miss Trisha charged.

Since the blackboard would be occupied for some time, Miss Trisha called an exercise class in place of arithmetic. "Now before we exercise," Miss Trisha began, trying to get control of her breathing, "I would like for someone to define loyalty for the class, in case we should forget."

Three hands went up. All the children burst out laughing when Mary Crawford stuck out her tongue at the teacher's back. But when Miss Trisha turned to check on the four, they were very busy. No one told on Mary.

"All right, Amy." Miss Trisha turned her attention to the class. "You may define the word for us."

"Loyalty is caring." Amy paused to carefully select her words. "Well…it's putting your friends before yourself."

"Good. Very good, Amy. I couldn't have said it better, myself."

After a shouting ovation for Amy, the class went into fifteen minutes for strenuous exercise. A must in Miss Trisha's estimation. By the time the exercises were over, the blackboard was covered with 'loyalty', and Miss Trisha went to help count.

The rest of the day, Shae and Jenny played together. Jenny told Shae about her baby brother and Shae shared stories of her father, Scar and Sandy. Surprisingly, they discovered they were both looking forward to school the next day.

Calling good-bye to Jenny when school was out, Shae walked briskly along the dusty road on her way home. She wanted to look for Scar, and yet she was anxious to tell her papa about her new friends, and ask if he'd gotten to see the pearl dealer.

Halfway home, she heard an engine coughing and sputtering for gas. Glancing over her shoulder, she recognized the hunter's truck. When it pulled up beside her, Jeff Locati leaned his head out the window and asked, "Would you like a ride home, young lady? I'm going as far as Murphy's store."

It was tempting but remembering that her papa had told her not to talk to strangers, Shae shook her head. "My papa said I shouldn't."

"That's all right," Locati said. He pulled the gas lever down and coaxed the worn-out truck toward home.

It was a half hour before Shae got to Murphy's. She saw Locati's truck parked near his tent. He was walking toward the river and Shae knew he must be going hunting. He was dressed in his black jacket, gum boots, and carried over his shoulder a gunny sack on the end of the forked stick.

Walking very slow until the hunter was well out of sight; Shae cut behind the store and took the path to the river. She couldn't resist stopping to look at a large reef knot he'd tied the tarp down with, but she didn't dare touch it. She did put her ear to the tarp and listened. She was sure he had something in there, but it was as quiet as a sunrise. Turning, she walked to his tent, raised the flap, and peeped inside. There she saw an old camp stove and a cot of sorts. Beside the cot was an orange crate with a lantern and a clock. On the dirt floor, she noticed an open book; one of the colored pictures facing up was that of a beautiful blue racer snake. She'd never seen one so pretty, but the book confirmed her suspicions. Now she feared all the more for Scar.

When she got to the water oak, a fox squirrel swung out on a limb and barked at her. "Be quiet! Can't you see I'm hopin' my friend will come out of his den? He wouldn't like you anymore than he does Jock."

While she was trying to quiet the squirrel, she noticed Jock sneaking down the path. "Go home, Jock! Get!" She slapped her hands on her legs and stomped her foot. "We don't need your help!"

But Jock stood glaring at her until she broke off a switch and moved toward him. Seeing that Shae meant business, he tucked his tail between his legs and crept back toward the cabin.

Shae stayed as long as she dared. Her papa had told her to come straight home from school, and she felt guilty about snooping around the hunter's tent. Then, too, she was anxious to see if he'd sold the pearl. She knew if he had, there would be a surprise waiting for her, and she loved surprises.

When Shae got home, she kindled a fire in the cook stove and put on a pot of beans. It was worth the extra work because she remembered how they'd been up all night pumping drinking water after the sardine supper. Her father came home, exhausted, but with a loaf of bread and a hunk of bologna.

"Oh, Papa," Shae said happily, relieving him of the paper poke. "This is just what I was hoping for."

"Good, Girly Shae. You remembered your 'G'. It shows you're learning at school. Did you have a good day?"

"All right, I guess. I made a friend. Her name is Jenny. I stopped at the water oak, but Scar wouldn't come out. I just know he's dead."

"Give him a few more days. He might be working on a new skin."

"Did you see the pearl buyer, Papa?"

"No, I didn't catch up with him, but I saw his price list at the store. It looks like the pearl will bring us enough to keep us in groceries for a while. I sure could stand a break from that filthy water. I think I will rest until the beans get done."

Crashing into his rocker, he was soon snoring.

When Shae called her papa to supper, he was ravishing hungry. After two plates of beans, a hunk of bologna, and half of a skillet of cornbread, he allowed he'd never tasted food as good. He helped Shae to clear the table, and then went outside to pump water for the herd of stray animals, which he knew would be pawing at the watering trough by dark. After a while, Shae came out to relieve him from the pump handle, and he sat on a stump to rest.

"Girly Shae." He took the pump handle. "We are going to have to tie some new bass flies. While I finish filling the trough, will you find a jar to put bugs in? I bought some red and yellow string today. When Dolly comes home, you can gather flies and gnats while I milk her. We have beeswax, and we will need some bird feathers. The bass will be running soon, and our flies are faded. If the bass aren't hungry, they won't come up for them."

When Dolly came home, she not only gave them a full bucket of fresh milk, but a jarful of bait from the cloud of bugs attracted to her hide. Later, Shae would fix up a bee or moth, beeswax and a few tiny feathers to make a moving, live-bug bait.

The next day when Shae got home from school, she and her father went to the dock to take the catfish hooks off the trotlines, and store the lines until later. They would be fly-fishing for the bass.

"Papa?" Shae removed the hooks from the trotlines. "Our number fourteen hooks are rusty. We will need some new ones, and some fox squirrel tails."

"I know, Girly, but I doubt that I can hold my shotgun steady enough to shoot a squirrel. Maybe we can clip some hair from Jock's bristles. He won't notice the difference."

"Maybe not, but animals are smarter than you think, Papa." Shae put the hooks into a jar and straightened the trotlines while her papa wound them around a stump. "If you notice, Papa, the bass bite some flies better than others."

"How about we take a rest and talk about your day at school. Did you have another good one?"

"Yes. Jenny told me more about her little brother, and she said she was going to ask her mama if I could spend a night with her. She said that her mama is real nice. Could I, Papa?"

Clay seated himself on a log and mopped the sweat from his brow. "We will think about it. You have never spent the night away from me. Do you think you want to?"

"Yeah," She said, and studied her papa for a moment. "I think I would."

🍁 🍁 🍁

It was almost sundown when Locati came home from his hunt, and it wasn't what you would call a success. He'd caught a friendly bull snake, which had all but crawled into his gunnysack. He was tempted to free it, but decided it would make a gentle pet for kids to play with at the zoo. Maybe tomorrow he would do better.

Putting the snake into a cage, he washed up. He was as hungry as a wolf, but he'd have to go to the store before he could eat.

Low and lonely, Jeff stretched out on his hard cot and thought about Sara, the girl he planned to marry some day. He needed to make some money, though, before he could ask her. He thought of his big, wide bed at home, where he could spread out his arms like an eagle's wings, and waking up to the aroma of his mama's hot cinnamon rolls. He was envious of the boy who'd taken his previous job, for he was begging to think that this job was a demotion. Finally, he dropped off to sleep, and when he woke up, it was dark, and the light was out at Murphy's store.

So much for that. He got up and drank a dipper of the slush water from the bucket. It tasted a lot like iodine, but it was all he would have before morning. He wasn't sleepy anymore, but if he lit the lamp, the mosquitoes would eat him up. He lay back on his bed and listened to the whippoorwills. Then he thought of the footprints.

He couldn't imagine why someone would be snooping inside his tent.

It was the wee hours of morning before he slept, and sunup when he again opened his eyes. He dressed quickly. Emptying the water bucket, he hurried to the store for cornflakes and milk. It was the fastest thing he could fix for breakfast, and he was starved.

With a polite 'good morning' to the crowd of crusty lumberjacks and squirrel hunters, he bought his breakfast and made a fast exit out the back door to pump a fresh bucket of water. He was ready to die of thirst.

After half a box of cornflakes with a can of pet milk, and a cold drink of water, he dressed for another hunt. Before he left the tent, he drank all the water he could hold. His canteen only held enough for a half day, and he sweated it out as fast as he could drink it.

Black snakes and moccasins were stirring, but there was no bonus on them. After a while, his boot starting rubbing his heel and he sat on a log and pulled off the boot to find a wrinkle in his sock. While he sat there, a tiny red-bellied snake slithered into a hole.

Hank Lang had told Jeff that the stinging snake had a red checkered belly. But the snake was so small and slithered so fast, Jeff couldn't be sure. He poked his forked stick around the hole. Two more slithered from under the leaves. They were too small to catch with his stick, but he kept poking in the hole, hoping to disturb the mother. The ground worked, but he found no sign of the other snake. As he sat in the blistering sun, he kept nipping at his canteen until he was out of water. He told himself that maybe it would be best to stalk the hole in the late afternoon—that was, if he could find his way back.

Shouldering his gunnysack, he eased on through the timber. After a while, he stopped by a tree to rest. As he stood there, he saw an ugly, dark lizard pawing its way along, casting skittish looks for anything edible. His book told him that it might be one of the *Iguanidae* order. If it was an iguana, it was a large one. As it crawled closer, Jeff held his breath until it was within three feet of him. When he clamped the forked stick on its neck, it struggled. It looked as if it would get away, but Jeff held tight, put the gunnysack down in front of it, let up on the stick, and it clambered into the bag. He quickly gathered the mouth of the bag up tight, and removed the hoop. He knew he would have to go back to the tent. It was too hot to wag a load that big around the woods.

When he got to the tent, he caged the lizard and reset his traps, wondering if the reptiles he was catching would be worth their keep until he got them to the zoo.

Tired, hungry and thirsty, he went to the store and pumped a long drink of water. Then he went inside and bought bologna for his lunch and a can of sardines and crackers for supper. He wanted to stalk the hole where he'd seen the baby snakes, and he didn't want to be caught without food again.

When Jeff returned to the tent, it was too dark to run his traps, and he hadn't fed the reptiles. By the time he got undressed, it was too dark to go for fresh water. He ate the sardines with crackers, drank the stagnant water, and lay flat on his back for an hour. Then he lit the lantern and picked up his snake book to see just what he'd caught that day.

The next morning, Jeff went to his traps and found he had caught four mice and a half-grown rat. The lizard made short work of the rat and two of the mice, and begged for the others.

"What a glutton." Jeff watched the lizard as it all but swallowed the small mice whole. "I only have six traps," he grumbled. "I might have to set you free."

While hunting religiously every day all week, he stalked the hole under the log. He doubted Hank Lang's tall tales of the Cache swamp, but he knew if he asked any of the blowhards around Murphy's store, they'd probably tell him a taller tale, just to make a monkey of him. By Friday night, Jeff had captured a beautiful blue racer and a coral snake. His book said the coral was a very poisonous snake, and colorful. But he couldn't imagine his boss shouting with glee over anything he'd caught so far.

A dark blood-clot cloud lay back in the west when Jeff went to bed. A light breeze rustled the leaves, cooling the air, and he got the best night's sleep he'd had since coming to the swamp.

On Saturday morning, he rose early with new expectations. He was in the woods by sunup, and went to a place where he had not been before, and hunted hard until long past lunchtime.

Without luck, Jeff decided to head back home. Another dark cloud was coming over, and he heard thunder rumbling far off. He wasn't much of a weather prophet, but it looked as if there could be rain in that cloud.

CHAPTER 10

❀

"Girly Shae," Clay said as he got up from the table after lunch on Saturday. "I'm going to the dock to shell the mollusks we left the other day. The cloud that's gathering looks as if it might become a gullywasher. When it rains in July, it always comes a cloudburst."

"Could I go with you, Papa? We need to find some bird feathers to tie on the bass lines. We need tiny ones."

"I wish you would stay around the cabin. You need to wash your hair. The filly hasn't been home since Thursday. If she comes home, put her into the lot and latch the gate. Hope she's not into trouble."

That sounded like a good idea to Shae. Maybe they'd have time to take a ride before her papa got back. She tidied up the cabin and waited for an hour. When Sandy didn't come home, she thought of a bluebird nest in a big sweet gum tree on the river. The only problem, it was at the top of the tree. Putting her shoes on, she headed up the river. When she got to the tree, she stood looking up. It was way up there. She measured her arms around the trunk, and then started climbing. The bark was old, and it bit into her knees something awful. She would climb a while and rest, then go from one limb to another. Finally, pushing one knee after the other, she made it to the top, where she sat catching her breath and admiring the construction of the bird nest.

If her papa could see how the birds had laid one stick after the other and had padded it with feathers, he would have to say they weren't dumb birds. They had built a soft, warm bed for their babies.

Shae picked feathers of blue, grey and white, and stuffed them into her overall pocket, then sat in the top of the tree. Her thoughts went to the taunting kids at school, Miss Trisha, and Jake Crawford. Nobody could get to her now.

When she started to climb down, the bark bit into her knees. She tried to use the soles of her toughened feet, but it wasn't easy. She had taken off her shoes before she'd climbed the tree.

"Uh-oh," Shae cupped a hand around her ear. "What was that?"

Listening closer, she recognized the cry of a peeper frog. She had rescued more than one from a moccasin's jaws.

She slipped into her shoes and waited between cries. As she walked toward the faint sound, she picked up a stick. It was the time of day when everything slept. Thunder rumbled away off, but it was the quiet before the storm. When the peeper cried again, she detected the direction it was coming from, and eased along the river bank. Fifty yards away, she came to a big, dead log. The bark had fallen down around it, and she knew the bark was a moccasin's camouflage. She picked her steps carefully. When she peeped over the log, she saw a big copperhead with a tiny, green frog swallowed up to its toenails, which it had clamped around the snake's mouth, holding on for dear life. She knew one more gulp and the peeper would be gone.

As Shae stepped closer to aim the stick, she forgot to watch her step. The baby moccasin she stepped on, retaliated, and bit her just above her shoe top. It felt like a bee sting, but when the snake thrashed around her feet, then slithered away, she knew she had a snakebite. She missed the copperhead. When she cried out, it burped the peeper out and leapt into the water.

For a moment, Shae stood stunned, and then she ran down the river toward the dock. "Papa! Papa! A snake bit me!" Her screams sounded far away. Her legs turned to water and she crumbled to the ground.

Hot and tired from the load in his gunnysack, Jeff Locati had stopped under a cypress to rest. He had drunk the last drop of water in his canteen. Thunder rumbled closer and lightning streaked through the timber. When Shae's faint cry came to his ears, he listened closer. It sounded like someone saying 'papa, then he thought of the girl he's seen at Murphy's store.

Jeff hurried in the direction he thought the cry had come from. He walked up the path on the side of the river he'd been hunting on. When he heard her again, he looked across the river and saw Shae lying on the ground.

"Papa! Papa!" she called again, then she lay still.

By the time Jeff got to Shae, she looked as if she was asleep. Her long, black eyelashes lay on her brown cheeks, and she lay very quiet.

"What happened, young lady? What scared you?"

Jeff knelt beside her and stripped off his gloves.

Shae knew the voice wasn't her papa's. She was even more scared when she opened her eyes and saw the hunter stripping off his black jacket.

"What happened?" Jeff looked into Shae's frightened eyes. "Can you tell me?"

Shae pointed to her ankle. "A snake bit me."

"What kind of snake was it?" he asked, examining the fang marks.

"It was a baby moccasin. Will you call my papa? He's at the dock."

Jeff gave a thunderous whistle, then pulled his bandanna from his neck and tied it around her leg, above the bite.

"What's that for? Will you get my papa? He's down at the dock. I want him to take me home. I'm so thirsty."

"I'm sorry, young lady. I'm afraid we don't have time to look for your father. Are you sure it wasn't a cottonmouth moccasin?"

Jeff opened up his snakebite kit and looked for the right essentials. The puncture marks had gone down and her leg was discoloring. He had to do something now! He raised her knee higher than her body, retied the tourniquet, and then took out his knife.

"What's that for?" Shae tried to get to her feet when he opened the blade and lit a match to it. "If you whistle again, my papa will come. He's not too far away."

"Don't be afraid," Jeff said in a comforting tone as he eased her back to the ground and waited for the yellow ooze to start. "I'm going to have to make an incision—cuts." He changed the word when Shae looked puzzled. "It will hurt, but it's what we have to do to suck out the poison."

"No! don't cut my leg! Whistle for my papa!"

Getting to his feet, Jeff put a thumb and finger into his mouth and whistled twice more and waited. But the wind had started to howl, and his calls went nowhere. He went back to his job.

Shae was shaking and her pulse was racing. Jeff wished he had some clean water to rinse her mouth, but his canteen was empty. After one more tie of the tourniquet, the yellow ooze started, and he knew it was time to make the incisions. Shae closed her eyes when he struck another match to the blade. She hardly flinched when he made the cuts. After he'd used the suction cup for five more minutes, he stood up and yelled as loud as he could, and finally someone whistled back.

"That's my papa." Shae opened her eyes. "I want him to take me home. I'm so thirsty."

"I know. I wish we had some water."

About that time, Clay called, "Girly Shae, where are you?"

Jeff looked up and saw a crusty, ill-kept Indian running and stumbling up the river. His skin was like leather, his hair blue-black. "We need help!" Jeff kept working the suction cup. "The girl has a snakebite."

"What happened, Girly?" Clay asked, falling to his naked knees beside her. "Are you all right? What kind of snake was it?"

"It was a baby moccasin, I stepped on it, or it wouldn't of bit me. I was trying to save a peeper from a big copperhead."

Clay's skin turned pasty-gray. "Was it a cottonmouth?" He looked at the fang marks when Jeff stopped the suction cup.

"I'm sure it wasn't a cottonmouth," Jeff said. "Mister, she would be *very* ill by now. It was a poisonous snake. The coloration isn't too bad, and the swelling could be worse. I believe I have most of the poison out."

"Take me home, Papa. I want a drink," Shae kept begging. "A real cold drink."

Clay consoled Shae, and then offered a friendly hand to Jeff. "I'm sorry. I'm Clay Upshaw. I don't know how to thank you for what you have done."

"Not at all." Locati gripped Upshaw's hand with a firm shake. "My name is Jeff Locati. I happened to hear the girl calling for help. I was on my way to my tent from a hunt. I'm here in the swamp, scouting for Forest Park in St. Louis."

"I suspected so. I've noticed your truck around." Clay patted Shae's hand. "Feeling better, Girly?" He brushed her long, black hair back from her face. The wind was blowing and she wasn't suffering from the heat.

Again working the suction cup, Jeff asked, "Do you think we should take her to a doctor, Mr. Upshaw?"

"The only problem is…." Clay thought the situation over. "The doctor would likely be three miles from his office. He has a lot of typhoid right now. I think I'd as soon risk a fatback poultice. It worked on a copperhead bite on the dog."

"I am sure you know best, Mr. Upshaw, but we should get her to water. Since we're guessing at the time of the bite, I'll work the suction cup five more minutes."

"We're a quarter of a mile from the cabin," Clay told him.

When he was done with the suction cup, Locati put his kit into his pocket and started to lift Shae into his arms.

"No!" She pulled away. "I want my papa to carry me. It hurts."

By the time they arrived at the cabin, Shae was asleep. Clay barely made it to the bed with her. Hobo, her cat, lay curled upon her pillow. Clay scatted the animal away, and laid Shae on the bed. Jeff raised her leg higher than her body, put a pillow beneath her knee, and then hurried to the pump to get her a fresh drink.

"It hurts, Papa. It hurts so bad."

"We'll fix it, Girly. Stay still. I'm making a poultice like the one we put on Jock when the copperhead bit him."

Clay got out the over-cured fatback he'd been saving for just this purpose. He sliced off a thin piece, laid it on her ankle and bound it up with a piece of flour sack. When Jeff brought the water, Shae drank a whole gourd dipper full, and then she asked for Hobo.

"Who is Hobo?" Jeff looked around and noticed the yellow kitten hovering around the bed.

Shae motioned to the kitten. "My cat. I want my…cat."

"Oh, I see." Jeff picked the kitten up and handed it to her. Shae thanked him and cuddled Hobo in her arms.

"Let's lie still, shall we?" Jeff pressed her back on the pillow. "You need to be quiet, or the poison will scatter into your bloodstream."

Jeff looked out the window. Lightning flashed. Thunder cracked. He had never been in the timber when a full-blown storm had hit, and it was frightening. Then he thought of his jacket, gloves and gunnysack with the second lizard in it. He'd forgotten about it during the commotion. He dashed out the door and made a run for the sack. Before he got back to the cabin, the rain came down in torrents. He was soaked to the skin, but it was too far to his tent. The trees were swaying. Limbs were falling all around and he wondered if his tent would blow away.

When he returned to the cabin, he stashed the gunnysack on the porch, hung his jacket on a nail, and darted inside, where Clay assured him that it was just a typical July thunder storm.

"Here." Clay lifted a worn pair of chopped-off overalls from a nail on the wall. "I'll close Girly's door. Slip into these, they are the best I have to offer, but they're dry."

Jeff stepped back into a corner and changed clothes. Upshaw picked up the wet ones and hung them behind the cook stove to dry. He had stoked the stove while Jeff was gone, and put on a pot of coffee.

"I must get to my tent as soon as the rain slacks off, if you don't mind me borrowing your pants."

"Why, you can't go out into this storm. The rain might not stop until tomorrow. I don't have much to offer, but I'm going to fry some spuds and a skillet of cornbread. I'm not a bad cook, and you are welcome." He laughed, adding, "It beats snowballs."

That was the best offer Jeff had heard since he'd left home. He took the cane bottomed chair Upshaw offered, straddled it, and crossed his arms over the back of it. He watched Upshaw peel spuds. When Upshaw sliced the potatoes into the hot bacon grease, Jeff took one whiff of them and was again homesick. They smelled exactly like his mother's.

While Clay whipped up the cornbread, Jeff knocked on Shae's door. "May I come in, Shae?" he called. "I want to check your ankle."

As he'd expected, she'd fallen asleep after the cold water.

"I'm afraid," he said, turning to her father, "she's asleep and that's not good for her. Would you like to wake her?"

When her papa opened the door, Shae opened her eyes. He went to her and lifted her leg again. "Feeling better, Girly?" He put a wrist to her forehead, and found it to be cool. "Could you stay awake for me, Girly?"

"I'll try, Papa. I want another cold drink."

"Here you are, Shae," Jeff said, handing her another dipper of water.

"Thank you." She emptied the dipper and then asked, "How did you know my name?"

"I heard your father call you Girly Shae. I was sure the Girly was his pet name for you."

After rearranging the pillow under her knee, Jeff went back into the kitchen to get another whiff of supper. Clay went to the safe to get dishes for the table, as Jeff dipped water into the wash pan and washed his hands.

"Could I help?" he asked his host.

Jeff took the plates and placed them on the table, one on each side. He wanted to talk face-to-face with the friendly Indian. He couldn't remember when he'd felt so at home, and he wondered why everyone had it in for the man.

Going back in his chair, he watched Upshaw scoop the cornbread dough into an iron skillet. He knew right away the Indian could fill him in on the Cache River, but he hesitated to ask him a personal question. Finally, he couldn't resist.

CHAPTER 11

❦

"Mister Upshaw, how long have you lived in Cache River?"

"Oh, I can't remember," Upshaw said as he turned the potatoes over in the pan. "It was soon after the turn of the century." He turned, washed the cornbread dough from the pan he'd mixed it in, then dried and put it into the cabinet. "There's been a lot of water down the Cache since I came here. Like most boys when they get to feeling too big for their britches, I wanted to seek my fortune."

"Hunting and fishing must have been good around here at that time," Jeff said, watching the Indian push the skillet of potatoes to the back of the stove, and look in on the cornbread.

"Yes, there was a good living to be made here. I found the Cache River swamp to be the hunting grounds of my dreams. I have never wanted to leave, until recently...."

Jeff was sure he knew why the Indian wanted to leave, but he wasn't one to pry. Instead, he said, "You must know the history of Cache River for miles around."

Clay lifted the skillet from the stove and scooped the potatoes onto a platter before he answered. "Well, one never learns everything, but I would be hard to lose around here. There used to be good money in mink and bobcat hides. They're about trapped out, now."

Jeff thought that trapping might be easier than the forked stick. "There was a market for them, back then?"

"Memphis was a good market. A buyer came every week. But no more. Women are not wearing fur nowadays. Pearlin' and cat-fishin' is about all there is to do. Not much money in that, unless you're lucky enough to find a pearl."

"Is that right? Have you ever been lucky?" Jeff was getting to know Upshaw from the friendly look in the man's big, obsidian eyes. He could see the man was starving for friendship. "I would love to see a real river pearl."

"A few times there has been pearls in the Cache, but she hordes them. I found a nice one when I first came here…like a fisherman. The first is always the biggest."

"I see."

Clay lifted the skillet of bread from the oven and turned it upside-down on a plate. "Pull up your chair, or if you'd rather sit on the other side of the table, on the bench…. Let's eat."

"Thank you." Jeff slid onto the bench, facing Upshaw, and waited to see if the man would offer up thanks.

"Help yourself," Clay offered. "It's not much. Poor folks have poor ways, but you're most welcome."

Jeff dug into the food. It had been a while since he'd had a home-cooked meal. It smelled like his mother's. He sat filling his mouth with one fork after another, while Clay held his fork halfway to his mouth, and kept talking. It had been so long since he'd had anyone interested in what he had to say. He talked on and on about his life at Cache River.

Finally, Jeff pushed his plate back and swigged the last of the big glass of water. "Mr. Upshaw, did you ever know a man around here by the name of Hank Lang?"

"Hank Lang?" Clay thought for a moment. "Did you ever hear him called Quack? We used to have a man who worked here—or he'd talked his way to a pay check—more or less. Was he a short, plump, jelly-faced fellow with a cigar hanging from his mouth most of the time?"

"That describes him well. I don't remember of ever hearing him called Quack, though. Why was he called that?"

"I can't say, unless he was always talking like nesting ducks."

Jeff laughed. "That's the best one I've heard. Anyhow, he worked as a flunky at the zoo. He told my boss there were stinging snakes, jointed snakes, and blue racers here. My boss is not going to be satisfied until I bring a pair of one or the others to the zoo."

"Yes, that fellow was full of those tales," Clay laughed. "I think he believes them."

"He made my boss believe them. He said a stinging snake stung an oak tree here in the swamp, and killed it dead as a doornail."

"Yes, I've heard that one." Clay went to the door and peeped in on Shae, but found her sleeping. "Did he ever tell the one about the blue racer chasing him for a half mile, before he thought to step out of its way? He told one about the jointed snake, too. It's supposed to gather up its joints after being hit with a stick."

"I don't think my boss believed that one, yet he expects the impossible," Jeff said.

"I'm afraid your boss will have to wait on that one. I've never heard of a jointed snake." Clay took another bite of potatoes, and pushed his plate back. "I have heard of stinging snakes, but I think it might be mistaken for a scorpion."

Jeff kept his eye on the platter of spuds. His mother had taught him good manners, but it would be a shame for the food to go to waste.

"Maybe you can clue me in on some of the tricks of the trade on snake hunting, Mr. Upshaw. My book knowledge just isn't working at all. They're either not the right kind, or they slip the stick. At the rate I'm going, I won't make gasoline money."

"Well...." Clay weighed his words. "They are a slippery subject. Girly has always been able to play with the kings and garter snakes. I think they're like people. They sense if you love them."

"Maybe so. I came down here with great expectations, but I'm beginning to wonder if this job is a promotion or a demotion. I was sure of a check when I worked at the zoo. Now it all depends."

Jeff sat listening to the Indian's life story until he noticed the wind had calmed and the rain had slacked. "I think I'd best be going." He lifted his dry jeans from the nail on the wall, backed into a corner, and slipped them on. "I wouldn't want it to come dark on me."

"Don't rush off, son. You're welcome to stay. Oh, yes, I forgot to show you the pearl."

Jeff waited as Upshaw went to Shae's room, lifted the lid on Dora's trunk, and took the Garrett snuff box from its secret hiding place. Jeff stood in awe when Upshaw lifted the ring tenderly from the box, his hand trembling, his eyes brimming with tears.

"It was our wedding ring. Dora's and mine. I have had to hock it for groceries two or three times, but I have always managed to get it out. Money won't buy it. It's for Shae's wedding." His eyes went sad and he looked away. Would Shae have a wedding if they stayed in Cache River?

Jeff's eyes blinked at the size of the pearl. "Did you find that in the Cache? It's so beautiful!"

"Yes, but it's been a long time since the Cache gave up another one this size. I have one the size of a black-eyed pea. For some reason, they don't grow like they used to."

Unwilling to intrude on Upshaw's thoughts, Jeff turned toward the porch. The lazy lizard lay like a sleeping baby in his sack, undisturbed by the weather. Jeff took his jacket from the nail, slipped into it, and pulled on his hip boots.

"Thanks for the delicious food." Jeff turned back to Upshaw. "I've never tasted better. Get a good night's rest. If you need anything...." He stepped off the porch into gumbo mud past his ankles.

"We will be fine. Thank *you*. But for your suction cup, Girly would have been one sick girl." Clay fingered the ring in his big, river-chapped hand, placed it into the snuff box, and took it back to its secret place.

"You lazy sucker," Jeff said to the lizard, rearranging the gunny sack on the forked stick. "You must weigh forty pounds!" He pulled one boot after the other out of the sticky gumbo mud, chiding "and you might have to swim before we get home, from the looks of that purple cloud coming over."

By the time Jeff got halfway to his tent, thunder rolled and lightning forked down into the timber. "Why did I ever come to a place like this?" Chills ran up and down his spine as he tried to hurry, but there was no way he could pull his feet from the mud any faster. Suddenly, there was a crash like a shotgun blast. A big oak burst into flames and split down the middle. Half of it fell to the ground in a flame of fire. The other half stood with smoke rolling into the angry cloud overhead. Jeff stopped in his tracks, his ears seeming to burst. Afraid to stay and afraid to go, he watched the flames shoot toward the heavens, lighting up the sky until the cloud burst and quenched the blaze. The rain poured down. He was soaking wet again, and still two hundred yards from his tent.

Once he came out of shock, Jeff worked his way on toward the tent in the driving rain. Surprised to find that it was still standing, he dropped the gunny sack—lizard and all—down and hurried inside.

The lizard wouldn't drown.

The storm had cooled things off and he was anxious to get into dry clothes. His bed looked to be dry, but if it rained this way all night, he would probably be looking for higher ground by morning.

There was one good thing…he wasn't hungry. Thanks to the generous Indian. Jeff lit his lantern, picked up a Zane Grey western, and read into the night. It was the wee hours of morning before he slept. As he lay there thinking of many things, he couldn't help wondering why Upshaw kept his daughter in this overbearing, prejudiced neighborhood. Deciding it must be to stay close to his wife's grave, he turned over and over as thunder rumbled, lightning flashed, and rain poured down. His bed felt like a rock. His clock read ten. When he looked at it again, he knew it must be Sunday morning, and he was hungry. All he had in the tent was enough cornflakes for breakfast and a can of sardines.

The rain was still pouring down. For something to do, Jeff picked up the book on snakes and reptiles. Maybe it was scorpions Hank Lang had been talking about. If there were stinging snakes around here, Upshaw would know about them.

About halfway through the book, he found a poisonous scorpion with a venomous stinger on the end of the tail. The name of it was *scorpionida*, and it looked as if it should be respected.

"I'm sure Mr. Upshaw will know."

When his hunger pains overpowered him, Jeff laid the book on the orange crate bed table, and fixed his breakfast of cornflakes and milk. About the time he was half finished, he heard an awful commotion outside. By the time he got into his jeans and had untied the flap door on his tent, he saw a big Red Duroc sow tearing across the swamp with his iguana swinging from her jaws. Her brood of pigs followed, squealing for their share.

"Oh no, what next?"

Not only had she snatched his iguana, but had torn his gunny sack up in the process. How would he mend it? He hadn't thought of needing a needle. Maybe Mr. Upshaw would have some fishing line with which he could thread it back together. One thing for sure, he would have to mend it or find another sack.

By the end of the day, the Cache was creeping over the banks, and Jeff wondered if it would swamp his tent before morning. He had noticed an empty shack up the road, but he couldn't move into it without asking somebody. Then, too, he was sure it wasn't snake proof.

Dark closed in on Sunday. He ate his can of sardines without bread, and lay back down on his hard cot.

🍁   🍁   🍁

Between keeping Shae's poultice changed and pumping fresh water, neither Shae nor her papa got much sleep. It was about four in the morning when she woke up asking for cold water, and Clay went for the third time. Before he got the slush water pumped off, he heard whimpering up in the sweet gum tree, near the pump. He looked up into a pair of big green eyes staring down on him, and he was sure it was not a house cat. About that time, Jock came growling from the cabin, with his bristles standing straight up.

Clay knew there was trouble.

As Jock stood snarling, showing his long tushes, the wildcat plopped to the ground. They went together in a clinch, which could only end in a killing. Which one it would be, Clay wasn't certain. He tried to run, but his strength all but gave away. Every way he turned, the two animals were at his feet.

The cat broke away and ran for the trees, but Jock caught it by the back end and pulled it to the ground, going again for the jugular vein.

By now, Shae was at the door, wailing, "Run, Papa, run!" But her papa stood leaning against the sweet gum tree, panting for breath. The cat came back screaming and tearing into Jock. Hair and blood mixed together, and Clay was sure Jock was done for. But another big slash of his tushes brought the cat down. It tried to get back to its feet. Jock stood over it, waiting for another move. When the cat relaxed and laid still, Jock sat back on his haunches with his tongue hanging out, laughing.

"Good boy, Jock." Clay wobbled to him and patted his head. "But for you, I would have been in a bad fix." He rolled the cat over with the toe of one shoe, and noticed she'd been suckling young ones. He felt bad about her death, but he reasoned that, since it was July, the kittens should be old enough to make it on their own.

After Shae got the cold drink of water, she and her papa went back to bed and slept late. It was eight o'clock when Clay woke up on Monday morning, but he'd had little sleep since Shae's snake bite. Before he could get into his chopped-off overalls, Dolly came bawling to be milked. It had been three days since she'd been for salt, and he was sure she had lost her calf to the timber wolves, or she would have brought it home by now. It was a sure bet he wouldn't get any more rest until he milked her.

When he looked in on Shae she was sleeping soundly. He didn't want to start rattling pots and pans. She needed her rest, but he also needed coffee to get him started. It was then the brainstorm hit him. He'd milk Dolly and then he'd test the 'possum grape wine. It needed to age for a spell, but it should taste pretty good by now.

Sure enough, Dolly's bag looked ready to rupture. He milked one bucket full, poured it into the cat's pans, then poured the next one on the ground, as it was still too close to her calving, and dark yellow, and no good to drink yet. After she's licked the salt block, Dolly ran back down the path, bawling for her calf. And that confirmed his thinking that the wolves had slaughtered it. Too bad, he thought. When she had a calf that he could pen up, she would come home every night, giving them fresh milk.

The rain the previous night had filled the watering trough half full. Clay went into Sandy's shed where he kept his wine hidden, and took a gallon into the cabin. It smelled powerful when he uncorked it. He drowned two tin cups without taking them from his mouth, then sat and sipped another. After a while, digging a hole to bury the wildcat felt like no chore at all. He picked up a shovel, dragged the cat out into the woods, and buried it. Then he came back to the watering trough and pumped the trough full to running over. He felt so good. He loved everyone in Cache River, even Jake Crawford. He couldn't remember when he'd felt so good. As he stood pumping water, a song came to his mind, one that he and Dora used to sing. He cut down on *Down In The Valley*. At first he could only remember a line or two and then it all came back to him. The more he pumped, the louder he sang.

Clay had forgotten all about Shae sleeping. She woke up and saw the jug of wine on the table. It looked as if it was down a quart. What was going on? She's never seen her father drink more than a small glass of wine. And she had not heard him sing since her mama had died. She went to the door and listened. His voice was so beautiful! But it wasn't to last.

Shae looked down the road and saw Jake Crawford half-dragging Sandy behind him. She knew now why the filly hadn't come home. She was in trouble again.

Shae knew Crawford was saying dirty words from the way his big mouth was working.

"Upshaw!" he bellowed, but her papa was singing so loud, he didn't hear.

Shae darted back into the cabin. She knew if he saw her home from school that her father would be in trouble again. But she was too late. Crawford's pig eyes never missed anything.

"Upshaw!"

Crawford was right at Upshaw now, who had stopped singing and looked at Crawford.

"If you don't keep this starvin' filly out of my cotton patch, I'm gonna put a load of buckshot into her behind. Between her and that black stallion, they've knocked out or ruined an acre of cotton!"

"I'm sorry, Mr. Crawford." Clay stopped the pump handle. "I was afraid she might be into trouble, but my daughter got a snake bite on Saturday, and I have been tied up, caring for her. How much damage did they do?"

About a bale of cotton, and I'm expecting pay for it."

"Ah, c'mon, Crawford!" Clay shot back at him. "That buckshot land of yours never made a bale to an acre, and you know it."

"Well, I guess I will have to hold the filly for damages."

Crawford held onto Sandy's rope as she snorted water from the trough.

"We will see about that, Mr. Crawford." Clay jerked the rope from Crawford's hand, led Sandy to the horse lot, turned her inside, and latched the gate.

Crawford stood by the watering trough, chewing a cud of tobacco. He spat it out as Clay walked toward him.

"I see your girl's out of school again today."

"That's true, Mr. Crawford. I told you that she got snake-bit, and I don't want her walking on her leg."

A smirk appeared on Crawford's face. "A snake bite, huh?" Then he ventured a little further. "You know, Upshaw, I'd like to believe you, but it's like Sheriff Brody says, 'When a liar tells the truth, nobody believes him.'"

Clay's black eyes flashed fire. Veins stood out on his neck, but he told himself he knew what a little fire water could do to an Indian. He said, "I have proof of it."

"Who?" Crawford snarled. "That other foreigner hangin' around here?"

Determined to hold onto his temper, Clay started to walk away, until Crawford said, I'm tellin' you now, if you don't have that young squaw in school tomorrow, I'm gonna have to have the sheriff…"

With the speed of a panther, Clay went after Crawford with his fists flailing. He caught him by the collar, held a fist to his jaw, and backed him against the watering trough. "Don't you ever dare insult my daughter!" He pulled the short, stubby man up to his naked chest. "She's an Indian princess, and you make sure you call her that from here on, you stinkin' skunk!"

"I-I meant n-no harm, Mr. Upshaw. It just slipped out of my mouth!"

"What do you mean, you meant her no harm?"

It was then that the wine took over.

In the meantime, Jeff Locati had started out on his hunt, but had to go by Upshaw's for the snakebite kit he'd left at the cabin Saturday night. He'd also hoped to find a needle to patch his gunny sack. When he heard the ruckus, he stepped behind the cabin. He certainly didn't want to tangle with Crawford again. He was already on Sheriff Brody's list.

Unless Mr. Upshaw needed his help he would stay out of it.

He watched from his ringside seat. He'd arrived in time to witness Upshaw shove Crawford into the watering trough.

"You dirty rat nose!" Clay pumped Crawford's head under two or three times. "I ought to drown you!"

Jeff stood watching from his amphitheater. He almost laughed out loud, thinking he'd paid thirty-five cents at the Fox Theater for less entertainment.

Clay stood over Crawford like a cat teasing a mouse. When Crawford tried to crawl from the trough, the Indian shoved him under again and again.

Mother Mary! Jeff's hand went to his heart. He's going to drown the man! And these people will string him up to a limb without a trial!

"Hold it, man!" Jeff ran toward them. "Hold it!"

CHAPTER 12

❈

Startled, Clay fell back panting for breath. Sweat streamed down his face as he stood trembling, watching Crawford wrestle himself from the watering trough. Until he caught his breath, Clay stood looking guiltily at Jeff Locati. Finally, he said, "Thanks, son. I don't know what come over me. But for you, I might have drowned a man."

Placing a friendly hand on Upshaw's shoulder, Jeff gave it a tight squeeze, assuring the shaken man that he understood. "But remember, Mr. Upshaw, you have a daughter to think of."

"You'll pay for this!" Crawford shook his stubby finger at Upshaw. "Wait till I get Sheriff Brody! You won't manhandle him!" He picked up his hat from the water. "He'll have a gun. Wait till I tell him that you threatened to kill me."

"Calm down, Crawford. I know all about Brody." Clay tried to control a grin playing around his generous mouth. "You will get your damages, as soon as I sell another load of mussel shells. I respect the law, but you can't get money out of a clam."

"You're mighty right I will get it, when I get back here with the sheriff." Shaking himself off, Crawford hot-footed it down the road, talking to himself.

"What happened to you, fella?" Jeff tousled Jock's fur after he limped to the cat's pan, and stood lapping milk.

"We tangled with a wildcat this morning." Clay examined the gash around Jock's eye, which had swollen shut.

"What happened to the wildcat?"

"I just finished burying her. I felt bad about her death. It looked as if she was still suckling young ones."

Clay did not give Jeff the usual invite to come in. He thought of the jug on the table. He'd hate for the young man to draw the wrong opinion of him.

"I came for my snake bite kit, Mr. Upshaw. Then, too, I am in need of a big needle. An old sow tore my gunny sack apart, and snatched my lizard." Jeff retrieved the tattered sack from where he had left it, when he'd rescued Crawford.

"Yes, I'd say it won't hold snakes, anymore." Clay walked toward the shed in the horse lot. "I don't have a needle, but I have a good supply of gunny sacks." He brought Jeff two. They were better than the one he'd been using.

"Thanks a lot." Jeff took the hoop from the tattered sack and laced it into the mouth of one of the others. "Otherwise, I would have to go to Murphy's before I could hunt. I had no idea hogs would eat reptiles."

Clay chuckled. "They will eat about anything, especially these wild hogs. They learn to live on the land."

"Was your daughter able to go to school, today?" Jeff asked as he turned to leave.

"She's doing fine, but I kept her home. I hope Crawford doesn't find out. It would be one more thing for him to hang on me, when he goes to the sheriff."

Jeff got a whiff of Upshaw's breath as they talked. It wouldn't take a mathematician to figure out where the Indian got his energy to handle Jake Crawford. Grinning to himself, he left for his hunt. He would have to hunt close by until the river went down.

The minute Jeff was out of sight, Clay went into the cabin. He grabbed the jug of wine, hobbled out into the woods, and poured the potent contents into the leaves.

Shae watched her papa rinse the jug at the watering trough. "Papa," she asked when he came into the cabin, "why did you pour the wine out? It made you feel so good. I heard you singing. It sounded beautiful!"

"It's not good for me, Girly." He went about kindling a fire in the cook stove to brew coffee. He was still happy, recalling the ruckus with Crawford.

Shae looked askance. Her papa had always made 'possum grape wine, but she had never seen him drink a quart before. "Papa," she asked reluctantly, "do you think Mr. Crawford will tell the sheriff that I'm out of school today? I heard him say…"

"We have a reason, Girly." He patted her shoulder reassuringly. "Sheriff Brody's a reasonable man. He's not going to lock your papa up for no good reason. What would you like to eat?"

"I'm not hungry, Papa." Shae sat in her papa's rocker, looking fondly at Hobo sitting on the bench at the table, waiting for her to feed him. Her papa didn't take too much to the many cats around the cabin, but they kept the mice down.

As the day wore on, Clay cleaned the cabin and changed the bed clothes. So far so good. Sheriff Brody had not shown up. The river was too high to do anything. He had not yet gotten around to seeing the pearl dealer, and his pockets were about empty.

❧ ❧ ❧

About three o'clock in the afternoon, the sun popped out, and the swamp began to smoke with steam. It was ninety-five degrees, next to unbearable. Jeff Locati had hunted hard all day. It had not been all bad. He'd bagged a beautiful blue racer. At least he had one that his boss had sent him for, but to capture a mate would be a miracle. Hot and tired, he came upon a stump, where a big tree had been cut down. He swigged the last drop of water from his canteen and laid his gunny sack down. As he sat there thinking of the Indian and the firewater, he couldn't help wondering what might have happened if he had not been close by. What a coward Crawford must be to start a ruckus and then let a man try to drown him without fighting back. But, he reasoned, if the Indian had a drinking problem, these prejudiced people would have had his hide long ago.

Jeff's stomach began giving off signals for food. He had left home without breakfast, and the water wasn't doing what his stomach expected. When he got up to leave, he noticed the ground working over by the log. The tail of a reptile protruded, and it had something on the end of it. Looking closer, it resembled the bill of a hawk. He stood like a statue until the tail was a good three inches out of the ground. It had a little color, so it couldn't be the stinging snake Jake Lang had spoken of. Unable to resist any longer, he jabbed the forked stick into the ground, and it went through the stomach of a rare-looking scorpion. Catching it by the tail above the stinger, he pulled it from the ground. Its mouth fell open, its legs relaxed, and it lay dying. Too late to be cautious, he decided to take it by Upshaw's. He would know what it was, that was, if he could get it into the gunny sack without losing his blue racer. He carefully opened the bag just enough to drop the scorpion inside with the snake, and headed toward Upshaw's.

When Jeff arrived, Upshaw and his daughter were working on bass flies.

"Well." Clay looked up as Jeff walked around the corner of the cabin. "Did you have a good day, son? Looks as if you have a full bag," said Clay as he laid a new bass fly on a board. It would have passed for a live swamp fly.

"Sorry to bother you." Jeff dropped his gunny sack. "I have something to show you. I'm sure you will have a name for it. Too bad I killed it. I got excited and punctured it with a stick." Jeff opened the sack just enough for Upshaw to peep inside.

"No." Clay looked over the oddity. "Can't say that I have ever seen anything like it. Too bad you couldn't take it alive. I'd hate for it to sink that stinger into me, whatever it is."

"What do you know about the shack down the road, Mr. Upshaw? If the Cache comes out another few inches, it will flood my tent. I'm afraid to go to bed."

"It belongs to nobody. The saw mill owned them. The owner just turned them back to the land. Most of them have gone to wreck the last few years. It's not snake proof, but gumbo mud will fix that. Help yourself to it.

🍁 🍁 🍁

The Cache started slipping back into her banks the next day, but Jeff decided that the shack would be better than the tent—if he could get his truck out of the mud. And the shack would be sow-proof.

Within three days under the sweltering sun, the swamp was dried out, and the river had sneaked back into her bed, leaving tons of grennel fish high and dry in mud holes, to bake in the ninety degree heat. Everything looked favorable for a good bass run. It seemed that something always happened just before Clay had to hock Dora's ring, he thought to himself, and he was grateful.

By Tuesday, Shae's ankle looked back to normal, but she wasn't ready to go back to school. She said it still hurt when she walked on it. She knew she was going to be behind in her arithmetic, and she dreaded to get a lecture from Miss Trisha for not catching up the first day.

"Just one more day, Girly, you have got to get back in school. I'm surprised that Crawford hasn't sent Brody out already."

"I'm going down the river," Clay went on, "and throw a few lines to see if the bass are running. You stay here and rest, and study your lessons."

Her papa was no more than out of sight before Shae bridled Sandy, led the filly to the straddling stump and headed for the dock.

If Scar didn't show up for her this time, she would know he was dead.

Sandy's hooves were clapping pretty well by the time she got to the dock, and Shae caught a glimpse of the king as he leaped into the river. Scar was alive! But why wouldn't he come to her? She waited around for a while and then sat down by the stump where Shadow had found her kittens. As she sat there, she heard old Tom—her big brindle cat—squall over by the mud hole. He had landed a two pound fish. She watched as the other cats gathered to get their share. When the tearing of flesh got to be too much for her, she closed her eyes and stuck her fingers into her ears to shut out the squalling and fighting as the poor fish struggled for its life. When the commotion died, she unplugged her ears and looked up. The stony eyes of a big man stared down at her.

"Why are you crying, child?" the sour-faced man questioned.

Surprised, Shae wiped her shirtsleeve across her face, and stammered, "I-I wasn't c-cryin'. I can't stand to hear the cats tear the fish to pieces while it's still alive."

"Where's your father, child?"

The man's hard eyes locked on her. She quivered as she looked at the star on his shirt and the gun swinging from his hip. It had to be Sheriff Brody, who Jake Crawford was always threatening her papa with.

Brody's six-foot frame, huge hairy hands, and cutting eyes made him look even meaner than he was. "Where in the world did you get all of the cats?" He watched as the mob of cats walked away licking their chops.

"The people from town drop them out here. Every time a mother cat finds kittens, the people sack 'em up and bring 'em out here."

"I see." Brody changed the subject. "What's your name, child?"

Child! Shae flinched at the word. Couldn't he tell that she was thirteen? "My name's Shae Upshaw, but my papa calls me Girly. It's my pet name, he says."

"By the way…" Brody picked up a handful of sand and let it sift through his fingers. "…why do you sift the sand?"

"Cause…sometimes the shells have a pearl inside them."

"Where is your papa? I want to talk to him."

"What about?" The words slipped out, "He won't be back before dark."

"It's not child's talk." Brody gave three loud whistles. When Clay didn't answer, he turned to go. "You tell your papa that Sheriff Brody was here to see him." He walked toward Murphy's store. "I'll be back."

Shae lost no time. She led Sandy to Shadow's stump, straddled her, and raced toward the cabin. She was supposed to have stayed home. *What will I tell papa?* She led Sandy into the lot, unbridled her, and hurried into the cabin. *If I tell papa what the sheriff said, he can be gone when he comes again. If I don't, Brody might take papa to jail while I'm at school. What would I do without my father?*

Shae had her arithmetic on the table when her papa came home, and she was pretending to be concentrating on problems.

"We're having fresh bass for supper, Girly!" her papa called from outside, where he went about scraping the fish. "If you will kindle a fire and put some grease into the iron skillet, it will be hot by the time I get the fish cleaned."

Shae did as he asked, without comment, and went back to her lessons.

"Why are you so quiet, Girly Shae?" Clay asked when he came into the cabin and took a knife from the rack to butcher the bass.

Without looking up, Shae said, "My ankle is hurtin' again," meaning that she wouldn't be able to walk to school tomorrow.

"Let's take a look." Clay laid the fish into a pan and lifted her ankle, finding no swelling or discoloration." Looks fine to me, you're just tired. It'll be fine by the morning. We must get you back in school, even if I have to take you in the cart."

That did it. Shae knew she would be back in school, behind her class, with Miss Trisha after her to keep her nose in that arithmetic every minute that she wasn't in another class.

Shea slept little that night, and went to school without telling her papa that she'd talked to Sheriff Brody.

All the kids had heard about her snake bite, and Miss Trisha inquired about it and then said, "I hope you worked on your arithmetic when you felt better."

Shae stashed her books on her desk and hurried outside to see Jenny. She had noticed her friend sitting by the catalpa tree when she'd gone inside.

None of the other kids acknowledged her, but Jenny was so happy to see her. She hugged Shae, and said, "I brought an extra cookie. I thought you might be back today."

When Jenny and Shae parted to go home that night, Jenny asked Shae when she could stay overnight with her.

"I will have to ask my papa." Shae tucked her arithmetic under her arm. Miss Trisha was sending her home with a note to her papa, saying that Shae was falling far behind in class.

Shae had supper started when her father came in from fishing. The bass were running early since the river had flooded. He had filled a fish box already, and they could use the money.

Clay sat down on the bench at the table and unlaced his brogan shoes. He was bushed for no good reason. He hoped he wasn't going to come down with the chills again. "Did you have a good day at school, Girly?" He dreaded to ask, but he had to know.

"Not too bad. Jenny was there. She likes me. Mary Crawford snickered when she saw me go to my seat, but I don't know why."

Clay got up and eased his tired, aching body into his rocker. He hurt as much as Shae from the taunting children. Having been brought up on the better side of the tracks, he had never been subjected to what Girly was going through.

"Jenny wants me to spend the night with her, Papa. Could I?"

Uncertain, Clay asked, "Does her mother know she asked you? Is Jenny as old as you are?"

"She's only twelve." Shae sat two plates on the table. "But she is already wearin' tight waists. She lets the strap fall on her shoulder, so the other girls can see."

"I see." Clay's face flushed. He had not heard the word, but was sure it had something to do with growing up.

When Shae brought home the note from Jenny's mother, inviting her to stay overnight, her papa was pleased. He packed her clean clothes in a paper bag when she left for school, and reminded her to watch her manners. To most people, 'homely' would have been the word for Jenny's mother, in her faded gingham dress and her brash brown hair pulled back into a grandma-knot. But to Shae, she was a mother and even more beautiful than Jenny had described her. Her soft amber eyes welcomed Shae before she opened her mouth, but when she said 'welcome to our home', Shae beamed like a glowworm to the tips of her water-chapped toes.

Jenny had quit playing with dolls when her baby brother came along. Now she was feeling like a teenager, since she found Shae to be thirteen.

After Jenny showed Shae her pet rabbit and two black kittens, they were called into the house to play with the baby while the mother cooked supper.

Shae was fascinated by Mrs. Steven's white starched apron. She'd never seen one before. She was sure it was the thing that made her so pretty.

When it came time to set the table, Jenny asked Shae if she'd like to help. Watching every move Jenny made, she placed the plates as Jenny placed napkins, knives and forks. Shae had never used a knife and she was dreading using it. She thought she'd never fill of the chocolate pudding. Remembering what her papa had said, she refused a second helping.

After lessons were done, the girls hurried off to bed, talked and giggled under the cover until Shae got around to asking which doctor brought their baby.

Stunned, Jenny giggled. "Don't you know where babies come from?"

"Sure I do. The doctor brings them. My papa said so."

"Honest?" Jenny giggled. "Is that what he told you?"

"Sure. I asked him one day and that's what he said."

"He was only spoofin'. I suppose he can't explain things like Mama can. My mama gave birth to my brother and me, too." Jenny whispered into Shae's ear, "She told me all about it before he was born. She said girls should know all about life before their twelfth birthday."

"Really?" All ears, Shae pulled the cover over their heads and listened closely while Jenny started from the beginning and told her everything her mama had told her.

In shock, Shae sat up in bed. "That's not what my papa said. I can't believe it. How could it be?"

"Nature, Mama said, its God's way." Fluffing her pillow, Jenny yawned and turned her back to Shae, leaving her to think on it until the wee hours of the morning.

Dumbfounded, Shae walked tongue-tied beside Jenny to school the next morning. If what Jenny had told her was true, her papa had told her wrong. She'd ask him again when she got home.

Glancing at Shae's somber face, Jenny shifted her lunch bucket to the other hand and reached for Shae's. "Did I do something, Shae? Are you mad at me?"

"No." Shae edged around the subject. "I was thinking about Papa. What if he has a chill while I'm gone…? Who would bathe his head?"

"He won't," Jenny assured her as they entered the schoolyard where the kids were playing hopscotch. It was time to line up by the time Jenny and Shae got their lunch stashed away. They went to the end of the line to await the sound of the march-in bell.

"Shae," Jenny whispered into her ear, "you won't tell anyone what I told you last night, will you? Mama said it's a secret just for girls."

For a moment, Shae stood bewildered, then said, "Of course not, if you say so." She crossed her heart. "I was goin' to tell my father, but I won't."

After Shae's cross-my-heart promise, Jenny added a little more everyday to the subject of the birds and the bees. By the end of the week, Shae felt like a full-fledged teenager. Many nights she lay in bed listening to the crickets singing on her window sill, and she started to figure by nature's arithmetic. Thanks to Jenny's mother, two and two added up to four. She said nothing to her father because of her promise to Jenny. It wasn't right to tell a secret someone had shared. Yet, she still wondered about some things.

The two girls learned to ignore the taunts of the other kids, and hurried to their secret place to share lunch. Shae loved the homemade cookies Jenny brought her, and Jenny shared Shae's butter-honey biscuit.

CHAPTER 13

❁

Shae dreaded parting with Jenny everyday, but she had a long walk and she had promised to have supper ready when her father got home. Then, too, she wanted to go by the dock. Scar would be showing off his new coat—if he ever got nerve enough to come out. Old Jock had scared him half to death the last time he'd caught him.

When Shae got to Murphy's store, she cut behind it to the river path. Thinking there would be no one around; she walked close to Jeff Locati's tent. If she could untie that strange knot, she would take a peep inside the back of his truck. She knew he was catching snakes. What right did he have to take them from the swamp?

It's not right to pen them up at a zoo, whatever that is.

Shae was almost even with the truck when Jeff raised up in front of the truck, where he'd been pumping up a flat tire. He stood for a moment, staring into Shae's guilty brown eyes.

Surprised and at a loss for words, Shae shifted her lard bucket to her other hand and turned away. Seeing her confusion, Jeff dropped the tire pump and asked, "Is there something I can do for you, Shae?"

"N-no," she stammered. "I…I was just takin' the river path home."

Jeff thought of what Upshaw had called Shae when he'd ruffed Crawford up, and Jeff agreed that she did look like an Indian princess in her red dress. She looked scrubbed as a slick potato.

Wheeling around, Shae hurried down the path toward home, leaving Jeff wondering what she could be looking for. She was curious about him for some reason.

Scar stayed in his den. For all Shae's coaxing, he was still afraid the wolf-dog would be waiting for him. She went straight home from there, kindled the fire and put on the skillet. Her father had dressed out a big bass for her to fry.

As Shae rolled the fish in cornmeal, she thought of what Jenny had told her. She wanted to tell her papa, but she had crossed her heart, and could not break her promise.

The grease in the skillet was smoking-hot when Clay got home. His luck hadn't been so good, and he was bone tired.

Clay planted himself into the cane-bottom chair, tossed his straw hat into the corner, and let out a big sigh. "Did you enjoy your visit with your friend?"

Shae dodged the question. "Don't you feel good, Papa?"

Shae dried her hands and felt of his flushed forehead. "I think I ought to stay home with you, tomorrow. I'm afraid you are gettin'—or getting another chill." She added the 'G' when her father raised an eyebrow.

"I'm just tired. I will be fine when I get some of that bass under my belt."

They had not had fish since the catfish had gotten muddy, and it was a treat.

"Girly…" Clay watched as she forked the fish onto a platter and lifted the cornbread from the oven. It was getting hot again after the storm, and sweat ran down Shae's face. "…I missed you last night." It'd been the first night he'd ever spent away from her, and it was almost like she'd gone like Dora.

"I missed you; too, Papa, but I had such a good time. I got to hold Jenny's baby brother. And Jenny's mama is so nice and pretty."

"I'm glad you have a friend, Girly. I have been worried about you. We must talk after supper."

After pushing his food around on his plate, Clay got up from the table and went to the rocker. Shae went about clearing the table.

"Papa, you left all your food. Wasn't it good?"

"Yes, it was good, Girly, but I guess I wasn't too hungry."

Shae scraped the fish bones into the stove. She wouldn't want Hobo to get one in his throat. Then she asked, "Papa, was my mother pretty?"

"Not pretty…beautiful!" He looked out the window as if he envisioned her mother. "Her eyes and hair was much like yours, but her skin was as fair as lilies."

"Did she sing me to sleep at night in your rockin' chair?"

"Every night, and daytime, too, when you were a baby."

"Papa, what was it that you wanted to talk to me about?"

Clay's chin came up. He had almost dropped off to sleep. "Some things we should have talked about before now. I guess I haven't made a good mother, Girly Shae. Remember you asked me where we got you, and I told you that the doctor brought you?" His face flushed a deep pink. "I'm afraid I made a mistake. There are things you should know. Some girls are women before they're fourteen." He stammered on, "and…I-I am bad at girl-talk. I was raised in an all-boy family."

"Oh, you mean I should know where babies come from? Jenny told me, but I'm not supposed to tell. I crossed my heart."

"It's all right. You don't have to tell. I'm glad you know."

Shae watched as relief spread over his face. Then he nodded off again. It had been a long day.

When Shae woke up the next morning, her father was stumbling through the back door with a bucket of milk. "Jump up, Girly!" he called to her. "I overslept!" He went for a clean cloth to strain the milk through. "Wash up and get dressed while I fix you a bowl of Post Toasties."

While she ate breakfast, Clay made a peanut butter sandwich and poured a pint of fresh milk for her lunch.

"You must go now. You will have to walk fast."

"I need a dime, Papa, for a tablet and pencil." Shae grabbed her books and lunch bucket from the table, and reached for the dime her papa held out to her. Grabbing another nickel from his pocket, he said, "Buy yourself a dill pickle, or a candy bar."

When Shae got to Murphy's store, she stopped a moment. She heard the hunters, tie hackers, and the loafers all talking at once. She had to go in. Her pencil was worn down to two inches long, and Miss Trisha had told her to bring a new one.

Two husky men stood bellied up to the counter, waiting for Murphy to open a new shipment of *Run John Run* tobacco.

"Whee-ee!" one of them whistled as Shae came into the store. "Look at that girl today!"

Murphy raised up from behind the counter, pulled down his specs, and asked, "What's for you, kid?"

"A pencil, a Big Chief tablet, and a dill pickle, please." Shae eased to the counter and laid fifteen cents down before he could ask if she had the money.

"I'm all out of dill pickles." He handed a nickel back.

"I'll take a Baby Ruth." She gave him back the nickel. When he handed her the candy bar, she rushed from under his stare and out the door.

The children were already in line when Shae got to school. Tracy Allen whispered something to Mary Crawford, and they snickered when Shae got into line. She did not see Jenny, and she knew she was in for another sad day under the catalpa tree.

Jeff Locati's tent had held overnight and today would be as good as any time to move to the shack. After a bite to eat, he loaded up his bed, camp stove, pots and pans, and hauled them to the shack. The tent and snake cages would make another load, but he would do that when he got back from his hunt.

The sun was blazing down by the time he got to the woods, but the river was backing into her banks, and snakes were stirring all over. He had gone no more than a mile before he captured a big copperhead, and two coral snakes of the most brilliant colors. They loved a naked tree, and Forest Park had plenty of those.

By the end of the day, Jeff had caught more snakes than he'd caught the whole time he'd been there. Along with his load, his hip boots were getting heavier.

'If I get my moving done tonight, I can get an early start, tomorrow," he thought.

He turned toward home.

Taking a half-dozen cages into the shack, he caged his catch, and marveled at his luck. The old sow was going to be disappointed when she found him moved.

It was six o'clock by the time he got the tent and the other cages moved. It was a long time until dark, but he had a lot of chinking to do before the shack would be safe to sleep in. But he was hungry. It seemed he was always starved out here in the swamp.

When Jeff got his truck unloaded, he cranked it up and headed to Murphy's, pumped a jug of cold water, bought pork and beans, bologna and crackers. He had just finished his supper when he heard a knock on the side of the exterior wall.

"Come in," he called from where he sat on an orange crate with a number two tin can of water.

"I thought you might need some help." Clay Upshaw pushed the broken door to one side and entered with a bucket of gumbo mud.

Dipping his big, bony hand into the bucket, Clay plopped a glob of mud into a knothole, squished it down with his bare foot, and repeated the motion.

"I think I can do that," said Jeff.

He watched Upshaw for a moment longer then, scooped out a handful of gumbo, and plastered it over the hole.

"Of course you can," Clay assured. "There's nothing like gumbo to chink cracks with. I used it on my cabin."

After another hour, Jeff stood to inspect the floor. "Looks as if we have it snake-proof, thanks to you, my friend. Mosquito proof, too, once I get that door fixed."

"Not quite, my boy." Clay put his hands on his hips and straightened his aching back. "You will never do that. Some of the critters are small enough to crawl under the door, and some are big enough to open it."

Chuckling at the best joke he'd heard since he'd left home, Jeff pushed an orange crate toward the old man. "Sit for a spell? I'm imposing upon you."

"Not at all," Clay eased his tired, rheumatic body down on the crate and slung a handful of sweat from his brow. "You chinked two holes to my one. I can't do what I used to. This slimy river's no good for a man."

Sensing that the old Indian wanted to talk, Jeff seated himself in the middle of the floor, pulled his legs under him, looked straight into Clay's water-burned eyes, and listened as a baby would to a lullaby.

After taking a moment to catch his breath, Clay began to talk. It had been such a long time since anyone had given him the time of day. Even Girly seemed to be preoccupied most of the time.

Hanging onto every word, Jeff sat without interrupting, only to say, "I'm sorry, or that's too bad," until Clay had poured out his life story. Tears mingled with sweat as he spoke of his wife's passing. Ashamed of himself for crying on the young man's shoulder, Clay wrestled his bony body from the crate and wiped his face with his muddy hands.

"I'm sorry." He gained control. "I didn't mean to spoil your day, son." He turned toward the door. "I'd best be on my way. Girly will need help with her lessons." Rolling the gumbo from his hands, he moseyed out the door and walked toward home.

Springing up from the floor, Jeff followed the old Indian outside. "I understand," he said. He placed a hand on Upshaw's shoulder and gave it a sympathetic squeeze. "It's all right for a man to cry. My mama says it cleanses the soul." When Clay made no reply, Jeff walked him a ways up the path, and then watched him grope toward home in the dusk of the evening.

Looking the dilapidated door over when he returned to the shack, Jeff allowed it was nothing that baling wire wouldn't fix. The door moaned and groaned as if he was setting an elbow as he forged the rusty hinge into place and slipped a wire through the connection. After twisting the wire up tightly, he stepped into the big, dark, barren room and slammed the door tight. Except for the moon shining through the holes in the roof, the room was ghostly dark.

For a while, Jeff didn't move from the door. Tears welled in his eyes as he thought of how it would hurt to see a wife and mother lowered into the cold, dark ground. Blinking, he reached up and turned the wooden button at the top of the door. He would hate for one of those ruffians from Murphy's store to barge in on him while he was crying. For the longest time, he stood there, pulling himself together. Even if his mama did say it was all right, she'd be shocked to find him like this.

Once adjusted to the darkness, he shoved his cot toward the corner where the lantern sat on an orange crate. Lighting it, he unfolded the legs of his cot and threw his bedroll on it. Mosquitoes buzzed in the corners. He knew they loved light and blood, but he just had to read and unwind before he went to bed.

❦   ❦   ❦

"Papa, where have you been so long?" Shae sat at the table with her English book opened. "Miss Trisha says I'm droppin' my 'G's' and she wants you to drill me on them."

"I've drilled you on that before, Shae. Why do you do it? Say going."

"Goin'—" She stopped and looked askance.

"No, you missed it. Say 'bring.'"

"Bring."

"Sure. It's the same thing, Girly, if you will stop and think."

"I know, Papa." Shae's long, black eyelashes fell on her cheeks and her chin quivered. "I just can't remember. I hate school. I'm old enough to quit and I'm gonna."

"Now, now, Girly," her papa calmed her. "You know you can't do that. You wouldn't want the sheriff out here again, would you?"

"*No.* But I hate the kids pokin' fun at me all the time. Miss Trisha never hears them. She hates me, too. She never says anything to Mary Crawford, just 'cause she's the director's daughter."

"See there, you used the 'G' on thing without even thinking. Your teacher only wants her pupils to do her proud."

"I still hate school when Jenny's not there."

"I understand," Clay said disparagingly. "You will be glad once you learn to add the G. Maybe we'd better sleep on it, and we will study before you go to school, tomorrow."

With an exhausted body, weary mind, and a clean pair of underwear, Clay moped out to the watering trough to take a bath in the water he'd pumped for Dolly and the filly. A dirty trick, he'd have to admit, but it served Dolly right for staying out. Today's milk would be soured before morning. That meant they would not have gravy for breakfast.

As the tall Indian measured the length of the cypress watering trough, he lowered himself up to his ears in milk-warm water, and thought about leaving the Cache River.

I guess thirteen must be the borderline between a girl and a woman. I can see a difference in Girly everyday, but to take her to a strange place, strange people....

She needs the guidance of a mother. Would my mother be willing to take care of a grandchild? If she's still living, will she be old and wrinkled?

When he thought about it, Girly Shae favored her grandmother more than she did her own mother.

If Girly keeps rebelling against school...?

Between her and Jake Crawford, they could drive a wooden Indian to 'possum grape wine!

I have to think things out.

CHAPTER 14

It only took five minutes for Jeff to decide that the light would have to go, or the mosquitoes would suck his hot, sweaty body dry of blood. The shanty was ghostly dark as he lay listening to the timber wolves howl, and a hoot owl hoot, "Whooo-whooo-whooo are you?"

Jeff hardly knew who he was. He'd always thought he had his head on straight, but tonight he wasn't sure. His hopes of making enough money to buy Sara a 'promise ring' looked hopeless.

It must have been three in the morning before sleep finally claimed him. When he awoke the next morning, he wrestled himself from the soaking wet mosquito net and pulled his tired, aching body from the hard cot.

"Holy cow," he blurted when he looked up at the sun shining through the holes in the roof. "It must be ten o'clock." Walking to the broken door, he turned the button and pulled it open a crack, rubbed his eyes, and looked again. He should have been in the woods by daylight. His mouth was as dry as cotton, and he was famished.

After gobbling down a bite of breakfast and a cup of coffee, he mustered the nerve to put on his hunting clothes. It was bad enough to wear clothes at all under the sweltering sun, but to put on a leather jacket and hip boots.... Was it worth it?

By the time he went to Murphy's, filled his canteen and bought a snack to take along, the sun would cook a lizard. He doubted that there would be many stirring. But he forged on.

It was late afternoon before the woods began to come alive with the creepy critters. The first thing he came upon was a big green Rana frog. He knew it on sight, but it was the brightest green one he'd ever seen. He knew there was none like it at the zoo.

The frog sat looking at him as if it wanted to be captured. When Jeff eased the gunny sack in front of it and touched its behind with the stick, it hopped inside as if it was a mud toad house.

A little ways down the path, a white-bellied garter snake slithered lazily along, going nowhere. It hardly fought at all when Jeff penned it down with the forked stick. The white belly on the garter snake was very rare. He had read it in his book. Not bad for one day, he thought, easing through the cypress. But he was running out of water, and so he headed toward home. He wasn't culling anything, not if it slithered, hopped, or crawled on four feet. He had to fill the cages in the next two days. He set mouse traps around that night, in hopes of catching enough mice for a good feeding for his catch, before he left on Friday morning.

The next two days proved to be good hunting. When he got back to the shanty on Thursday, he had a reptile for every cage except two. After caging all his catch, he looked his truck over, re-twisting a few bailing wires here and there. When he could stand his thirst no longer, he headed toward Upshaw's for water, and to let the old man know he would be leaving early the next morning. He was a hundred yards from Upshaw's cabin when he heard an awful groaning.

Striking into a long lope, he entered the cabin without knocking. Upshaw lay sprawled across the bed, moaning, "Oh my head! My back! Oh!"

Jeff had never seen anyone so sick. Rushing to the man, he asked, "What's the matter, Mr. Upshaw? What can I do for you?"

"A cold drink of water," the Indian gasped. "Oh…my head, I think I'm dying!"

"No, you're not." Jeff calmed him before going to the pump for fresh water. He wasn't sure that the old man wasn't dying, but as long as he was talking, he was still conscious.

Finding the pump had lost its prime, and the stock had knocked the priming water over, he had to go to the river for water to prime with. When he got back to the cabin, Upshaw had worn himself out, and lay exhausted on his rumpled bed. He weakly raised up when he heard the bucket bail drop.

"Water…water," he called weakly.

"Here we are fella." Jeff lifted Upshaw's head with one hand, and held the dipper of water to the man's lips with the other.

Grabbing the dipper with a trembling hand, Clay emptied it and asked for a cold towel to cool his brow.

Jeff wondered what to do as he searched for the towel. He couldn't leave a sick person alone. Unable to locate a towel, he found the straining cloth hanging behind the stove. He wet it in cold water and laid it on Upshaw's feverish brow.

"Ah." The groaning man lay back. "That feels so good. I wish Girly Shae was home."

"I'll stay with you," Jeff assured. "Should I call a doctor?"

"No. No, it's just a river chill."

By four o'clock, Jeff had the man's fever cooled, but it kept him busy wetting the rag. It was time Shae was getting home.

Jeff had a lot of time to think as he sat fanning flies and keeping the rag cold. His mama and papa were about Upshaw's age…. Could this happen to them? A wave of homesickness swept over him, and he couldn't wait to start home.

Shae was half an hour late getting home. She had made friends with an old mother opossum on the way. Seeing that the mother had been suckled to a shoestring, she opened her lard bucket and offered the brood the sandwich she'd taken for Jenny. After watching them enjoy the biscuit, she then hurried up the road.

When she came to Jeff Locati's new home, she looked around. Sure there was no one about, she stopped at the truck. She quickly pulled the rope untied and peeped inside the backend. When she found the truck all but empty of cages, she knew that he had moved them into the shanty. But she didn't dare go inside. If he caught her there, he would tell her papa. Then she would be in trouble.

Shae heard voices before she got to the cabin. Thinking that her papa was talking out of his head again, she ran. When she stepped onto the porch, she saw Locati bathing her papa's head.

"Oh, Papa!" She dropped her books and lunch bucket, and ran to his bed. "I wanted to stay home with you."

"It's all right, Girly. I've had good care. Our friend has been with me all afternoon."

After thanking Locati, Shae brushed him aside, dipped the cloth into cold water, and bathed her papa's brow. "Maybe the worst is over." She patted his cheek. "You're not shaking now."

"Atta, girl," he smiled when she added the 'G'. "You will make Miss Trisha proud."

Sure that Upshaw was going to be all right when he saw the man smile at Shae, Jeff pumped another bucket of water, then said he'd be going if it was okay.

"We will be fine, son. Much obliged for your help. Maybe I can repay it, someway."

"I am returning a favor," said Jeff. "Remember, you helped me dob rat holes the other night. I will be leaving for St. Louis early tomorrow. I will return on Sunday."

Jeff walked away, wondering where Shae had been the half hour she was late. Then, too, he thought of what she would do if her father had another chill like the one he'd had today.

When Jeff got home, he noticed the knot in the rope on his tarp had been retied. He found nothing missing, but what could that girl have been looking for?

Jeff had heard that mosquitoes did not like smoke. He found an old lard bucket, added some rags, poured some coal oil on them and then set the bucket inside the shack. He would open the door and light a match to it before he went to bed. The smoke would be better than more mosquito bites. They had been pure torture the night before.

After loading the cages into the truck, he checked his traps. He didn't catch enough mice to go around, but he first fed the snakes he'd trapped, trusting the others would be fine until he got to the zoo.

Once everything was ready to travel, except filling his gas tank, he went into the shanty and lit the coal oil rags. He opened the door for the mosquitoes to go out, but he was outside first. With no windows, the room filled with smoke, choking him.

He sat the can outside after a time. It was an hour before he could go inside, but the smoke had chased the critters out. He quickly closed the door and turned the wooden button. He knew it was going to be another long, long night.

❦ ❦ ❦

"Girly." Clay woke up before dawn. "You will have to go to the store for chill tonic before you go to school. This awful gall taste in my mouth tells me that I will have another chill without it. Murphy should be opened by the time you get there."

"Do you have any money, Papa?" Shae slipped into her chopped-off overalls, shoes and shirt, and re-braided her hair.

"I'm sorry, Girly. You will have to ask Murphy to charge it. I'm flat broke. Maybe the pearl buyer will come to Murphy's this weekend, or the minister will come for fish."

❦   ❦   ❦

Being so anxious to leave the swamp, Jeff was up early. About the time he was ready to leave, he noticed Shae cutting down the river path in a half-run. Where would the girl be going this time of morning? He should check, but he needed to get away as soon as possible. The truck started without a hitch, and he drove toward Murphy's.

When Jeff got to the store, the usual gang was there, talking loud and spitting tobacco at the wash pan of ashes under the front of the king heater.

All the way to the store, Shae hoped she'd beat the crowd there, but the first person she saw as she eased into the store was Jeff Locati. He was talking to the minister. She walked quietly toward the counter, hoping that Murphy might take pity on her, since she needed to get back home and get ready for school. Instead, he motioned her to the back of the line.

"You will wait your turn, kid." Murphy went about waiting on the squirrel hunters who wanted to get into the woods before the squirrels went into their dens.

Lowering her head, Shae went to the back of the line. The minister sat staring daggers at Murphy, and Jeff Locati wanted to punch Murphy in the nose. Jeff had never known a sister, but he could see where they needed a protector.

Anderson broke Jeff's train of thought. "How is the job going?"

Jeff didn't answer until he saw the man's eyes on him. "I'm sorry," he apologized.

Reverend Anderson repeated the question and Jeff replied, "I'll have to admit, I'm not getting rich." He forced a laugh. "My book knowledge doesn't seem to be what it takes. I'm leaving for St. Louis, today. I would like to ask a favor of you."

"Just name it. I'm here to help," Anderson assured.

Jeff spoke in a whisper. "Mr. Upshaw had a real bad chill yesterday. Would it be too much trouble for you to look in on him?"

"Not at all, Mr. Upshaw's having a rough time of it, right now. I will be glad to give him a call."

About that time, Shae made her way up to the counter. "My papa's sick, and he needs a bottle of chill tonic." She rushed on, "And you will have to charge it till he sells some shells."

"I still don't have any chill tonic," Murphy growled. "I have quinine." He waited for an answer. "It will do the same thing."

Debating a moment, Shae said, "I guess I will take it."

Murphy handed her the bottle and wrote it down in his ledger.

Shae stuffed the bottle into her pocket and rushed out the door. Maybe, she told herself, I ought to stay home with papa, in case he has another chill.

In her haste to get home, Shae wouldn't have noticed Locati's truck parked to one side of the store, had it not been for Jock smelling her out and following her. When the wolf-dog saw Shae head for the shortest way home up the river path, he went to the back of the truck, sat on his haunches, and beat a tattoo on the ground with his tail.

"What is it, Jock?" Shae turned and walked stealthily toward him. She had not seen Scar since the day he had leapt into the river, and the hunter had been out there all week. Seeing that the tarp was only tied with a slipknot, she jerked the rope, raised the flap, and was inside the truck before thinking. If Scar was there, she would take him. The scout had no right—

Venom stung her eyes as she tried to adjust them to the darkness. The only light came from the tiny window in the back of the cab. The caged snakes hissed through the screen wire, but she had to find out if Scar was trapped there. She had heard Locati tell her papa that he was going to the zoo today. If Scar was there, he'd be gone forever.

Shae examined three cages. One held a big lizard. She could tell that the other two held snakes by the way they hissed. As she turned to a cage in the back of the truck, she stumbled over a big heap of canvas, which had to be his tent. Maybe he was going to stay…? But he'd told her papa he'd be back on Sunday.

Before she could get her balance, she heard voices.

"Oh-oh," she moaned. "What if the scout catches me in his truck?"

Then she heard the minister say, "I'll go right away and check on Mr. Upshaw. Don't worry about him."

When Shae felt the truck spring give, she knew someone had stepped on the bumper.

"Oh!" she moaned under her breath. "Why did I do this?"

Her heart trip-hammered. Like a mole, she darted under the canvas and flattened herself out. As she lay breathless, she kept asking herself, who will bathe papa's fever down? He will be worried sick about me!

"Papa…Papa…."

CHAPTER 15

Jock went crazy when Jeff stepped up on the bumper. He started after him like a rabid wolf. Then Jeff noticed the rope was untied and yelled as Jock came after him, "Out of here!" He looked around at the minister. "A pretty smart dog," he added. The minister didn't comment.

Though she had not been gone from the store two minutes, Jeff's thoughts ran to the Upshaw girl. What had she been looking for in his truck? He'd been asking himself that same question for a week.

Jock kept trying to get into his truck, so Jeff decided to try to calm him. "Come on, fella. You don't want in there with those poisonous snakes. You would be laid up with a fatback poultice like the girl was for two or three days."

When Jock kept snarling, his lip up over his long, white tushes, Jeff stepped up into the truck and picked up the forked stick.

"Best not to crowd him," Anderson advised when Jeff started to get out of the truck. "He's one vicious dog, I'm told."

Unable to talk to the dog, Jeff stepped back to think the situation over. Looking at Anderson, he said, "I think the girl untied the rope, but why?"

Anderson thoughtfully replied, "That's a good question."

Jock's bristles raised and his growl sank deep in his throat. When Jeff made a move toward the truck again, the dog went savage, leaving nothing for Jeff to do except whack him across the nose. Jock kept coming toward him. Jeff turned his hand sideways and hit the dog just under the right eye. When Jock went howling behind the store, Jeff went into the truck.

Shae almost screamed out when she heard Jock howl. But when she felt a big boot touch the canvas at the very edge of her foot, she lay petrified. She was sure the scout could hear her heart beating. Sweat stung her eyes. She had to get out, even if she had to scream!

Shame flooded her conscience as she thought of the day the hunter had saved her from the moccasin bite. What would her papa say when he found out she had sneaked into Locati's truck? She heard the cages being shuffled around. She almost spoke out, but her voice was gone. The words would not come out.

Finding nothing disturbed, Jeff walked back to the rumpled tent in the corner and climbed out of the truck, still puzzled.

"It would have to have been an accident if the dog untied the rope." He looked inquisitively at the minister. "If the girl did it, we must have scared her away. But why would she get in there with those snakes?"

"Can I be of help?" Anderson asked.

Jeff flapped the tarp two or three times, and tied it down hard and fast with a reef knot, which would take some real know-how to untie. "Thanks, Preacher." Jeff turned to the minister. "You might stand by, if you're not in a hurry. It takes a lot of tender loving coaxing to get this rack of bailing wire on the road sometimes." Jeff went to the back of the seat to get the crank. "I've got to have gasoline, if Murphy ever gets time to pump it."

As Jeff stood talking to the minister, Murphy came shuffling out, wiping his hands on his denim apron. "I think I'm about out of gas, buddy. The delivery man will be here anytime, now." He turned and went back into the store.

Jeff and the minister stood talking for fifteen minutes, but the delivery man did not show. About that time, Murphy came out and said that the gas would not arrive for another two hours. The delivery man's truck had broken down. "I'll pump what I have."

Jeff knew he had not gotten more than a gallon of gas, but Murphy hung up the hose and said, "That'll be twenty five cents." He held out his hand impatiently.

"How much is gasoline a gallon, Mr. Murphy?" Jeff asked.

"Fifteen cents, he replied."

Jeff held onto his change. "The register only shows a fraction over a gallon."

"All right!" Murphy barked. "Twenty cents!"

Jeff handed him the change and watched as he crammed it into his apron pocket. Though he knew that he had been gypped out of a nickel, Jeff was too flustered to argue with Murphy.

"What do I do now?" Jeff stuck his thumbs under his belt and looked at Anderson for an answer. "I'll never make it to State Line on a gallon of gas."

"I don't have a lot of gasoline," Anderson said, going for his siphon hose, "but I'll give a friend half of anything I own."

After Anderson had siphoned another gallon into Jeff's truck, he stood back, feeling good about himself, while Jeff wheeled the crank around and around in the gut of the model T. When the engine didn't turn over, Jeff went and pulled the gas lever down a notch, and cranked and cranked. Finally, the engine shimmied and coughed like an asthmatic child...and died.

Anderson suggested, "You get in and give it the gas. You know her nature better than I do. I'll crank."

"But you'll get your nice clothes dirty, Preacher." Jeff cranked a half-dozen more rounds without any luck.

Taking Anderson up on his offer, Jeff crawled into the cab. Anderson gave the crank a swift spin around. The engine hit on three cylinders. Jeff quickly gave her more gas, and she started hitting on all four.

Thanking Anderson over and over when he brought the crank to the truck window, Jeff then hesitated to ask one more favor of the minister. But he had to make sure someone looked in on Mr. Upshaw. Since he had seen Shae buy quinine, he was afraid her father might be sick again.

Jeff sat still, letting the engine idle. Anderson said, "Good luck, friend." He waved to Jeff and started to walk away.

"I'm sorry to keep pestering you, Preacher, but Mr. Upshaw was really sick with a chill when I left there last evening. Would you be sure to remember to look in on him today?"

"Not at all, I'll be glad to. I'll go by before I leave for home."

"Thank you…and thanks again for the gas."

Jeff nosed the jalopy out to the washboard road and headed north. If he could only make it to the state line….

Jeff assured himself he'd be all right.

🍁   🍁   🍁

Though it was already eighty degrees early in the morning, Shae sat shaking after she'd crawled from under the tent. The truck threw her from one side to another as it hit the chuck holes in the worn-out road. She wiped tears from her face with her shirttail. Who would bathe her papa's fever down?

As she wondered what she could do, she could see the top of Jeff's head through the back window of the cab. What if he should see her in the rear view mirror? She ducked back under cover and lay smothering. Then she heard Jeff humming a tune, a happy tune.

I bet he's thinkin' of his girl. I'm sure he has one. He's too good-lookin' not to. Maybe he has two or three girls….

❦   ❦   ❦

Puzzled, the minister stood watching the wolf dog trailing the truck. What? He asked himself, can that dog be after? If it's snakes, the woods are crawling with them.

When the truck went around a corner out of sight, Anderson thoughts shifted to Upshaw.

God works in mysterious ways. I have been wondering what excuse I could find to visit the man. The daughter needs to be in church—but I don't want to make a nuisance of myself.

But somehow, Anderson had to bring it to pass. He wouldn't be happy until the girl had the upbringing she deserved.

Hoping he'd have enough gas to get to Upshaw's and back to the store by the time the delivery truck came with a refill, Anderson cranked his Overland, crawled into it, and drove toward Upshaw's.

"Hello…hello," he called at the door. When there was no answer, he called louder. "Are you there, Mr. Upshaw?" He looked through the screen and saw the long, bony Indian sprawled across the bed. Hurrying to him, Anderson asked, "Are you all right, Mr. Upshaw?"

Finding the Indian's brow to be hot to the touch, his eyes half open, and making no response to his visitor, Anderson told himself Upshaw was seriously ill.

What should I do first…?

He decided to go to Murphy's and call Dr. Bond, but Upshaw began to breathe shallowly, and Anderson knew he couldn't leave him alone. The girl should be home, anytime. Frank Murphy had made it clear that she'd bought quinine, and she wasn't dressed for school. Where could she be?

Maybe she had taken the river path….

The sick bed being one of Anderson's close associates, God had given him the touch of an angel and lips that dripped honey. But a mere touch or words wouldn't help Upshaw. He needed a doctor.

Loosening his tie, Anderson rolled his shirt sleeves to his elbows and went to work.

When turning Upshaw lengthwise on the bed had brought no response, Anderson pressed an ear to the man's chest and found the heartbeat to be very weak. Upshaw was scorching with fever and the stench was unbelievable.

Finding the water in the bucket warm enough for bath water, Anderson stripped Upshaw down to his underwear and looked around for a wash cloth. Finding none, he took a well-used towel from a nail and bathed the leathery skin of the near-skeleton until his fever had cooled. Then Anderson waited—waited and waited for the girl to come home.

When an hour had passed with no sign of Shae, Anderson knew what he had to do. Making the patient as comfortable as possible, he got into his car and drove as fast as he could to a telephone, only to find out that the doctor was two miles past yonder with a sick child. The next best thing he could think of was to get his wife, who made a good nurse. By the time he chased her down at the Ladies' Circle, Dr. Bond had received the message. Within fifteen minutes after the Andersons arrived at Upshaw's cabin, the minister answered a knock at the door.

"Good morning." A smile spread over Dr. Bond's tired, wrinkled face. "Good morning, Mrs. Anderson," he added, stepping inside and tipping his hat to her. He hung it on a nail and sat his black bag on the stand table. He looked over at the rack of bones on the bed.

"Looks as if we have a very sick man on our hands." The doctor looked over the situation, as if he knew without doubt what they were facing.

"Very sick, I'm afraid," said Anderson, and went on to explain that the scout had asked him to look in on Mr. Upshaw while he was gone. "This is how I found him when I got here."

Rolling up his sleeves, the tired doctor moved over to the bed. His deep sigh, bloodshot eyes, and uncombed hair showed that he'd had little sleep in the last twenty-four hours—yet he had come straight from one bedside to another.

"Phew!" Dr. Bond thumbed his nose as he neared the bed. "I smell typhoid."

After giving the Indian the usual going over, the doctor opened his bag for a needle to draw out a sample of Upshaw's blood.

Anderson glanced at his wife, Vivian, who stood ghostly white. Her look as much said, what have we gotten ourselves into?

"I can't be sure," Dr. Bond said, "but the man has all the symptoms."

He shot the vial of blood into a bottle and screwed the cap on tight. "If the analysis comes back positive, he should be quarantined. Does Mr. Upshaw have relatives close by?"

"Only a daughter...eleven or twelve years old. She was at the store early this morning. She bought quinine and left. She should be home at any time. She wasn't dressed for school."

"I see." Dr. Bond labeled the bottle of blood. "Do you know anything about his financial situation? He should be in a hospital."

"Bad would be the only word for it." Anderson looked straight into Dr. Bond's tired, inquisitive eyes. "He's a good, hard-working man, but luck has been down on him, recently. Bringing up a daughter alone can't be easy."

"If the man's illness proves to be typhoid, there will have to be a mass inoculation. The daughter, you, your wife, the scout and, last but not least, me. It's too bad, but if the man has no money, the Red Cross is the only alternative. But they take time. I don't want to predict anything, but this man is very ill." Then he added, "Would it be possible for you and your wife to stay with the patient until I get some sleep? I have hardly closed my eyes for two days."

"Sure thing." Anderson looked at his wife for assurance. "As I told the Locati boy, we're here to help. We will be here when you get back."

"It might be morning." The doctor lifted his hat from the nail on the wall and made ready to leave. "All you can do is keep him comfortable, give him plenty of cold water, and a capsule of quinine every three hours around the clock." He measured out the quinine and then walked to the door, saying over his shoulder, "Be sure to keep the girl home until I get back. And thank you so much for your help."

After the doctor left, Vivian went about cleaning up the cabin. The patient's bed needed a change. One change depleted the clean bedclothes and then she needed to wash laundry.

Fred Anderson went out on the porch and looked down the road. There was no one in sight. The wolf dog came to mind.

Why was he so vicious when Locati stepped into the truck? Could the girl have been inside?

🍁   🍁   🍁

Locati had gone no more than three miles before the radiator started to steam. The cross-tie cutters had worn the ruts down six inches with their iron-tired wagons and the rank weeds had bedded down in the middle of the road. Jeff soon found the truck high centered and was barely able to move at all. The wolf dog still worried him. He didn't want him to stray away and get lost.

Cutting his engine, Jeff got out and slapped his legs. "Go back home, fella. Your feet will be bleeding if you follow me on the gravel road."

Inside the truck, Shae listened until she heard footsteps. Darting back under the tent, she started her sweat-bath all over again.

Jock stopped and looked at Jeff, but made no move to turn back. Deciding that he'd better fill the radiator before the road wandered too far from the river, he turned toward the backend of the truck to get a bucket.

Lowering his head wolf like, Jock raised his gray and black bristles and tore to the backend of the vehicle. By the time Jeff got there, Jock met him from the opposite side. When Jeff touched the rope on the tarp, the dog came at him with lips curled up over long, white teeth, and Jeff knew he meant business.

"Hey, fella, what's with you?" He dropped the rope and held out a friendly hand. "I'd like to be your friend, but this is no way to go about it. What is it you want of me?"

Lowering his lip, Jock calmed and accepted the pat on the head, as long as Jeff kept his hand off the rope.

"Fella, you'd better go home. I know someone who will be wondering about you."

Jock made no attempt to turn back. When Jeff reached for the rope, the wolf dog went for the jugular. Unable to get away from the dog, Jeff kicked him a good one in the ribs and laid him low until he got back into the back of the truck.

Petrified, Shae glued her skinny body to the floor of the truck and lay motionless. She knew Jock had taken an awful kick. He lay howling outside the truck.

Shae wanted to pray, but the only prayers she'd ever heard were the ones Miss Trisha prayed when school opened.

Oh, Papa, I'm so scared!

Finally, Jock quit howling. What if he had died, she wondered? She would never find her way back home.

CHAPTER 16

Shae had no idea why the hunter had stopped, but when she felt the backend of the truck spring, she knew he had left. Then she heard footsteps. When she dared to peep out the window of the cab, he was going toward the river with a bucket. Jock limped around near the truck. He could hardly walk and she knew he was hurt, but she could not help him. She wasn't mad at him anymore. He was her only hope of getting back home, if she ever got out of the truck.

When Shae saw the hunter walking back toward the truck with a bucket of water, she darted back under the tent. If he got back in there one more time, he'd be sure to find her. Then what? But Jeff decided that he would not go to the backend. That seemed to be the dog's problem.

Jeff knew he had badly hurt Jock. He tried again to make friends with him, but Jock tried to get away. He filled the radiator and threw the bucket in the cab. The engine started the first time he turned the crank.

Jeff was sure he could outrun him now. He hopped into the truck and took off as fast as he dared over the bumpy road. If he hit an underground stump, he would burst a tire and really be sunk.

❧   ❧   ❧

Fred Anderson looked down the road as he pumped cold water to bathe Upshaw's fevered brow. He still saw no sign of the girl.

After wetting the towel in cold water, he laid it on Upshaw's forehead and turned to his wife, Vivian. "We'll wait fifteen more minutes. If the girl isn't home by then, one of us will have to go to the school."

Without waiting for his wife to respond, he went on, "I'm puzzled. Why would the dog follow that truck? Could the girl have been inside there? She left Murphy's not two minutes before Locati and me. He found the rope untied…. And the dog went after him when he started to get inside the truck. He suspected that the girl might have untied the rope. But why?"

"Maybe I should go to the school," said Vivian. "I can do the laundry when I get back. You can handle the situation here much better than I can, and I would like to talk to her teacher."

"That will be fine, but you'll need to get some gas. I divided with the scout before he left."

School was out for recess when Vivian arrived. The children were running all over the place, but she would not know the Upshaw child if she saw her. Her husband had said the girl was a beautiful child with long black braids and dark reddish skin. She did not see a girl of that description.

Walking quietly into the schoolroom unannounced, Vivian Anderson found Miss Trisha. The teacher was at the blackboard, working on an assignment.

Miss Trisha turned at the sound of a step. "Good morning. May I help you, Mrs. Anderson?"

"Yes." Vivian admired the teacher from her dark wavy hair to the hem of her cool, cotton dress. "I'm sorry to intrude, Miss Wilson, but I'm here to inquire about the Upshaw girl. Is she in school today?"

"No. I'm afraid she isn't. I suppose she decided to skip."

The teacher looked past Vivian Anderson. "It's too bad. She was about to catch up with her class. Why do you inquire, Mrs. Anderson?"

"Do you think she would do that?" Vivian looked surprised. "It's important that we find her. My husband said she was at Murphy's to buy quinine early this morning. She hasn't returned home and her father is very ill. We are worried about her."

"I wasn't surprised to find her absent today." Miss Trisha shrugged. "She was very disappointed when her friend Jenny wasn't here, yesterday."

Puzzled, Vivian primped at her marcelled hair before she asked, "Does she only have one friend?"

"You see, Mrs. Anderson…" The teacher weighed her words. "The girl stands out here, if you know what I mean. Being the only mixed-blood, it's very hard for her. I hear Sheriff Brody is looking into her home life. Mr. Crawford tells me that she lives much like the animals out there on the river. She's without a mother, and alone much of the time, which is bad for a thirteen-year-old girl—"

Taken aback, Vivian cut in, "Are you sure the child is thirteen? My husband guessed her to be eleven, twelve at most."

Catching Mrs. Anderson's disbelief, Miss Trisha opened the drawer of her desk and took out her registration book. Tracing a finger down the names, she said, "Shae's record shows she was thirteen on July twenty-third. The age a girl needs a mother most." She thought for a moment and then added, "Sheriff Brody thinks with help from the community, he could get her into an orphanage, that's where she really belongs."

The teacher stood staring into Vivian's eyes for agreement, which she did not get.

Being a minister's wife for fifteen years had taught Vivian to think before she spoke, and she prided herself on the system. Would her words hurt someone? Were they true or false? She had on occasions agreed to something she did not believe in. But on this day, she was hot, tired, and disturbed over the Upshaw situation. There was a very sick man and a missing child to think of, and she almost forgot to weigh her response.

"I am sorry to disagree, Miss Wilson. There are other places for the child besides an orphanage. My husband and I would be happy to give the girl a home until her father gets back on his feet." Vivian straightened her five-foot seven-inches to full height, as if she was proud she had spoken her mind.

Shocked, Miss Trisha said, "Do you mean you would take a half—"

"That's exactly what I said." Vivian Anderson picked the last word off Miss Trisha's tongue. "The girl had no choice of color. We would never be a party to Sheriff Brody's plan."

Turning on her heel, Vivian took two or three steps toward the door before she turned around and said, "I'm so sorry, Miss Trisha. I did not intend to be rude."

"This is a free America," Miss Trisha muttered. "You have a right to your own opinion, but I think you would live to regret it. I'm sure she would be best off with her own kind." She hurried to ring the five minute bell.

It was not like Vivian to have the last word, but she turned to the teacher and said, "Who could be so cruel to take a child from her father while he's unconscious?" Walking hastily toward her car, she vowed it would never happen again.

Vivian was still fuming when she got back to Upshaw's. Her husband was surprised. He had never seen her lose control.

"You didn't quarrel with the school teacher, did you?" he questioned after she had told him about Brody's plan. A disagreement with the community could lose him his job, and they weren't easy to find.

"I'm afraid I said some things I shouldn't have," she admitted. "I was so shocked at Miss Wilson's feelings. She as much as said the

Upshaw girl had one friend in the whole school. We can't stand by and let this happen to the child…can we?"

"Of course not," Anderson assured. "But there are other ways of handling it. If the girl isn't home soon, we'll have to notify the sheriff."

"I know." Vivian went about gathering the laundry. "First thing, we will change the bed."

Anderson went to Upshaw's bed, rolled him to one side of the bed, pushed the clammy sheet to the middle and then rolled the helpless man over on the clean sheet, which Vivian had placed on the mattress.

Once the patient was comfortable, Anderson filled the wash kettle and kindled a fire under it.

🍁   🍁   🍁

The river road had straightened out and Locati was going at a pretty good speed. Shae lay choking for water, wondering what she would do if and when she did get out of the back of the truck. She had heard the scout say that he was going to St. Louis, wherever that was. She could just hear her papa whistling for her.

"Oh no," she moaned under her breath.

Why did I do it? Without his quinine, he will be shakin' with a chill by now.

And if she should be caught in St. Louis, she was sure to be put in an orphan's home, and she would never see her papa again. Even the old school house was better than this!

As Shae lay cooking alive, she thought of what Miss Trisha had said about Jesus. All you had to do was ask, and he would give it to you. But she couldn't see Jesus, and how could she ask him to get her out of here? One thing she was sure of…Scar was not in one of the cages. She would still have her friend when and if she ever got back home.

❦   ❦   ❦

As Jeff jogged along over the washboard road, he could hear the traffic on the main highway to St. Louis. He was sure he would make it to the state line, where he could buy gasoline. Then he'd be on his way. He had gone no more than a hundred yards before the ruts got deeper and he was soon high centered again. The radiator started boiling over. The cap blew sky high and landed in tall grass.

Jeff sat for a minute. When he looked out the window, the wolf dog was close beside him. He had to get out of the truck to push it to the lower ground. He reached down and picked up the crank. Even if he didn't have to use it on the dog, he felt safer holding it. And he didn't want to use it. It would be pure cruelty to hit a dumb animal with a weapon like that, but he'd best be prepared.

Surprisingly, Jock made no move toward him as Jeff retrieved the radiator cap, took the bucket from the cab and walked to the river. The dog even accepted a pat on the head from Jeff. After he'd filled the radiator, he noticed that Jock stood by as calm as a clam. But when Jeff walked toward the back of the truck to check the tires, Jock tore into him.

Jeff was at the wolf dog's mercy until he hung a tush up into Jeff's pant-leg. Jeff folded up his big fist and whacked the dog across the nose. Jock fell over howling. When he finally got to his feet, he wandered into the woods, out of sight.

Hoping he could get the model T going before Jock got mean again, Jeff gave the crank two or three swift spins, but the engine sputtered a few times and died, which told him he was out of gas. There was only one thing to do. He'd have to walk to the State Line station for gasoline. It couldn't be over a mile. Thank heaven his gas can was behind the seat, for he would never be able to get into the back of the truck. If the dog could still walk, it would come after him.

Jeff looked around as he picked up his can and started walking toward the highway. Maybe, he told himself, I can thumb a ride. But when he thought of the way he looked, he doubted that anyone would take the chance.

🍁   🍁   🍁

Shae had crawled under the tent when the truck stopped. She heard Jock attack Locati, and had crammed a fist into her mouth to keep from screaming out when Jeff hammered her dog over the head with his fist.

When everything went quiet, Shae was sure the hunter had killed Jock. Without him, she'd never find her way home, even if she ever got out of there.

When she could no longer stand the suspense, she dared to ease from under the tent and peeped out the tiny window. She almost shouted when she saw Locati walking along the road with a can in one hand. Suspecting that the truck was out of gas, she waited until she was sure he was out of ear-shot, then she called out, "Jock, come get me out of here!"

When there was no response, she went to the backend and beat on the tarp. "Jock! Jock, come help me!" She tried every way to find a way to get to the rope, but it was hopeless. "Oh, Jock, please help me! I'm starvin' for a drink. And if that man catches me here…h-he might give me what he did you."

Giving up, Shae sat down and wiped the sweat from her face. Her shirt was as wet as a wash rag and then she did what Miss Trisha had said to do. She prayed.

"Oh, Lord, please help me. My Papa will be so worried about me. I will never do this again if you will only help me this once!"

Shae felt better after she'd prayed. If what Miss Trisha had said were true, she'd be out before the man got back. But where was Jock? Maybe he died…. If he did, which way would she go?

"Jock! *Jock!*"

Exhausted, Shae sat with her head propped on her knees, wondering if the Lord had heard her prayers. Her mouth was so dry she could spit cotton, and she was hungry. She had no idea when the hunter would be back.

What if he doesn't come back?

She got up and tried to reach the rope again.

And what if he does…?

🍁   🍁   🍁

Looking back over his shoulder as he stepped off a yard at a time, Jeff saw no sign of Jock. Maybe the stupid dog had decided to go back home.

Again the old Indian came to his mind. He thought of the girl being in the store for the quinine. Upshaw must have had a chill coming on.

I'm sure the minister will look in on them.

Jeff thought back over the time he'd been in the swamp. It had been a miserable time, but he felt as if he'd made a friend in Upshaw. But the girl, what was going on there?

I can't figure her out. She acts as if she thinks I'm trying to steal something. Heaven forbid.

They would be the last people he'd steal from, if he were a thief.

Jeff could see traffic buzzing along the highway as he got nearer. If he could only catch a ride. Each car and truck passed him by as if the drivers thought he was out for a walk. The sun seemed to rise higher by the minute. He would be lucky to get home by dark.

CHAPTER 17

❀

Sure there had to be tie cutters, squirrel hunters or fishermen somewhere close to hear her. Shae screamed, "Help! Help!" until her throat would bring no sound above a whisper.

Licking the sweat dribbling down her face to soothe her throat, she sat back on the piles of canvas, pulled her knees up and folded her arms over them. She was suffocating from the venom the snakes hissed, but there was no place to go. She sat waiting for the worst to happen.

After forever, she made her way to the back of the truck. Someway, she had to untie that knot. She could untie any of her papa's, but this one was different.

Hearing something breathing hard, she darted to the tent and wormed under it. Then she thought she heard Jock whine. Could it be? She was sure he'd turned back home or was dead. Easing up, she peeped out the window. Sure enough, there lay Jock, spread out on the ground with his tongue hanging out as if he'd had a hard time catching up, and was wondering what had happened to the hunter.

"Jock! Jock!" She tried again and again, but Jock didn't even prick his ears, until she hammered on the window. Rolling his tail into a donut, his ears went straight up and he ran barking toward the river.

"No! No!" Shae dropped back on the tent, pulled her knees up under her chin and gave way to dry sobs.

What would they do to her if they found her there…? Put her in the orphans' home for sure, and her papa would never know where she was.

It was a long time before Shae heard Jock whining at the back of the truck. Jumping up, she ran to the back end, yelling, but it came out a whisper again. When she slapped on the tarp with both hands, Jock reared up on the tarp and started clawing with all his might. Though the canvas was tough, he finally punctured it with a toenail, giving her hope. But Jock soon gave up and lay panting by the side of the road.

"Please, Jock," she begged as loud as she could. "Get me out!"

Of course, Jock couldn't hear her.

What would the snake hunter do if he caught Jock back there?

If she could only make him hear!

Once more, Shae hammered on the tiny window, bringing Jock back to the truck. Rearing up on the side of it, he glimpsed Shae working her mouth. Racing to the back end, he clawed and clawed. Once the hole was big enough to hang a tush in, he went to work with his long teeth and ripped a hole large enough for Shae to run her hand through it. She tried with all her strength to rip it open, but in her weakened condition, she couldn't. It was hopeless.

Once, Jock stopped long enough to go to the river for water. He came back and didn't stop until he'd ripped the tarp wide open. When the light shined through, she looked through the window to see if Locati was in sight. She saw no one, and turned the snake cage around to the light. A big king snake lay facing her, but it wasn't Scar.

All this for nothin' she thought.

She pushed the cage back into the corner and skinned out the hole, while Jock stood by, thumping his tail on the ground. She hit the ground running and didn't stop for a half mile. Finally, she sat on a stump. Jock licked her face and she tousled the thick, gray fur on his head.

"Good ol' Jock," she murmured. "I never thought you could get me outta there."

Shae was more than out of sight when Locati got back to the truck. After sitting for a few minutes to cool off, he poured the gallon of gasoline into the tank and went around the truck, checking the tires.

"What the…?"

Then he guessed it. That dog had caught up after all. He thought of the inch-long tushes and knew with no one there to check on him, he could soon tear the whole tarp off.

Climbing inside, Jeff looked things over and found them much as he'd left them, except the tent, which was scattered at the corners.

What, he asked himself again, could the dog be wanting in my truck? The snakes were calm and the cages in place. It didn't make sense. And he didn't have time to stand around wandering. He'd be after dark getting to Forest Park now. It had to be ten thirty.

It took several cranks to get the jalopy going. Once it hit on all four cylinders, he threw the crank under the seat and headed north.

Locati filled the tank to running over when he got to the State Line station. Airing up his tires, he filled the radiator and handed the attendant the last green money he owned, secretly hoping there would be enough change for a hamburger and a milkshake. If he waited until the middle of the afternoon to eat, he could make it until breakfast. Just thinking of food made his mouth water for his mama's buttermilk biscuits and gravy.

Counting the quarter, dime and two nickels as he crammed them deep into his pocket, he cranked up, threw the crank onto the seat beside him, and was once more on his way to Forest Park.

Jock trotted circles around Shae as she sat on the stump. He was telling her to come on. It was a long way home. Getting to her feet, she followed as he sniffed the air and loped faster. She knew he smelled something good. When she caught up to him, he stood lapping from a gurgling creek. It was only a trickle, but it gurgled into a beaver dam. The water was so clear; she could see the sand on the bottom. It didn't look to be over waist deep. Flopping down on her stomach, she drank until she felt as if she would pop.

After drinking his fill, Jock pricked up his ears and ran barking across the creek, where a skinny opossum sat high in a tree, helping itself to a vine of summer grapes. Like herself, Jock had missed his breakfast. He sat waiting for the opossum to make a run for it, while she rushed over and filled her stomach with grapes more green than purple, but she was so hungry.

"C'mon, Jock," she coaxed. "We've got to get home. Papa will be worried."

Jock went right on thumping his tail.

Knowing she'd have to wait, she went back to the cool, clear creek. She dropped her shirt and eased into it feet first, happy knowing old Jake Crawford or Sheriff Brody wouldn't be sneaking around watching her. She didn't even have to use her G's. Miss Trisha couldn't hear her.

Cupping her hands, she washed her face and drank her fill again. This water wasn't muddy like the Cache. When she called Jock again, it came out loud and clear. Jock didn't come.

Deciding she'd have to wait on him, she waded out a few steps further and found it to be deeper than she thought. It felt so good up around her neck. Gradually, she felt a creeping sensation around her feet. The sand was quivery. When she pulled one foot out, the other sank deeper. She began to panic. Before she realized what was happening, she was in quicksand halfway to her knees. It pulled her down...down...down.

"Jock, help me!" she screamed, and started treading water. The sand wouldn't let go. Flopping around like a hooked fish, she strangled out, "Papa! Papa!" Holding her breath, she turned around and went after her feet. When she pulled one out again, the other sank even deeper.

"Jock! Jock...*help!*"

By the time Jock got to her, she'd dipped beneath the surface. But he was confused. He'd seen her frolic in the Cache with Sandy, her pony, and he sat for a split second, grinning at her. When she came up and started down again, he made one long leap into the water. His first grab caught her gallus and ripped it off. Slinging it to one side, he caught her by the overalls, but she instinctively fought him off. When she came to the surface, he grabbed a braid, sinking a tush into it, and hauled her halfway out on the sand. He stood helplessly by as she hunkered on her hands and knees, heaving water from her lungs. Exhausted after she'd pumped her body dry, she crumbled on the hot sand and lay shaking. Jock lay nearby.

It was an hour later when Shae looked around, disoriented. Where was she? What was she doing in this strange place? She couldn't figure it out until Jock jumped the creek and picked up her shirt. Wagging it in his mouth, he dropped it at her feet and tugged at her overalls. Then it all came back to her.

"What would I do without you, Jock?"

Struggling to her feet, she tied the shirt sleeves around her waist and looked at the sun, which was bearing to the west. It was after noon.

When Jock curled his tail and crossed the creek above the sinkhole, she followed. She had to run half the time to keep up, but she hoped at any minute to find the Cache, and she knew it would take her home. She had to get her papa's quinine to him before he took another chill. To be sure she had it, she felt into her pocket to find it gone.

"Jock!" She slapped her hand over her mouth. "I've lost Papa's quinine!"

Thinking she'd lost it in the sinkhole, she knew it was hopeless to find it. She'd just have to hurry home in time to buy some more, if Murphy would let her have it.

❦   ❦   ❦

It was two o'clock when Reverend Anderson left for Murphy's store. Telling himself there had to be something wrong; he drove down the river road. Several times, he stopped and whistled as he'd heard Shae's father do, but there was no answer. When he got to the store, a dozen loafers sat on the lazying bench near the front door, chewing tobacco and catching up on gossip. Jake Crawford was one of them.

"Lo, fellas," Anderson waved to the group and slid over to where Murphy worked on his charge book. "Have you seen the Upshaw girl since she was here this morning, Mr. Murphy?" he inquired when Murphy finally looked up.

"No. She bought some quinine and left here in a run. I figured the old man had another buckegger chill. Why?"

"He does. He's real sick. The girl never came home with the quinine. She's not at school. We checked."

Seemingly undisturbed, Murphy went on figuring in his book. "Ah, she's probably skipped school again. You can never tell about that kid. Brody's been on to the old man several times, lately, about her absence from school."

"Is her pony home? She comes by here like a bat from a chimney, sometimes."

"No. The pony was there for water. I didn't have time to pump it. But the dog hasn't been seen since he left here tearing at the hunter's truck. I don't know what to think. I feel there's trouble."

"Give her time." Murphy grinned. "She'll be home."

"I think I should report it. Since she came for medicine, I believe she would have brought it home."

"There's a phone." Murphy nodded toward the wall. "But I doubt that Brody will bother to come out."

Picking up the receiver, Anderson rung two longs and a short.

"Hello, sheriff. This is Reverend Anderson." He hesitated. "We have a problem at the Upshaw place." He listened a moment. "But this is different, sheriff. Mr. Upshaw is dangerously ill, and the girl hasn't been seen since early this morning. I'm afraid there's something wrong. Would you contact me at Mr. Upshaw's place as soon as possible?"

Dropping the receiver into its cradle, Anderson stalked outside, got into his car and drove back toward the river. If he found her boat there, he'd know there was trouble.

As he suspected, he found the boat tied to the root of the water oak. All he could do was go back to Upshaw's cabin and wait.

It was five o'clock when Brody showed at Upshaw's, and barged in without knocking.

"You should have knocked, Mr. Brody." Anderson looked up from where he dipped a towel into a wash pan. "The doctor thinks this man has typhoid fever."

Brody edged back toward the door cursing his stupidity. "Guess it's too late now." He walked over and took a closer look at Mr. Upshaw, then started quizzing Anderson about the girl.

After asking every possible question, he shrugged. "I'll see what I can do, but I still say she'll be home before dark."

"That might be true." Anderson's eyes dressed Brody down. "But it will be too late to search by then. I'd like to see someone out there right away."

"I'll see what I can do." Brody turned toward the door.

"Do about what?" Clay opened his eyes for the first time all day, and stared at Brody. "What…what are you doing here, Brody?" Exhausted, he fell back on his pillow. After catching his breath, he weakly asked, "Where is the girl?"

"She will be here soon, Mr. Upshaw," Anderson said, calming him down. "Lie down and get some rest, doctor's orders."

"D-doctor? What doctor?" His blank eyes searched the room for Shae.

"Doctor Bond was here this morning. Do you remember?" Turning the old man's head to a more comfortable position, Anderson added, "He says you're going to be just fine, but you need rest."

"R-rest," Clay muttered. "Where…is…girlie?" Suddenly, he looked up at Anderson and said clearly, "You will take care of my girl?" Then, closing his eyes, he slept.

"You bet we will, Mr. Upshaw. You bet we will."

"To my way of thinking," Brody said, approaching Anderson, "an orphanage is the place for the girl. That old gentleman is in bad shape. This swamp is no place for a girl child." Brody turned toward the door.

"You heard my promise, Mr. Brody." Anderson followed the sheriff outside. "My wife and I will be glad to give the girl a home until her father gets back on his feet. I agree this is no place for her, but she is all he has. I'm afraid—"

"Do you mean to tell me," Brody blurted out in disbelief, "that your wife would mother a half-breed?"

Anderson's cerulean blue eyes dressed him down for a moment before he said, "She wouldn't be a Christian if she refused. That's what Christianity is all about."

Brody hot-footed it to his car, rummaged under the seat and got his crank. Looking Anderson straight in the eye, he said, "I've never put much stock in religion." Shrugging, he added, "I never thought there was one to fit a sheriff."

Anderson stood grinning his get-around-grin as Brody whirled the crank around two times and stood listening to the engine purr. Chuckling, Anderson said, "We all have our sizes, Mr. Brody. Our revival starts on Sunday. Why don't you come over and try one on? It might look good on you."

Without promise or rebuke, Brody pitched the crank into the car and crawled behind the wheel. "I'll drive down the river road and look around. My guess is she's off in her boat with that pet king snake."

With an important grin on his face, Brody pulled down the lever and turned toward the river.

"Her boat's tied to the water oak!" Anderson called. "Why do you keep stalling?"

Anderson's eyes flashed fire. "There are enough men at Murphy's store for a search party. It's only three hours till dark. I'm sure there's something wrong. The girl would never leave her papa sick! She takes good care of him."

"I'll see what I can do."

Brody drove away.

Anderson stood looking helplessly after the sheriff, muttering, "I pray the Lord will grab you by the nape of the neck some day, and bring you down to size."

CHAPTER 18

❀

Finding no trace of the girl along the river, Brody felt forced to do something to get the preacher off his back. When he returned to the store, he found tongues wagging, and everyone had a different opinion. Some said she'd only skipped school. Others said she'd be home when dark came.

Wrestling his big, fat body from the lazying bench, Jake Crawford allowed he had to get home. He had an important meeting to attend at seven-thirty. "But," he advised Brody, "the first thing I'd do would be to locate that young wop." Going to the door, he spat a mouthful of tobacco across the porch. "He's been hanging around Upshaw's place. He's up to no good. We ought to tar and feather every foreigner that comes here."

"You had better be careful with your tongue, Crawford. What do you know about that young fella?"

"I know he's too quick on the trigger. He pasted me in the mouth the other day, just because I asked to be waited on before the darkies. I don't think that's asking too much."

"It's a matter of opinion." Brody surveyed the crowd. "Do I have any volunteers? From the looks of that cloud coming over, we could be in for a cyclone. We only have three hours before dark."

"My ol' lady's out of cook wood," one man edged. Another said he had a sick child and had to get home with chill tonic. The excuses went on and on.

By the time Brody got a search organized, the cloud was boiling over the swamp. Lightning forked all around, warning danger to the tender, dry territory, and irritating mosquitoes to an unbearable state.

"It's odd to me that the Upshaw dog would follow that scout's truck away," Murphy broke into the conversation. "He never leaves that girl. Wherever you see her, you see him. For some reason, that boy was in one big hurry to get away from here."

"It's funny," Brody said, latching onto the information, "Anderson didn't mention that to me. Just what are you saying, Murphy? Do you think the girl might have been in the truck?"

"I'm just saying the dog was tearin' at the tarp when the truck went out of sight. I only had a gallon of gasoline to sell him, and the preacher siphoned enough out of his car to get him to State Line. He was in a big hurry."

Thinking that was the first good clue he'd had yet, Brody told the men to spread out over the swamp. He would join them after he'd questioned Anderson again.

Back at the cabin, Anderson was pumping water for the filly and two range cows when Brody pulled up. "How come you didn't mention the Upshaw dog followed the Locati boy's truck off this morning?" the sheriff barked.

"I'm afraid you're jumping to conclusions, Mr. Brody." Anderson kept the pump handle moving. "The dog was chasing the Locati truck, but I'm sure he smelled the snakes. Locati was delivering his catch to Forest Park. Then, too, dogs chase cars like flies chase garbage."

Brody walked closer and eyed Anderson. "I've been told that the boy has been seen hanging around Upshaw's place."

"I'm sure I wouldn't know about that. If I'm any judge of character, the boy could be trusted. From what I've found out, he's from a nice Christian family. No doubt you've been talking to Jake Crawford. He dislikes anyone who isn't of his breed. He thinks blood is thicker than water…if you follow me."

"Just how much do you know about the boy, besides him being from a Christian home? Kids don't always follow Christian training, you know. I'd a little rather not have to put up with foreigners."

"I know the boy saved Crawford's hide when he happened up on Upshaw ducking him in the watering trough. From what I've heard, Crawford asked for it."

"When did that happen? Crawford didn't mention that."

"He wouldn't. Bully's like a gambler." Anderson grinned in spite of himself. "He only talks when he wins."

Brody stood thinking for a moment. "I think I'll have the boy picked up. It can't hurt anything." He rushed to his car when lightning fingered around the pump. He'd left his car running. Pulling the lever down, he stepped on the gas and left Anderson fuming for the second time in less than an hour.

"I'll see what I can do," Brody called back to the preacher.

While men searched the swamp, Shae ran frantically along the rut-gutted road, which she hoped would take her home to her papa. It wouldn't be long until dark and the storm was raging by the minute. Lightning cracked around her, and tree limbs fell in her path. If she could only find a hollow tree. Her papa had warned her to stay away from trees when it was lightning, but she had to get somewhere.

She heard Jock barking a quarter of a mile ahead. What if it's a wolf? She asked herself. Wolves and wildcats were two animals her papa had told her never to trust.

"Oh, Papa…Papa," she groaned as she pushed one foot in front of the other. "I'll never make it home before dark."

When she rounded a curve in the road, she saw Jock barking at what looked to be a big mound of dirt. As she drew closer, she saw it was an old, rotting-down shack. The back corners squatted close to the ground and berry vines covered the door. About the time she got within a hundred yards, a small red fox made a break from the berry vines, with Jock in close pursuit.

Shae could tell the shanty had long since been abandoned. Luscious blackberries hung ripe on the undisturbed vines clinging over the half-open door. She was hungry and thirsty again, but she needed shelter more than food, and the smooth earth floor felt so good to her aching feet. She felt safe within the walls, and she wouldn't be afraid with Jock there.

The only window in the shack had been nailed up with boards. When her eyes got accustomed to the dark inside, she noticed two rusty steel traps hanging on the wall and a burned out king heater in one corner. Other than a battered coffee pot, there was nothing that would hold water.

For an hour, Shae sat against the wall of the shack with her knees pulled up into her stomach. It seemed to help when the pain hit. Every once in a while the green grapes creeping up into her throat folded her over, and she was sure she would have to vomit.

Finally, the pain let up enough that she dozed off. She had no idea how long she slept. When Jock came back and forced his way into the shack, she got up and looked out. It was pitch dark. The wind was blowing. Hail stones as big as quail eggs bounced against the door, causing her to shiver.

Pulling the door closed as much as she could, she looked around for a way to fasten it. It had once had a latch, affording a hole to tie something into it. A shoe string would do, but she needed them in her shoes. It was either use her remaining gallus, or tear up her shirt, which would feel good since the hail had cooled the air.

Tearing the gallus off, she tied one end into the hole in the door, pulled it shut and crammed the buckle into a crack of the door facing. The shack wasn't snake proof, but it would keep the wolves out.

Full and contented, Jock stretched out on the dirt floor and lay snoring by the time Shae cuddled up close to him.

The hail storm was over in a flash, but the wind howled and a hoot owl sat in a tree nearby, hooting whooo-whooo-whooo are you? And wolves howled across the river.

For a long, long time, Shae lay stiff with fear. She'd never slept out alone before. She wondered about Jeff Locati and felt terrible about accusing him of stealing Scar. He had been nice to her, and the only man who called her a lady. Everybody else called her the Upshaw kid, or little squaw.

While she lay safe in the shack with Jock watching over her, five men combed the swamp until the hail storm drove them back to Murphy's store. One man declared he'd tracked Shae to the river, two miles from home. Another swore he'd heard the wolf dog barking about six o'clock, but the wind was so strong, he could never get the direction.

Persuading everyone to be back at Murphy's by daybreak, on horses for another search, Brody went to the telephone and dialed the St. Louis sheriff.

"Yes," he said when the sheriff answered, "this is Sheriff Brody, Cache River, Arkansas. I'd like you to pick up a suspect…a man of about twenty-two or twenty-three. He's traveling in a Model-T truck, on his way to Forest Park in St. Louis. He left here early this morning. We think he may have taken a girl from Cache swamp. He should be there by now."

"What's that? Oh, the man's Jeff Locati."

"No, I don't have his license number, but he's a tall, dark-complected fella with black curly hair. Call me at Murphy's store if you pick him up." Giving him the number, Brody hung up the receiver and went home for the night.

At the cabin, the Andersons faithfully watched over Upshaw through the night. They drank black coffee and pumped cold water to bathe Upshaw's fever down, and waited for news of Shae.

Several times the old man looked blankly around the room in the dim coal oil lamplight, and asked for Girly, muttering, "She ought to be home by now."

"She will be home soon," Anderson calmed him each time. With a fresh, cold towel on his head, Upshaw would fall back into a deep sleep.

In the shack, it must have been twelve o'clock before Shae dropped off to sleep, only to wake up screaming with a nightmare. She dreamed a monster was pulling her by the hair of her head, down in to a deep, dark hole.

"Papa! Papa!" she screamed, fighting at the air.

Jock was on his feet, ready to do murder, but everything smelled normal. He heard the eerie howl of the wolves. He was used to them, slept through the noise every night.

When Shae finally decided it was a dream, she sat as close to Jock as she could get, staring into the darkness of the dungeon. She trembled with fear, thinking any minute that something would break in at the door and swallow her up.

Assuring her that everything was all right, Jock sprawled down for another nap and Shae cuddled down beside him. But she didn't sleep. Hot liquid kept boiling up in her throat and she felt sick to her stomach. Then it suddenly happened. A green grape cramp hit her in the pit of her stomach, doubling her over in pain.

"Oh, Jock." She doubled over again, holding her stomach with both hands. "If only I had a drink of water. If Papa could be here, he'd give me some Red liniment." She'd never been so sick since she had made a pig of herself on fresh pigs' feet. Her papa had to wash bedclothes in the overflow that night. What if she got in a mess like that out here alone? Finally, the pain got so bad, she crawled to the wall and upchucked. For the longest time, she hunkered there with the dry heaves. Her mouth was so dry she could hardly swallow.

Jock stood by, whining his sympathy until he crawled back to the center of the shack and sat choking for water.

The door creaked and groaned. She imagined she heard something scratching at it, but Jock didn't move. Exhausted from heaving so long, she stretched out beside Jock and succumbed to some much needed sleep.

CHAPTER 19

❈

It was dusk-dark when Jeff Locati pulled up to Forest Park. Ralph Boyd, the park attendant, was closing the gate for the night. "Hello there," he greeted Jeff cheerily. "I was about to give up on you. Did you have trouble?" Boyd opened the gate for Jeff to drive inside.

"Yes, I did." Jeff pulled the truck inside the gate and crawled out. "I left Cache River early this morning. Should've been here hours ago, but my radiator kept boiling over and a wolf dog followed me most of the way to State Line. I couldn't chase him back. I knew he would be lost and he belonged to a friend in Cache River."

"Have you had any supper?" Boyd started to close the gate when he noticed a marked car driving toward them.

"No." Jeff kept his gaze on the car. "I've only had a coke all day, and I'm famished." He started to say more, but stopped when he noticed 'County Sheriff' written on the side of the car.

The vehicle had hardly stopped rolling before a big, burly hunk of a man bounced out and swaggered toward them. His face reflected a give-me-no-lip look, and the pistol strapped on his waist—a mean-looking one—hung lower than necessary. He lost no time flashing his badge, saying, "I'm Bob Morris, the county sheriff."

Something told Jeff the big man was after him. Struck dumb, he stood waiting for his boss to speak.

"Yes, sir," Boyd looked over at Jeff. "What can we do for you?"

The sheriff cut a mean eye toward Jeff. "Does your name happen to be Jeff Locati?"

"W-why...yes, sir," Jeff stammered as a lump came up in his throat. "That's my name, sir."

"Does this boy work for you, Mr. Boyd?"

"He does," Boyd said, nodding. "He has for three years."

"I'm told by the Green County sheriff that you left Cache River early today. He says he has reason to believe that you had a girl with you."

Stunned, Jeff opened his mouth to say something, but no words came. Looking helplessly at Boyd, he swallowed, his Adam's apple working overtime, and he stood speechless.

"Well, did you?" the sheriff barked.

Jeff's face blanched as he finally responded with, "I don't understand what you're talking about, sir."

"I have a warrant to search your truck." Morris produced the legal document.

"Yes, sir," having nothing to hide, Jeff went to the back of the truck and untied the tarp.

The sheriff looked it over suspiciously. "What happened to the tarpaulin?"

"A dog ripped it up, sir. I ran out of gasoline. While I walked to the station to get a gallon, he tried to get at the snakes in the truck."

"Where is the dog? Who does it belong to?"

"He belongs to Mr. Upshaw at Cache River, sir. I tried to chase him back home two or three times. While I was gone, he left, but not before he ripped the back end of my tarp."

The sheriff had raised a leg to hop into the truck, until Jeff mentioned snakes. Stepping back, he smirked, "Get into the truck and take everything out."

Obediently, Jeff hopped into the back end, lifted the snake cages out one by one, then hauled the tent from the front corner and shook it vigorously. As he did so, a bottle of quinine rolled near the sheriff's feet.

"What's this?" Sheriff Morris scooped up the bottle, unscrewed the cap and looked inside. "Quinine.... Where did this come from?"

Jeff swallowed hard when Morris unscrewed the lid. "I'm sure I don't know, sir." But he had seen the Upshaw girl buy quinine at Murphy's store earlier that morning. So that's why the dog was following me, he thought.

"Oh, lord." He silently prayed as blood rushed to his temples. "How will I ever explain this?"

"You have the right to keep silent," the sheriff informed. "Anything you say could go against you in court. But…" Morris pulled a pair of handcuffs from his pocket. "…I'll have to take you in."

Dumbfounded, Jeff looked toward Ralph Boyd to see him standing with his mouth open. Finally, Boyd said, "I can't believe this. Jeff would never break the law. There has to be a mistake, sheriff."

"Sorry." The sheriff locked the handcuffs around Jeff's wrists and motioned him toward the car. "We will talk about that in the court room, sir."

"Is there anything I can do for you, Jeff?" Boyd followed him toward the sheriff's car. "Should I call your father?"

"No, please, I would appreciate you calling Reverend Anderson at Cache River. He is the only one who can clear me of this horrid accusation. He knows I was alone when I left the swamp. He loaned me gasoline to get to Stateline."

"I've warned you of your rights, young man." The sheriff impatiently opened the car door. "You'd do well to remember it." He slammed the door before Jeff got seated, got behind the wheel and drove toward the jail.

Nodding to Jeff that he would call Anderson, Boyd stood unbelieving of what he'd heard. What could have happened?

❧   ❧   ❧

The stench of unbathed bodies stung Jeff's nostrils as he entered the jail. He could feel hard, criminal eyes glaring at him through the iron bars on each side as he walked down the hall to cell eighteen. He had never been inside a jailhouse, much less slept in one. A knot hit the bottom of his stomach and he felt as if he would vomit there in the hall.

The forty-year-old jail offered a sight for Jeff's young eyes. The inside conditions were inhumane. The finality of the experience gripped him when the guard clicked the lock on the huge iron door. Looking around the pigsty, he noticed a dirty cot in one corner with a naked pillow at its head. A few dog-eared books lay scattered over the floor. What Jeff supposed to be a bathroom lay behind a door hanging by one hinge, and the odor coming from it verged on the unbearable. Unable to make sense of the situation, he made two laps around the eight foot room, crumpled on the cot, and lowered his aching head into his hands.

"Oh, Lord," he prayed softly to the God he'd been taught to believe in. "What have I done to deserve this?"

For a long time, he sat staring at the dirty floor. What would his parents think? Finally, raising his head, he saw a little old man grinning a toothy grin through the bars.

"Sonny," he sniggered, "if you're waitin' for someone to rock you to sleep, they don't do that in here."

Jeff had never been a violent person, but clinching a hand into a fist, he told himself if he could get to this monkey, he would cram his fist down the man's throat. Knowing he couldn't go further than the dirty bathroom, he again lowered his head into his hands and sat wondering what his girlfriend, Sara, would think.

It was long past suppertime. He had no appetite, anyway. His mother's mouth-watering biscuits and gravy, which he'd thought about all the way to the park, all but turned his stomach. What he wouldn't give for a cold drink of water.

Going to the washbowl, he washed the tobacco rings from the lip of the cup and forced down two cups of the slow flowing water, then made a few more laps around the room.

It must have been midnight when Jeff decided he was in for the night. Until Ralph Boyd got in touch with Reverend Anderson, he had no way of proving his innocence. Moping back to the cot, he took off his shoes and dropped his head on his knees, which gouged him under the chin as he sat there. For the longest time he listened to the crickets chirping. Mulling his situation over in his mind, he went over all the events of the long, hot day. Several times, he asked himself, why me?

Finally, the thought struck him. Oh my Lord! What if the girl was in the truck when I crossed the state line? They will stick me with white slavery. Those people will tar and feather *me*!

"Oh," he groaned. "How will I ever get myself out of this mess? She had to be under the tent!"

His thoughts wandered on and on. How could she have hidden under the tent? It had to have been at least a hundred degrees under there.

Giving up the ghost, Jeff slung the foul-smelling pillow to a far corner of the cell, stretched out on the naked cot with his hands under his head, and fell into exhausted sleep.

❋   ❋   ❋

Finding no one at Anderson's home number, Ralph Boyd gave up and finally called the only business number in Cache River.

"Murphy's store," Frank Murphy grumbled into the receiver five minutes before opening up. "What say?" He listened with a hand behind one ear. "Do I know a Reverend Anderson? Yes." He hesitated, then, "But he lives three miles from here. Call his number. He has a phone."

"Oh? Not home? Maybe he's still with the sick man."

"You say it's urgent? Yes, sir, I'll give him the number—just a minute! Anderson just now stepped in the door." To Anderson, he said, "A long distance call for you, preacher." Holding the receiver out to Anderson, Murphy stood close by, so as not to miss anything.

"Ralph Boyd, did you say?" Anderson asked into the receiver. "From Forest Park," What can I do for you, Mr. Boyd?" Anderson listened intently into the phone.

"Sure, I know Jeff Locati. Why?" He stood dumbfounded for a moment. "You have to be mistaken, sir. What happened?"

When Anderson heard what the charges were, he stood stunned so long; Boyd thought he'd been disconnected. Finally, he said, "I will have to call you back, Mr. Boyd. Could I have your number?"

After writing down the phone number, Anderson turned to Murphy and asked for the pound of coffee he'd come for, hoping he could get away without answering any questions. But he had no luck.

Delaying him by dipping up too much coffee, dipping some out, then tying it extra well, Murphy pulled his specs down his nose and asked, "What's that young wop into now?" He looked Anderson in the eye for a straight answer.

"I wouldn't want to say until I get the facts." Anderson picked up the coffee and his change, just as three of the fellows from the search party rode up and tied their horses to the hitching post. Knowing he'd been with Upshaw since yesterday morning, one of them asked, "Has the old Indian kicked the bucket?" Another one said, "I don't suppose the young squaw has made it home?"

"No to both of your questions." Anderson cut over to the side of the porch and went to his car without making any small talk with them. He saw Sheriff Brody driving up. He didn't want to talk to him, either. He was sure Brody was the instigator of the boy's trouble. There was nothing he could do for Jeff until the doctor came to Upshaw's, and maybe not even then. He was pretty sure Mr. Upshaw would be sent to the hospital, but there'd have to be arrangements made, and that would take time.

Three of the search party waved at Anderson as he got into his car. Seeing he was in a hurry, they went into Murphy's store to buy lunch to take along on the trip. Anderson was in the act of driving away when he heard Brody's horn tooting. Pushing his brake in, he sat waiting as the sheriff pulled to a stop, crawled from his car, and swaggered toward him.

"Good morning, sheriff." Anderson made no move to get out of the car. "What can I do for you?"

"I was wondering if the Upshaw girl has made it home. I was on my way up there, before we start the search."

"No, she hasn't, sheriff. My wife and I have been there with her father all night. I'm worried. She would never go away and leave her papa sick. She came to the store for medicine early yesterday morning, and left here in a run. That's why I went to see about Mr. Upshaw."

"Do you know what kind of medicine she bought, preacher?" Brody kept his eyes on Anderson as he hesitated.

"I heard the girl ask for chill tonic. Murphy was out, but said quinine would do the same thing. She took the quinine and left here in a run. I'm sure she was going home."

"I've been told that you left the store with Locati, and was seen talking to him before he left," Brody probed. "Did you happen to see inside the back of the truck?"

"No, sir, the Upshaw dog was scratching at the tarpaulin when we walked out there. He'd pulled the slipknot loose and was trying to jump into the truck. He smelled the snakes. I think Locati suspected that the girl might have untied the rope. He crawled inside, but apparently found nothing disturbed. But the dog was still following the truck when it went out of sight." Anderson weighed the situation in his mind. "It puzzles me."

"We have reason to believe—" Brody chewed his cigar over to the other side of his mouth. "—that the girl had been in the back of the truck. The sheriff who picked him up found a bottle of quinine when the boy shook out the tent. Somewhere along the way, the dog ripped the whole back end of his tarpaulin."

"Maybe I'm not a good judge of character, sheriff, but I just can't believe that boy would do a thing like that. He's a great personality, very interested in other people's welfare."

"That will be all for now, preacher." Brody wheeled on his heel and sauntered into the store where a covey of men stood huddled together, lighting up a smoke of Bull Durham.

What should I do now? Anderson sat watching the sheriff as he disappeared into the store. Finally, he drove toward Upshaw's place with a lot of gut-tightening questions on his mind. It looked bad for the boy. But there was little he could do until the doctor came back to take care of Mr. Upshaw.

"Well, fellas," Brody called across the store to the group of men, "how many of you are going on the search? It's gonna be hotter than hot out there. Water your horses and carry a snack with you. The Cache is poison with typhoid. We will search as far as the state line. From there on is Missouri's jurisdiction."

"State line!" one fellow yelped. "That's eighteen miles from here! My horse can't make it in this weather!"

Walking back toward his car, Brody directed the men to mount and scatter over the swamp. "Cover as much ground as possible. I'd like to get this situation solved as soon as we can. There will be clean drinking water ten miles up north." Then Brody called over his shoulder, "Make your canteens last until you get there."

All the men knew the swamp well, but none of them knew it any better than Shae. All opinions were against the scout, and they were after his hide. It wasn't so much that they wanted the young squaw back, as they wanted the wop gone from Cache River. The old timers would like nothing better than having the dark-skins out of the county, and they would go to any means to make it come to pass.

The searchers rode for three hours. Their horses were in a lather when one man held up a hand. Everyone listened for a moment, and the man said, "Hold it! Did I hear a dog bark?"

CHAPTER 20

❧

Fighting her way out of another blood-curdling nightmare, Shae uncurled her sore, aching body and opened her eyes. For a minute, she looked around her strange surroundings, wondering where she could be. Then it all came back to her. She was lost, miles from home. If Jock was going the wrong way, there was no telling where they would wind up, and she would never see her papa again.

When she finally came out of her stupor, dawn had cracked and Jock stood scratching at the door to get outside. Shae had only slept a few fitful naps all night and she could hardly hold her eyes open.

If I only had a drink of cold water.... She licked her dry lips and coaxed Jock to quit scratching at the door so she could get some sleep. Now that it was daylight, she wasn't afraid. "The snakes will be crawlin' everywhere, Jock. We can't get out till after sunup. I sure don't want another snake bite." Jock kept scratching at the door. Struggling to her aching feet, she untied the gallus. The door fell back and Jock bound outside.

When Jock came back from the creek with his whiskers wet, Shae opened her eyes again and she knew she had to have water. She limped toward the creek on her swollen feet. The stream was only a trickle running from a beaver dam, but it was cold and it soothed her parched throat as she lay flat on the ground and drank. It felt so good to her feverish stomach.

When Shae looked around, Jock crossed the creek and went chasing after a cottontail rabbit. She knew he would not be back until he'd caught his breakfast. Hobbling back to the shanty, she tackled the blackberry briers climbing over the broken down porch. After picking a big handful of the juicy berries, she sat down and thumped the stink bugs from them, then gorged herself on the overripe berries.

It was a half hour before Jock returned and she was feeling much better, telling herself the berries would make her well. She remembered when she'd stuffed herself on pig's feet. Her Papa had given her berry juice. It always made her feel better.

When Jock came back licking his chops, Shae knew he had caught the rabbit, and they both felt like traveling. "We gotta get goin', Jock." She tousled the long, black bristles on the wolf dog's neck. "Papa will be out lookin' for us, if he's not in bed with a chill. Unable to get her swollen feet into her tennis shoes, Shae tied them around her waist, then followed Jock down a path along the creek, which she was pretty sure would take them to Cache River.

Shae thought about many things as she limped along. It was all she could do to keep Jock in sight. Her mind wandered back to Jeff Locati. What had he thought when he'd found the back end ripped from his tarpaulin? He's probably back to the swamp by now, she supposed, never dreaming that he was sweating it out in jail in St. Louis.

🍁 🍁 🍁

"Outa the sack! Outa the sack!"

The bellow of a grizzly guard brought Locati up with a start before daybreak the next morning. Getting to his feet, he ambled to the washbowl. The faucet was dripping, and the bowl was full. After catching water in his hand to wash his face, he combed his hair with his fingers, stumbled back to his cot, and sat waiting, for he didn't know what.

The orange, August sun was blazing through his tiny barred window. The guard opened the door a crack and pushed a tray toward him, with what looked like a bowl of cornmeal mush, two cathead biscuits and a cup of muddy coffee.

"May I have a glass of water, sir?" Jeff slung a handful of sweat from his brow. "There's no drinking glass at the sink."

"Glass!" the guard responded with a big, belly laugh. Use your tin cup. We don't serve crystal around here." Leaving Locati staring at whatever it was in the bowl and the day old biscuits, the guard rolled the cart on down the hall to the next door.

Jeff dumped his muddy coffee into the commode, turned on the faucet, and drank stagnant water from his tin cup. At least it was wet.

It was an hour before the guard came back for the empty dishes. When he noticed the untouched food, he turned cold, surly eyes on Jeff.

"Whatcha waitin' fer, Buddy, candlelight and roses?"

"Thank you, sir," Jeff said, recoiling from the guard's angry eyes, "but I'm not hungry."

"You will be before you get outa here, boy. There won't be nothin' else until you eat this, be it a day or a week." Wheeling on his heel, the guard left.

Without blinking an eye or opening his mouth, Jeff watched the guard roll the squeaky cart back toward the kitchen. Then he piled himself back on the hard cot and dropped his head into his hands, wondering if he had one friend in the whole wide world.

Oh, God in heaven…Surely Minister Anderson knows by now I'm locked up! He rolled his head in his hands. Only he and God can save me.

Voices in the hall brought Jeff's head upright. Maybe it was help coming. But it was only the sheriff escorting another prisoner to the next cell. Then Jeff heard a paperboy up the hall yelling, "Read all about it! Read all about it!"

Suddenly, Jeff thought of his parents. His father would be having his coffee with the St. Louis Globe in his hand.

What will he think? And Mama will be horrified!

🍁 🍁 🍁

The sun was just peeping over the treetops when Dr. Bond arrived at the Upshaw place to find his patient sleeping fitfully and Fred Anderson nodding in a nearby chair. He had spent the whole night changing the cold towels on Upshaw's forehead.

"Better than I expected to find him."

Dr. Bond woke up Anderson, talking to himself. "Morning preacher, I can see you've been a busy man through the night." He went about taking Upshaw's temperature. Reading the thermometer, he found the man's fever down three points, which helped, but Upshaw was still a very sick man. "Mr. Murphy was good enough to let us have a small chunk of ice. It helped a lot."

Anderson pulled himself from the chair, stretched and yawned. "Sorry, but we used up the last of the coffee early in the night."

"Why don't you and your wife go home for some rest?" the doctor suggested as he opened the patient's eyes and checked his pupils. He listened to Upshaw's heartbeat. "The Red Cross promised to meet me here at ten o'clock. I have hopes of getting this man into a hospital soon."

"That sounds good." Anderson yawned again. "I promised Locati's boss that I'd call soon."

"Have you heard from the child yet?" Dr. Bond asked as he went about making his patient comfortable.

"Not a word. They're holding Locati in jail. His boss informed me that the sheriff met him as he pulled into Forest Park about dusk last night. While searching his truck, the sheriff confiscated a bottle of quinine."

The doctor's eyes bugged. "What do you make of that? Didn't you say the girl bought quinine and then left for home? That sounds bad to me, Preacher."

"I'm at a loss for words, Doctor. I'd swear on a bible that the boy was alone when he pulled out from Murphy's store, unless he picked the girl up on the road home. I know she bought quinine." Anderson scratched his head. "It's a mystery to me."

Walking out to where Vivian stood over a washboard rubbing a sheet, Anderson took the linen once she rung it and hung it on a line. "The doctor says we should go home for a few hours rest," He told his wife. "He'll be here to meet with the Red Cross. We might have to stay again tonight."

Vivian did not argue with that. Her eyes could hardly stay open and her feet were swelling out over her high-heel pumps.

"Just a moment," Dr. Bond said, staying Anderson when he stuck his head in at the door to say they were leaving.

Anderson did not have to wonder long what the doctor wanted. Dr. Bond picked up a needle from his black bag, stuck it into a bottle of alcohol, and asked Anderson to roll up his sleeve. After drawing blood from both Anderson and his wife, Dr. Bond put it into a bottle and labeled it. "Thanks for your help, folks. Now go home for some much needed rest. I'll stay until help comes."

The minute Anderson got home, he went to the wall telephone and rung Ralph Boyd's number. "Is Mr. Ralph Boyd there?"

"Yes."

"This is Reverend Anderson from Cache River. Sorry I've been so long, but I have been with a very sick man all night, and he doesn't have a phone. What is the situation with Jeff Locati?"

"Sorry, I can't tell you much. But the Globe made it sound bad. They haven't allowed anyone to talk to him yet. I'm sure there has to be a mistake, but he is going to have to prove it." Ralph Boyd sighed. "I just don't understand how this happened."

"If we could only locate the Upshaw girl," Anderson assured, "I'm sure she could straighten the situation out."

"Please, call me the moment you hear anything. Meantime, I'll see what I can find out from the sheriff." Boyd hesitated to say more.

"I promise…if the girl is in the swamp, the searchers will find her. She can't very well hide with the wolf dog along, and he won't leave her. Good-bye, Mr. Boyd."

Vivian Anderson was sound asleep by the time her head hit the pillow. It had been a long twenty-four hours for her. After placing the receiver back in the cradle, Anderson sat for an hour mulling the situation over and over in his head. Could the man have picked the girl up on his way out? Nature could play tricks on the best of minds. No, the Locati fellow was not that sort, and he wasn't dumb.

Unable to solve anything, Anderson's head dropped to the back of the chair, where he'd planted his weary body after talking to Boyd. After another hour, he fell into a deep sleep.

❦ ❦ ❦

Jeff Locati's father picked up the morning Globe from the porch, and opened it up while his wife cooked breakfast. Jeff's picture stared at him from the front page. Shocked, he looked again before he moaned, "Oh…no! No! Mama! This can't be true! Our Sonny's in bad trouble!"

"What? What is it, Papa?" Jeff's mama grabbed the paper her husband shoved toward her. She read it while she limped around on her rheumatic leg, cooking breakfast and making ready to go to work at the garment factory, where she'd worked all of her life. "Our Sonny's in jail!" she gasped, and crumbled into a chair beside her husband, where he sat with his head in his hands.

"This can't be true, Papa."

She read the headline on the front page of the trembling paper. "Sonny would never do a thing like that. What will we do, Papa? What will we do?"

"Don't know, Mama. It'll take money to bond him out, and we still owe for last week's groceries."

Jeff's father wiped a tear from his cheek with a withered hand. "I'll go to the bank and see if I can mortgage the house." Taking the paper from his wife's trembling hand, he read the article again, not believing his eyes. "Call my boss and tell him that I can't come in today."

After calling her husband's boss, Jeff's mother stood listening to the clock tick the minutes away. It was time for her to leave for work, but how could she face all those people? Finally, she picked up the phone and called her boss. "I'm sorry," she quavered, "I don't feel well today. I won't be in for work." Dropping the receiver back into the cradle, she moaned, "Oh, Sonny!"

"I have a feeling that this is all a mistake, Mama. Everything is going to be all right. It's just going to take a little time, but I'm sure Jeff can prove his innocence. Take it easy, Mama." He patted her cheek and then hurried out the door before he remembered that the bank would not be open for another two hours. He walked around the block to control his nerves, and came back home to find his wife sobbing uncontrollably. "Now, now, Mama, bad luck comes to everyone. Don't make yourself sick. It won't help anything."

The clock had ticked away another hour before Jeff's mother got control of her dry-retching sobs. She finally sat quietly, thinking of how she'd worked and prayed to bring her boys up to be gentlemen. So far she had never been disappointed. And of all her sons, Jeff had always been the most thoughtful.

Jeff's papa spent the longest two hours of his life, waiting for the bank to open. He was at the door when it opened.

Mama sat asking herself, What if the bank will not lend the money on the house? It was old. The bank had refused to loan money to repair it five years ago. The roof leaked, and the paint had long since worn away. She looked at the clock. He'd been gone two hours. Drying away her tears, she limped to the window and looked out. He should have been back long before now.

Shae was sitting on a stump, resting her swollen feet, when she heard Jock give a throaty growl. "What is it, Jock?" She jumped up from the stump just in time to see a big grey wolf flash out of the creek and head straight for her, Jock in close pursuit. The wolf was within ten feet of her when Jock tore into its back end. Turning, the wolf went for Jock's jugular. The two went together in a savage fight. Over and over they rolled, while Shae went skinning up a sweet gum tree. Once she was safe, she sat on a limb watching the two animals tear each other apart. It looked as if Jock would lose the battle. She could tell he was wearing down, and blood streamed from his nose. But the last rollover, Jock got his chance. Hanging an inch-long fang into the wolf's neck, he ripped it wide open. The wolf came back with all the fight left in him, but as its blood flowed freely, it fell back, giving Jock full control. Jock never let up until the wolf lay staring flat on the ground, with blood gushing from its jugular vein.

Jock stood over the wolf, with his tongue hanging out. When he was sure of his kill, he sat back on his haunches and thumped his tail on the ground and waited until the last drop of blood drained from the wolf's neck. Shae clambered down from the tree and ran to the wolf dog.

"Jock! She crimped the gash on his nose with her fingers. "You're bleedin' to death! Oh, what will we do, Jock?"

Jock had not faired much better than the wolf, but he was still alive. His shoulder was cut up, one eye and a nostril was ripped open, yet he stood up to lick Shae's hand. Shae kept the gash on Jock's nose crimped until the blood slowed.

"Let's go to the creek and wash your face, Jock. The cold water will stop the blood." As Shae splashed cold water on Jock's nose, he pricked his ears and raised his bristles.

"What was that, Jock?" As she listened, she heard a car struggling along the pot-hole road. "Be quiet, Jock."

Coaxing Jock down under the creek bank, they lay very still. The car jogged past. When it was a hundred yards up the road, Shae peeped over the bank and put her finger to her lip. Understanding, Jock lay still.

Hunkering down beside Jock, the two of them lay motionless, when another car came into hearing. As it came into view, she recognized Sheriff Brody at the wheel. She had only seen the man once, but he had a face she would never forget.

"Quiet, Jock. It's old Sheriff Brody. If he catches me, he might put me into the orphan's home. That's what Jake Crawford wants him to do."

Jock lay very still, enjoying the cold water on his nose, until a horn blared on one of the cars. Raising his head, he let out a howl that would awaken the dead.

CHAPTER 21

❀

"Quiet, Jock." Shae slapped him across the sore nose and the blood started to flow. "I'm sorry, Jock." She pinched the wound tight with her fingers as a petrifying spasm of fear gripped her. "They will come after us for sure. We've got to get out of here!"

Coaxing Jock to his feet, Shae crossed the creek and ran down an old tram-road, which led her into deep timber. Her heart pounded and her side pained terrible as she stopped behind a big cypress tree.

❦   ❦   ❦

Jim Brody stepped from his car and looked around; sure he'd heard a dog howl. Tucking a hand behind his ear, he listened for a minute. It wasn't likely to be a timber wolf. They never howled in daytime.

Brody was not about to walk in the heat, for it could give a fella a sunstroke. The kid was likely home by now, anyhow. Getting back into his car, he drove slowly on north until he found a place wide enough to turn around, which took some doing. A logger's road a half-mile on up the road afforded a place to back up. He worked at it until the radiator boiled over. He would have to wait for the engine to cool now. He sat with one ear cocked toward where he thought he'd heard the dog howl, but the woods were calm. Not a leaf stirred. Taking off his straw hat, he sat fanning himself.

When the radiator cooled off, Brody took a bucket from the car and walked slowly toward the creek for water.

❦ ❦ ❦

The slap across the nose had served its purpose. When Jock caught up to Shae, he cowered down beside her. She kept a finger to her lips, and sat holding her breath every time Jock pricked his ears.

The big cypress tree Shae was hiding behind told her she was into the Cache River swamp. What little water trickled down the creek was running in the right direction, but she had no idea how far she was from home.

The springy ground under her feet felt so good. Her feet were still swollen and she couldn't get up on them. She sat like a manikin as Brody's car passed back by, and she knew he was on his way home. When the car finally went out of hearing, she sat thinking of what her papa would say when he found out that she'd not only sneaked into the hunter's truck, but had lost the quinine. If he had another chill, he would roast alive, with no one to bathe his fever down.

It was sometime before Shae dared to venture from the heavy timber. She knew there had been two cars that had passed. If one happened to blow a horn, Jock would howl. He could never stand a car horn, or a wolf-whistle. His ears were sensitive. He looked as if he was going to take a nap.

When she could stand her thirst no longer, Shae listened closely and eased from behind the tree. The creek was a good hundred yards away, but she had to have water. Her throat was parched, and Jock's nose was still bleeding.

"Jock, we gota stop that bleedin'." Shae sighed. "There I go again, droppin' my G's." "I will remember them when I get back in school," she thought. "Blast 'em anyhow. Why do they have to hang on to the tail of every word?"

Flopping down on her stomach when she got to the creek, she drank nearly a quart of water. Then she washed her sweaty face in the cold stream. Jock stood cooling his sore nose before he lapped thirstily. Once they were cooled off, he turned down stream, and Shae knew he was headed for home.

It was sometime before the locale looked familiar. Birds twittered and a cottontail jumped from a brush pile along the way. Shae stopped when she thought she heard a cow bell far off. Then Jock stopped, curled his tail into a donut, raised his bristles, and braced a foot, ready to attack.

"What is it, Jock?" Shae whispered as she caught up to him. As they both stood motionless, she heard a horse whinny. Another one answered. Pretty soon the clip-clop of hooves brought Jock's ears straight up.

"No…no!" Shae shushed him. Then she saw a man riding slowly along the road. What if he was looking for her?

"Come, Jock."

She coaxed the wolf dog behind a tree and kept quieting him until the man passed on.

For the next two hours, she had to run to keep in sight of Jock, which made her think that he knew where he was going. The sun was straight overhead, and she had sweated the last drop of water from her body.

Finally, exhausted, Jock stretched himself out on a mound of grass and refused to move. Unable to coax him to his feet, Shae hunkered down beside him. As they sat there, she gazed around for some sign of the swamp. When she saw what she thought to be a water willow, she thought they must be near the Cache. Surely, she could find her way home now.

Jock's nose had stopped bleeding, and the gash over his eye had swollen shut. If they didn't keep moving, he would get so stiff; she knew he wouldn't be able to walk. She remembered the time he'd fought with the wildcat and how she'd had to carry his food to him under the cabin for three days.

"C'mon, Jock." Shae got to her feet. "You wouldn't want to stay out here with these wolves another night, would you?"

For a while, they struggled through underbrush so thick, Shae's shirt was in shreds. Her hair fell over her body, and she was faint from thirst.

It was away in the afternoon when Shae recognized Persimmon slough, where she'd gone many times with her papa to dig mussel shells. She knew now she was at least five miles from home. Her papa had always packed lunch to take along. He had once found a nice pearl in one of the big mollusks. But the slough was only a hog-wallow now, covered with green slime. She was tempted to skim it back and drink from it, but she thought of typhoid. Instead, she grabbled around the edge and loaded her pockets with big purple shells.

🍁 🍁 🍁

Jeff's mama sat in the same chair she'd crumbled into after she'd called their employers. Dry sobs wracked her overweight body, until her husband came home from the bank with the news they had both expected.

"Mama," he laid an arm around her shoulder. "The bank adviser allowed that our rundown house would not be worth what it would take to bond Sonny out of jail, even if kidnapping was a bondable crime."

The word 'kidnapping' brought Jeff's mama up with a start. "Oh, Papa! That can't be true." She twisted her gnarled hands into her apron. "Sonny would never do a thing like that. We have got to get him out of there, some way. We've just got to!"

"I know, Mama, but until the child is found, anything we say is fruitless. We know he would never do a thing like that. They don't. I'm sure he can prove his innocence, but it will take time. They will have to prove him guilty. The minister from Cache River promised to call the sheriff here, the minute he has any news of the child. All we can do is wait for that to happen."

For the longest time, Jeff's father sat silently by his devastated wife. What was there to say? When he could stand the suspense no longer, he decided to go to the jail. If he could only talk to Jeff, it would help.

As expected, the jailer turned Locati away, saying there would be no visitors for Jeff until after the hearing in the afternoon. With a burdened mind, he rode the trolley back home to sit out the most miserable hours of his life, while Jeff paced the eight foot cell, and Shae walked the cow-path, which would finally lead her home.

❦ ❦ ❦

Reverend Anderson caught a few fitful naps in a chair, without taking his clothes off. When he opened his eyes and glanced at the clock, he couldn't believe it was three o'clock.

"Vivian? Vivian!" He shook his wife awake. "I'm going to the store to see if the search party is back. I promised to call the boy's boss." Pulling on his shoes, he added, "We will have to relieve the folks at Upshaw's by six o'clock."

When Anderson got to Murphy's store, Jim Brody was watering his horse at the trough.

"Any news of the girl, sheriff?" Anderson waited anxiously as Brody chewed on a big cigar.

"Not a word, preacher. I was sure I heard a dog howl once, but I found no tracks, nothing."

As the two men stood talking, two more of the search party rode in on hot, thirsty horses, with the same news. Within the next hour, all the searchers were at the watering trough, and not one had a clue as to Shae's whereabouts.

❦   ❦   ❦

While Jeff Locati walked the jail cell, wondering how Sara Rainey, his girlfriend, would react to the awful situation he'd gotten himself into, Sara had answered an emergency call from her uncle. Her Aunt had given birth to their fifth child two months premature, and would be off her feet for ten days. Since Sara was on vacation from her job at the hospital, she couldn't refuse to go for a week. The family lived so far out back in the Ozarks, they had no phone, and the newspaper only came once a week. Sara had no way of knowing Jeff was in trouble. Then, too, Jeff wasn't supposed to be home for another week.

Sara had dreamed of becoming a nurse, but money had been out of the question. So she had taken the next best job. A job at anything was a plus in the nineteen-thirties.

A beautiful Italian girl, Sara could have married into the upper-class families, but she had chosen to wait for Jeff.

❦   ❦   ❦

Fred Anderson knew he had to phone the bad news to Jeff's boss, but decided to go to Upshaw's first. Not one of the searchers had inquired there. When he got to Upshaw's, he found Jock lapping water from the horse trough.

"Hello, there, fella." He hurried to the wolf dog. "Where's the girl?" He looked the tattered dog over sorrowfully, and wondered if the girl would be in the same shape.

When Jock satisfied his thirst, he limped to the cabin and climbed carefully up the step, limped across the porch, and scratched on the screen to get inside. For a minute after Jock had gone inside, he stood confused. Finally, he limped over, and laid his head on the bed. Disappointed when there was no response from his master, he licked the old man's face and then stretched out on the floor for a long needed nap.

"Come, fella," Reverend Anderson coaxed Jock. "You look as if you've been cornered by a wildcat. Let's see if we can find something for that nose." Before he got the dog off the floor, Shae came running to the cabin door with her hair hanging down her face and her clothes barely hanging on her body.

"Papa! Papa!" she yelled. "I'm home!"

Like Jock, she fell back at sight of the strangers, but when she saw her papa still and pale on the bed, she rushed to his side. "What is it, papa? Did you have another chill? Papa? Papa?" She cradled his head in her arms. "It's 'cause I lost the quinine. I couldn't help it. I got lost."

"I'm afraid your father isn't hearing you, child." Reverend Anderson laid a hand on her arm to lead her away. "Maybe later, he needs to rest now."

"No. No!" Shae stood waiting for her papa to speak. "It was my fault he had the chill. If I'd gotten home with the quinine…"

"Where did you get lost, child?" Reverend Anderson couldn't help asking.

"I…I just got lost, I went to the store and…" Her chin trembled and she turned away.

Guessing she didn't want to discuss the situation, Anderson turned to Mrs. Daily. "Would you please help the child get cleaned up and feed her? She must be famished. I'll go for my wife and make a phone call to St. Louis."

Too tired to argue that she wasn't a child, Shae went to her room for a change of clothes. Bathed, combed and fed, Shae didn't look anything like the waif Sheriff Brody had described to the welfare case worker over the phone. He had made sure that the Green County Red Cross knew the full situation of the Upshaws. He also listened in on the conversation Anderson had related to Ralph Boyd, Jeff Locati's boss at Forest Park in St. Louis. After giving all the information of the girl's arrival back home, the preacher had assured Boyd that he was sure the girl would clear everything up as soon as she knew the Locati boy was in trouble over her.

"I will be right out to question the girl," Brody called after Anderson. "Then I will contact the sheriff in St. Louis."

"I would appreciate it, if you would wait an hour or two, Mr. Brody. The child is exhausted and terrible upset about her father."

"Crime won't wait, preacher!" Brody barked. "I have a duty to perform, you know."

By the time the Andersons returned to Upshaw's, Dr. Bond was busy with his needle. Shae stood petrified as the Daileys got their shots and the doctor refilled the syringe for her. She'd never been to a doctor that she could remember.

"Young lady," The doctor walked cautiously toward Shae. "I'm going to have to give you a preventive. We don't want you to catch what your father has. It will only take a second." "Which arm?"

Neither of the Daileys had hardly flinched at the needle, but Shae was so scared, and so tired, she just wanted to go to her room and rest. But feeling cornered, she held out her left arm and looked away. She hardly felt the sting, until Dr. Bond removed the needle and then she asked what was wrong with her papa.

"Typhoid fever, we certainly don't want you to get it. We are taking him to a hospital, where he can get well soon."

"No! No!" Shae broke down crying. "He's goin' to die like my mama did! Please, don't take him away!"

"Young lady, I have to tell you that your father is very ill. We must take him where he will get special care, so he won't die."

"Oh Papa, Papa!" Shae ran to the bed and hugged her papa's bony body to her. "Please don't let them take you away! What will I do without you?"

For the first time, her papa stirred. He opened his bleary eyes, and whispered, "Girly Shae." He reached for her and opened his mouth as if he had more to say, but fell back on his pillow and lay still.

True to form, Sheriff Brody came to the door, knocked, and barged on inside. He was just in time to hear the word typhoid, and started to back away.

"You're next, sheriff." Dr. Bond winked at Reverend Anderson and then sterilized the syringe.

"But…" Brody kept backing toward the door. "…I haven't been near the man."

"Which arm?" Dr. Bond followed Brody. "I'm inoculating everyone who comes into this room. I don't want this typhoid to get ahead of me. I have enough already to keep me busy twenty-four hours a day." He glanced at the low-hanging pistol on Brody's hip. "We wouldn't want to be without a sheriff around here," he added, unable to hide a grin.

Reluctantly, Brody stood still for the shot, mumbling that he'd only come to question the kid. He cut his gaze to Shae.

"I would appreciate it if you would wait until we get her father off to the hospital, sheriff. He needs his medication and a milk toddy before we leave. He's going to need all the strength we can give him for the trip, and it takes a while to get it down him."

"I'll be back in one hour." Brody turned to the door. "Make sure the girl is ready to talk. The sheriff in St. Louis will want a full report the minute he hears she's home."

"Don't be afraid, honey." Vivian Anderson circled a friendly arm around Shae's shoulder. "We'll take care of you."

When Clay began to stir in bed, Dr. Bond broke an egg into a glass of milk, beat it vigorously with a wooden-handled fork, and stirred some quinine into the mixture. It had been four full hours since Upshaw had medication, and he needed the toddy badly.

Noticing her papa stir in bed, Shae ran to his side and stroked his fevered brow. "Feeling better, Papa? I brought you a big purple mussel shell from Persimmon slough. Like the one you found a pearl in from Gum slough."

For a moment, Clay didn't respond. Then suddenly, he raised up. A weak smile broke over his face and he said, "Girly." It was all he was able to say, but he recognized her and that pleased the doctor.

Backing away when Dr. Bond laid a hand on her shoulder, Shae watched anxiously as the doctor raised her papa up in bed, pressed a pillow behind his back, and held the milk toddy to his lips.

"C'mon Clay, drink just a little for me. I made you a special one, this time. The doctor coaxed until the old man sipped a swallow, then Clay's head fell to one side.

"I think he'll drink it for me." Shae looked to the doctor for permission, "after he rests for a minute."

Dr. Bond raised Upshaw up again, and handed Shae the glass. Shae's papa looked up, smiled at her, raised a shaky hand to the glass, and drank thirstily.

"Atta, boy." Dr. Bond eased Upshaw back on his pillow, and made him comfortable. The full impact of the situation had not hit Shae until the ambulance attendant brought the stretcher inside and placed it near her father's bed.

She turned tearful eyes on the attendant. "Please, don't take my papa away! I can take good care of him. I do it all the time."

"I'm sorry, young lady." The man looked sorrowfully into Shae's pleading brown eyes. "Its doctor's orders."

CHAPTER 22

Wilting in defeat, Shae fell back on the shoulder Vivian Anderson offered, and closed her tear filled eyes as the attendants carefully carried her father away.

"How long will Papa be gone?" Shae wiped her eyes. "I know he is goin' to die like my mama did."

"No, he won't, honey. That's why we want to get him to a hospital soon. He asked us to take care of you while he's gone. You will go home with us, won't you?"

"Oh, no, I couldn't do that. Dolly's bag would sour, and Sandy has to have fresh water. Jock won't be able to chase rabbits for days, and he would starve. I can take care of myself." Wheeling around, she ran to her room and closed the door.

Agreeing with the Andersons that Shae would be best off in her own environment, the Red Cross case worker went back to her office assured the girl was in good hands.

The dust had hardly settled from the wheels of the ambulance, before Sheriff Brody's car pulled up outside. Swaggering to the door, Brody knocked twice before Anderson answered.

"Could I speak to the child now, preacher?" Brody stood with his hat in his hand. He twisted it around nervously when the minister turned scalding eyes on him.

"Would it be possible to wait another hour, sheriff?" the minister asked without opening the screen door. "The child's all choked up over her father. I doubt that she can give a straight story."

"Preacher…" Brody held onto the door handle. "…I don't want to be hard nosed about the situation." Softening under Anderson's cold accusing eyes, he went on, "But I have got to have some facts. There's a man in jail for possible kidnapping, white slavery, or whatever. Feelings are running high. The St. Louis sheriff called for me to come for our prisoner. If the girl says he had nothing to do with her being inside his truck, then we have no case against him. But if he is guilty, and we hold him seventy-two hours without a hearing, we've lost the case, guilty, or not. See what I mean?"

"All right, sheriff." Anderson motioned Brody inside, and turned to his wife, Vivian. "Would you see if the girl will talk to Mr. Brody?"

"I'll try." Vivian walked slowly to Shae's bedroom door and knocked softly. When there was no answer, she pulled the latchstring and let herself inside to find Shae cowering behind the door like a cornered animal.

"Girly Shae," Vivian used the only name she'd heard so far. "Brody, the sheriff, is here. Will you talk to him, now?"

"No! I don't want to talk to him. He scares me to death."

"But we have to, sooner or later, Girly." Vivian hesitated, not knowing what to call Shae. "Is Girly your pet name, honey?"

Hesitating, Shae looked deeply into Vivian's inquisitive eyes, wondering why they wanted her to talk to the sheriff.

Finally, she said, "My real name is Shae."

"What a beautiful name, Shae. It sounds like a name for a princess."

"My mama named me for my papa. His middle name is Shane. The kids at school never call me by my name." Shae choked up.

"They call me awful names. I hate 'em all, and Miss Trisha, too."

"I'm so sorry, Shae. Children just don't understand sometimes."

Vivian kept leading Shae along, trying to gain her confidence. "Shae." "Shae." She repeated the name slowly. "Such a beautiful name for a girl and you are as beautiful as your name. Now..." She brushed Shae's hair from her eyes again. "Do you feel like telling me where you spent the night?"

"I don't want to talk about it." Shae dropped her head into her hands and clammed up.

"Don't be afraid to tell me, Shae. I'll be your friend, whatever. Mr. Brody isn't going to hurt you."

"I don't want to talk to that mean old sheriff." Shae cowered back into the corner, and thought of Brody's scalding eyes crawling over her body when he'd come to the boat dock to talk to her papa about sending her to school. Looking up with hate in her eyes, she said, "I don't want to see him again, ever!"

"Hon, you can tell me," Vivian coaxed.

Without another word from Shae for the longest time, Vivian probed from every angle, while Shae sat as if she were deaf, dumb and blind.

Shae about jumped out of her hide when Brody knocked loud on the door. Then he barked, "If you don't bring the girl out, Mrs. Anderson, I will have to come in! I can't wait around. The Locati boy's guilt or innocence all depends on the girl's testimony. He has already been in jail twenty-four hours."

"Who's in jail?" Shae got to her feet. Guilt washed over her paper white face.

"Jeff Locati," Vivian informed her. "He is the man who works for the park, here in the swamp. You do know him, don't you?"

"Yes. Why is he in jail? Is it 'cause..." Catching herself, she refused to finish what she'd started to say.

"Yes." Vivian took the words off Shae's tongue. "It's because Mr. Brody thinks you were in Jeff Locati's truck when he left Cache River yesterday. Were you? Mr. Brody thinks the man took you away against your wishes."

"No, he didn't!" Shae searched for the right words. "I got lost."

"Where were you all day yesterday and last night?" Vivian kept stroking Shae's hair. "Don't be afraid to tell me."

"I just got lost." Shae stuck to her guns until, seeing that it wasn't good enough to satisfy Vivian Anderson, she added, "I had to go see about my friend. I was afraid somethin' had happened to him."

"Where does your friend live? Why are you afraid for him?"

"I-I don't want to tell. I'm afraid someone will hurt him. He's almost blind in August."

Hoping to trick Shae out of an answer, Vivian asked, "Who do you think would hurt your friend?" She wondered what it could be. "Has anyone threatened your friend?" Even if she had known that the friend was a snake, she probably wouldn't have known about a snake being unable to see just before they shed.

"No. I went to Murphy's store to get Papa some chill tonic, and I saw the hunter there. I heard him tell the preacher that he was goin' to St. Louis to take his snakes to the zoo, wherever that is. I went back by the dock to see if my friend was there. Someone has been chasing him, and he won't come from his den."

Thinking that Shae might lead them to the truth if they let her talk, Vivian asked, "Where did you go from there?"

Shae thought for a moment and then said, "I went across the river and got my clothes all wet and muddy. My friend fights with a mean old moccasin sometimes. I was afraid Papa would be mad if he found out I'd been in the river, and I got lost."

"Hon, he would have understood if you had explained. Everyone has been worried sick over you."

"I know." Shae chewed at her fingernails, "I heard the minister tell the hunter that he would go check on my papa, and I was afraid if he saw me all dirty, he'd be beggin' Papa to let him take me home with him. I don't want to leave my papa."

Vivian knew the sheriff was eavesdropping at the door, though she kept talking, hoping that Brody would respect Shae's bedroom, but she didn't know Jim Brody.

Finally, at the end of her rope, Vivian asked as patiently as she could, "Are you ready to talk to Mr. Brody?"

"No!" Shae hid her face in her hands. "I don't want to."

Stiffening into a statue, Shae grabbed onto Vivian. "Please don't let him come in here. I don't want to talk to him."

"We have to, Shae. Until you tell him different, Mr. Brody thinks Jeff Locati asked you to go with him. He could be charged with a terrible crime. Understand what I mean?"

"Oh, no, what will they do to him? I didn't mean to…"

"We know that, Shae," Vivian said, cutting her short. "It was only a mistake. We all make them."

When Vivian opened the door, she found the sheriff standing with his shoulders thrown back, and his big beefy arms crossed over his chest.

Glaring down on the frightened child like a hungry chicken hawk stalking its prey, he hissed, "Are you ready to talk, child? Tell me where you were all day yesterday, and last night."

Lifting frightened eyes to Brody's hostile stare, Shae stood numb, shifting from one foot to the other. Finally, she stammered, "I got lost, I was lookin' for…"

"You were in Locati's truck when he left Cache River." Brody pointed a finger at her. "Why? Did he know you were there?"

Taking the bottle of quinine from his pocket, he looked Shae square in the eye. "Where did you lose this quinine?"

Taken aback, Shae gripped Vivian's hand, and looked for mercy.

"Go ahead and tell the truth, honey," Vivian coaxed. "You have nothing to hide. It was all a mistake."

"I…I don't know. I had to swim the river, and I thought I lost it in a sinkhole." Lowering her eyes to the floor, she repeated, "I think I lost it when I got into a sinkhole."

"You think," Brody growled. "Don't you know? Where was the sinkhole?" He stood waiting for a straight answer.

"Could she have a minute to get control, Mr. Brody?" Reverend Anderson asked as he came to the door. "She needs a drink of water. She's only a child. Have a little mercy, please?"

"But the kid's not telling the truth, preacher." Paying no never mind to what the minister said, Brody held scalding eyes on Shae's quavering body without blinking, for a full minute.

"Here, Shae." Anderson brought a dipper or cold water to her. "Drink this, and you will feel better." He stood by while Shae drank thirstily, then she cowered away from Brody.

"I only have one more question, preacher, then I will let her go. But she's lying." Finally, he asked, "Why couldn't you find your way home from Murphy's store?"

Shae was trembling, and completely out of control.

"It's all right, Shae." Vivian patted her shoulder. "Just tell us the truth. Did Jeff Locati ask you to go away with him?"

"No! I didn't talk to him. I just got lost."

"Huh," Brody said, "don't give me that stuff. I'm told that you know this swamp like a trapper. Now, where were you for twenty-four hours?"

Shae stood with her lips clamped tight. Her big brown eyes shot daggers through the sheriff.

Wheeling on his heel, Brody started toward the door. Looking over his shoulder, he barked, "Young lady, you're going to talk, even if I have to take you to jail!"

CHAPTER 23

The word jail did it. Shae started screaming and crawled under her bed. Completely out of control, she begged, "Please don't let him touch me. I'll tell you where I was."

Sheriff Brody heard the commotion and looked back.

"Just a minute, sheriff," Anderson called after him. "Shae says she will tell everything. Please, be patient with her," he asked as Brody hastened back to Shae's room. "She's at the breaking point."

Sensing that Shae was in trouble, Hobo scurried under the bed and Shae cuddled him to her as if he was the only friend she had at the moment. She had lost all trust in humanity. They'd taken her papa away and she might never see him again. Now Sheriff Brody was about to take her to jail.

"Shae," Fred Anderson said, coming into her room, "if you will tell Mr. Brody why you were in Jeff Locati's truck, and where you were afterwards, he will go and we can take you home with us, where you can get some rest and get back in school."

The word school did not make Shae happy, but she came from under the bed and stood stroking Hobo under Sheriff Brody's scrutiny, who stood with suspicious eyes locked on her.

"The first thing I want to know, young lady, did Jeff Locati know you were in his truck when he left Cache River?"

"No, he didn't. When I started home from the store, I saw his truck outside and I heard him tell the preacher that he was takin' his snakes to the zoo." She stalled for a second. "I was afraid he had Scar in the truck. I-I untied the tarp and climbed inside to see if my friend was in there. Before I could get out, he came outside, and Jock jumped on him. I was scared and I hid under his tent. He tied the tarp down, and I couldn't get out, until his truck ran out of gasoline and Jock tore the back from the tarp."

"Then where did you go?" Brody kept a sharp eye on her all the time, wondering if she was telling the truth.

"I-I started back home, but it was a long way and it got dark. I slept in a trapper shack and I got sick on green grapes."

Every now and then, Brody tried to trip her up by asking an offhand question, but she stayed with her story. Finally, after asking the same questions two or three times, he said, "All right, young lady, I understand you are to stay with the Andersons while your father is gone. I want to see you in school every day, and I'm sure you will be in church on Sunday. No more scouting around the swamp by yourself. Understand?"

"Yeah," Shae answered without looking at Brody.

He turned and hot-footed it toward his car, motioning the preacher to follow. "You'd better keep a close eye on the girl, Anderson. She'll most likely run away back to the swamp, the first chance she gets."

"Mr. Brody, what do you think now?" Anderson asked anxiously. "Will they release the boy on her word, or will they still hold him for testimony?"

"I don't know. He may tell a different story. All I can do is to relate what the girl told us."

"I think she's telling the truth." Reverend Anderson watched as Sheriff Brody pulled out a big cigar and bit the end from it. Shae's a nice little girl. All she needs is some tender loving care. Her father does the best he can, but it will be a while before he can do anything for her. If the children at school would only accept her for what she is. She had no choice of blood. God made all people equal. Only people make the difference."

"Maybe so." Brody took the crank from the car, stuck it into the front of the overland, and spun it around. Then he smirked.

"But he didn't say we had to mix."

"Where did he say not to?" The preacher asked impatiently.

Brody turned his car toward home and Anderson hurried back into the cabin to give Vivian a hand.

"Can you rush it up a little, girls?" Anderson looked around for some way to help out. "I have a sick call to make."

Shae sat bewildered in her papa's rocker, cuddling Hobo as if she wasn't planning to go anywhere.

"You're going home with us, aren't you Shae?" Vivian went about gathering up her belongings.

"Who will pump water for Sandy and Dolly?" She moved from the chair and asked, "Could I take my clothes in my mama's trunk?" She thought of her mama's wedding ring and the pearl her father had not sold. She couldn't leave them here.

Shae took two dresses from nails on the wall, walked to the trunk, and raised the lid.

"Let me give you a hand." Vivian took out several dresses, including some of Dora's, which had been squashed into the trunk. When she started folding them neatly, Shae pointed to a white organdy one with yards of lace around the scalloped edge.

"This was Mama's weddin' dress. Papa says it will be mine when I get married. Her weddin' ring, too."

"Wedding ring," Vivian corrected kindly.

"I know. I'm always leavin' my G's off. I just can't remember."

Suddenly, Shae made a break for the door when she heard Sandy whinny at the watering trough. "I'll pump water for her and Dolly before we go."

Vivian folded all of the dresses back into the trunk, thinking how beautiful Dora must have been on her wedding day. She did not pry into the articles in boxes. After finishing the packing, she walked to the door to rush Shae up. Time was slipping away, and Fred was in a hurry. When she got to the door, she was just in time to see Shae straddle Sandy from a stump, goose her in the ribs, and take off down the river path, her braids flying out behind her.

"Fred!" She called to her husband, who was closing the windows. "The child has left on the pony. Where could she be going?"

Seemingly undisturbed, Anderson went to the door, and watched as Shae rode out of sight. "She's probably going to the dock to tell her snake good-bye. We will give her a little time."

"Do you mean to tell me that she actually talks to a slimy snake?" Vivian's eyes grew suspicious. "You didn't tell me that."

"Why not?" Anderson shrugged. "I once kept a creepy lizard in my room. It was a nice pet to tease the girls at school with."

"Ugh!" Vivian shivered. "But then, you were a boy."

"Anyway, we'll have to go find her. She might do as the sheriff warned…keep going." Anderson turned down the path, leading to the boat dock. He was pretty sure he'd find Shae there.

Scar was coiled up near the water oak. When he heard the clip-clop of Sandy's hooves, he made one dive and was inside his den. Shae tied Sandy a hundred yards away, hoping she'd be quiet, but the pony kept pawing the ground, wanting to wallow in the river with Shae.

After much coaxing, Scar ventured from his den, but Shae had to pull him from the water. He was scared to within an inch of his life of Jock. "Scar," Shae said, holding him close, "I'm goin' to have to leave you. My papa had to go away and the old sheriff is sendin' me to live with the Andersons. But I'll be back to see you, and I'm takin' Jock with me, I hope. And don't go out lookin' for a fight with that mean old water moccasin."

Shae stroked the snake's new coat.

❦   ❦   ❦

"Why can't we drive to the boat dock?" Vivian hurried to catch up to her husband, tiptoeing along in her patent leather pumps.

"We would never get near her in the car. In her state, there's no telling where she might go."

"Wait for me," Vivian whimpered. "You're walking too fast."

"Quiet," Reverend Anderson shushed her, a finger to his lips. "We'll have to handle her easy."

For another quarter of a mile, they whispered along. Then they saw the filly tied to a sapling, switching mosquitoes with her long, yellow tail.

"Oh no," Vivian said, as she stumbled into a half ripe cockle burr stalk, and a dozen burrs tangled in her silk hose. "Oh my gracious! Help me, Fred. I've ruined my good stockings. I don't know about this."

"We'll buy another pair." Her husband quieted her when he heard Shae talking. For a time, they stood listening.

"Oh, my, my, my." Vivian looked at her stockings. Then she saw Shae with Scar gathered into her arms. "I don't know if we can take that child into our home, or not."

"It will be all right." Anderson stopped and worked at the cockle burrs hanging from long threads on Vivian's stockings.

Sensing that someone was around, Sandy whinnied. Scar leapt from Shae's arms and into the murky river.

"Now, look what you've done!" Shae stormed at the filly. Then she glanced around and saw the Andersons. "I was gonna come back. I had to tell Scar I was leavin'…I was…"

"It's all right." Reverend Anderson edged toward her. "We understand."

He wasn't sure Vivian did, but she'd get used to the child.

Calmed by the smile on Anderson's face, Shae said, "Scar has a new coat, just like papa said he would. And he's all healed up where Jock ripped his back."

For a moment, Fred Anderson stood looking at Shae, realizing what she was going through. Having her father taken away suddenly was bad enough, but to have to leave her friends, the only ones she'd ever known, was almost too much for her. Finally, he asked, "Are you ready to go, now? We're late for my meeting already."

"Could I take Jock and Hobo with me? They'll starve out here. Jock is too stiff to chase rabbits, and Hobo likes to eat from the table."

"Yes, and I will pen the pony up in the lot and come back for her tomorrow. How would that be?"

"Oh, would you?" Shae's eyes shone. "But where will we keep her?"

"We'll rent a pasture nearby for a while," Anderson assured.

"This is where Shadow finds all her kittens." Shae led Sandy to the stump, crawled upon it, and straddled her. Looking Vivian's swollen feet over, she offered, "You can ride behind me if you want."

"Me?" Vivian couldn't suppress a giggle. "Ride the filly? I've never been on one."

Vivian shucked her pumps and crammed the stockings, cockle burrs and all into them, and limped along behind her husband, while Shae loped Sandy back to the cabin. Impatient, Anderson walked a hundred yards ahead. Vivian hot footed it along in the dusty rut. The hot sand squishing up between her toes was almost more than she could bear, but there could be a snake hidden in the grass. When she finally got to the watering trough, she stepped over the side of it and stood soaking her feet in the cool water. Her hair was soaking wet with sweat and her dainty voile dress stuck to her sweaty body. She shivered at the thought, Oh, if I have ever been so uncomfortable, I don't remember it.

"Make haste, Vivian." Fred Anderson rushed her when she lingered at the watering trough. He coaxed Jock into the backseat of the car and turned toward the cabin.

"Have you forgotten that we have to load Shae's trunk?" Vivian called after him.

"Get into the car," he said impatiently. "I'll get it."

"I have to get Hobo." Shae hurried into the cabin and picked the kitten up from where he lay coiled upon her pillow. "We've got to go away, Hobo. I know I'm gonna hate it there, but if I don't go with the Andersons, Sheriff Brody will put me in the orphans' home."

When Anderson got back to the car, Jock lay slobbering on the seat, and Vivian sat staring at him in disgust.

"I'll clean it up." The reverend took a rag from under the seat, wiped up the slobbers, and tucked the rag under Jock's head.

Vivian removed the stockings from her slippers and worked them onto her swollen feet without comment, while Anderson cranked the car, got in, and headed toward home. There was little conversation on the way home. Shae sat cuddling Hobo and stroking Jock's head as he lay half asleep beside her. What, she asked herself over and over, if Papa dies like Mama did and I have to live with the Andersons forever? I'm not gonna dress up like a princess. I won't!

After what seemed a very long time, Anderson's car pulled up to a pretty white cottage and stopped.

"We're home, Shae." Vivian had regained her composure, and smiled back at Shae.

Shae sat for a minute, thinking she'd never seen such a pretty house. Morning glory vines covered the porch and starched curtains hung at the windows. Would Mrs. Anderson let Hobo sleep with her there?

"You may carry Hobo." Vivian broke Shae's train of thought. "I'll carry your books, and Fred will bring your trunk inside."

"Could I bring Hobo inside with me?" Shae hesitated before getting out of the car.

"Sure. Misty comes in the house all the time. Fred will take care of the dog."

Pretty sure she'd made a good impression, Vivian led the way into the house, and Shae followed uneasily into a room unlike anything she'd ever before seen. She looked around in awe at a bureau with an uncracked mirror, a bed dressed in pink ruffles, and curtains to match on the windows.

When Anderson brought Shae's trunk inside, Vivian pulled out one of the dresser drawers. "You may put your undies in this drawer."

"My what?" Shae stood confused when Vivian took her bloomers from the trunk and handed them to her. "Do you mean my bloomers?" Shae stood holding her under things in her hand, waiting for an answer.

"Yes, dear." Vivian took a dress from the trunk, and hung it onto a hanger, telling herself that the child would catch on eventually. Noticing that her husband was tightening up his tie, before leaving on his sick call, she rushed out into the kitchen, thinking that she needed two more hands.

"Just a minute, honey. You can't leave without supper. It might be midnight before you get back."

She was about to make sandwiches and lemonade, when she returned to Shae's room. "Excuse me, Shae. As soon as you get your dresses hung up, come into the kitchen. We'll have a snack and then we'll finish later."

Shae had been fed when she came home from her overnight journey, but so many things had happened since then, it seemed like another day, and she was hungry all over again. Thinking that she'd never tasted food so good as she sat at the kitchen table, she wondered what it would be like to eat in the dining room from a white tablecloth, fancy china and silverware.

Shae and Vivian were up late, washing Shae's tennis shoes and pressing her best dress for church on Sunday.

"We'll go to town the first chance." Vivian hung the shoe strings up to dry. "You need some pretty Mary Jane slippers to wear to church, Shae, and a nice sun bonnet hat.

Shae looked confused for a moment and then asked, "What are Mary Jane slippers?"

"They are pretty black patent leather slippers, with bows on the toes. You will love them."

Shae held the 'ugh' on the tip of her tongue. She knew the slippers would hurt her feet, but she was so tired. It was long past her bedtime, and she wanted to get to sleep and forget about Sheriff Brody. It made chills run up her backbone every time she thought of him.

Long after Shae crawled between the soft, white sheets, she lay wondering if her mama looked anything like Vivian Anderson. Her papa had said that her mama was as fair as the lilies.

Shae thought "If she had only lived. I wouldn't have to live with strangers and Papa could stay home while he's sick. She could take care of us."

Hobo had hidden out as soon as he'd seen the new room and she doubted that he would ever come near it again. She wondered if Scar was missing her like she was missing him.

It was away in the night when Shae heard Reverend Anderson come home. She heard them talking in low tones, then she heard them praying. She was sure she heard her papa's name, hers, and they prayed for Jeff Locati.

Finally, Shae closed her eyes and prayed to the Lord Miss Trisha had told her about. "Dear Lord, please make my papa well, and get the hunter out of jail. It was all my fault. Why did this have to happen?"

Meanwhile, Jeff Locati lay on his hard, jail cot, wondering the same thing.

CHAPTER 24

❀

Worn and weary after pacing around his eight-foot cell for the most devastating twenty-four hours of his young life, Jeff was hungry enough to partake of the rabbit stew the jailer had served him for supper on Saturday night.

With nothing more to do, he went to the dirty washbowl, washed his face and raked his fingers through his hair. After making a few more circles around the cell, he fell back on his cot and dozed off into exhausted sleep, only to wake up from a horrible nightmare. Hooded men were chasing him on horses and he was struggling with a noose around his neck. In a lather of sweat, he jumped from his cot and ran over to the tiny barred window, to make sure it was only a dream.

A big, yellow moon was peeping over the treetops and a mockingbird sat on the limb of a sweet gum tree singing, as if all was well with the world.

How? He asked himself, can a moon shine and birds sing with me locked up in this filthy jail?

Edgier than a razorback shoat on hog-killing day, he fell back on his cot, dropped his head into his hands and sat for a full half-hour fingering the stubble on his chin. He hadn't shaved in three days. His beard itched awful and his stomach wrestled with the rabbit stew.

"Oh-oh," he groaned out loud. "What I wouldn't give for a glass of Mama's ice cold lemonade. If only I had stayed with my old job. Guess this is what I get for getting greedy."

Remembering that his papa always told him that big boys didn't cry, he wiped away a tear creeping down into his sideburn. If the Upshaw girl would only show up home safe, and tell the truth, maybe they would let him out of there.

I can't believe she'd say I took her against her wishes. Why didn't she go home? Her papa needed the quinine. If she wanted something from me, why didn't she ask?

As Jeff sat twisting the situation around and around in his mind, the rabbit stew kept boiling up into his throat. He felt as if he would have to vomit, but the commode wouldn't flush. He would just have to hold it as long as possible.

❦   ❦   ❦

While Jeff lay wondering why nobody came to help him out of the rotting jail, his mama walked the floor, wringing her gnarled hands, pleading with Jeff's father to do something, anything, to get their son out of jail.

"Even if it takes our home," she argued, "we can't just sit here and do nothing. We've got to get Sonny out of there. There's no telling what those white folks might get into their heads."

"But, Mama," her husband consoled, "I'm doing everything I can. The sheriff told me if I didn't go home, he'd lock me up in a cell down the hall. They wouldn't even let me see Jeff. Something will have to break. When the girl shows up, the truth will come out."

After Sheriff Brody had heard what he thought were the facts of the situation, he headed home to call the sheriff in St. Louis.

"St. Louis County Jail, this is Sheriff Morris speaking."

"Jim Brody, from Cache River, here."

"Yes, Brody, what's the news from there?"

"Good, sheriff. The Upshaw girl made it in home about four o'clock this afternoon. I had to threaten to take her to jail, but I'm sure I got a true statement from her. She slipped into Locati's truck to see if he had her pet snake. Thinking she could get out after he started the truck, she found he'd tied the tarp down and she was trapped there until he was miles from home. The wolf dog finally tore the back end from his tarpaulin when the truck ran out of gasoline. Locati had to walk a mile to get a can of gas. While he was gone, she got out, but she lost the bottle of quinine under the tent where she was hiding."

"Well…" Sheriff Morris hesitated. "…that's good news, if you're sure she's telling the truth. We have no case. The boy can go home."

"I'm sure of it, sheriff."

"Thanks for calling. I'm glad to hear the girl in good hands, and I'll let the man go. It's not the nicest place in the world to be locked up in."

Jeff's mama and papa were sitting at the table, pushing their food around when Jeff opened the door and walked inside.

"Oh, Sonny!" His mama worked her enormous body up from her chair, "Sonny!" His papa got up to clasp his son's hand. "I came, I tried to see you, but they wouldn't let me in. All we could do was wait. Thank God you're home. I knew you were innocent, but we had no way of proving it. Maybe it would be best if you stay here and work. No kind of money is worth what we've all gone through the last two days."

"I'm so sorry this happened." Jeff hugged his parents. "I'm sure Mr. Boyd will give me my old job back. Cleaning cages isn't such a bad job after all."

Jeff reached for the pitcher of lemonade on the table and poured a full glass. Sitting down at the table with a long sigh, he drank the whole glass without taking it from his lips.

❧   ❧   ❧

Shae's first night with the Andersons was a long, restless one. Mrs. Anderson knocked a second time before Shae stirred. She had wondered about her papa into the wee hours of the morning, and the place was so strange to what she'd been used to all her life.

"May I come in?" Vivian cracked the door as Shae bounced from the bed and started skinning into her chopped-off overalls. She had one leg into the overalls, and stood with the other leg half-mast when Vivian pushed a dress toward her.

"No, no, honey. We don't wear overalls to dine. Only to ride your pony."

Dine? Shae looked confused. She'd heard the word before, but didn't know if it meant breakfast or what. Reluctantly, she took the dress and slipped it over her head, letting the overalls drop to the floor.

Pretending to tend the bacon, Vivian rushed back to the kitchen, giving Shae her privacy. She couldn't help but remember how, as a young girl, she had liked to stand before the mirror and primp.

Once Shae's dress was buttoned and her sash tied, she turned herself around before the uncracked mirror.

If them smart alec kids at school could see me now! She unbraided her long, black hair and let it fall down her back. They wouldn't call me Cache trash, or…squaw!

After a minute of spinning herself around in front of the mirror, she thought of her papa, Scar, and the swamp. She would be caged in like the animals in the St. Louis zoo. As she stood thinking, this must be what a princess looks like; she heard another knock at the door.

"Breakfast is served, Shae." Vivian cracked the door and added, "When you're ready."

Pulling her hair back, Shae tied it with the fish cord she'd brought along and crept into the dining room, where the Andersons sat with hands folded in their laps. Easing into the chair she was motioned to, she folded her hands and bowed her head for grace.

"My, my." Reverend Anderson looked across the table at Shae as she raised her head. "You look like a grownup, young lady. Did you sleep well?"

"Yeah." Shae looked around at all the extras. She had never used silverware, only the time she had spent the night with Jenny.

Raising an eyebrow at the word 'yeah', Vivian decided there would be plenty of time to correct Shae's English.

Accepting the biscuit offered her, Shae sat awaiting the next move and then she asked the most urgent questions on her mind. "Is my papa gonna be all right? How long will he have to stay in the hospital?"

"Not too long," Reverend Anderson assured her as he pushed his scrambled eggs around on his plate. He was upset over Misty, his twelve year old Maltese cat, who had taken the place of children in their home up until now. She was almost blind and her teeth were gone. He doubted that she could catch a mouse if it stepped on her tail. She owed them nothing. She had paid her dues, though he would miss her terribly.

As soon as Anderson could excuse himself properly, he took his plate and went outside to look for Misty. She lay near her pan of water, sleeping.

"Misty." He scratched her along her ribs to wake her up. Turning sad eyes on him, she pulled her frail body up on trembling legs, sniffed at the plate of food, then feebly turned on her back for a tummy rub.

"C'mon, Misty," he coaxed as she purred under his massage. "Just a few bites. You're getting as skinny as a summer 'possum."

Following her husband out back, Mrs. Anderson stood listening as her husband pampered his favorite pet. Finally, she chided, "You didn't eat either, Fred. What did the sheriff tell you last night?"

"Nothing, but he was going to phone the sheriff in St Louis. I can't see how they can hold the boy after Shae's statement."

Jim Brody had made no effort to phone the Andersons after hearing Jeff would be let go. They kept praying all day Sunday for news, but none came. When the minister could stand the suspense no longer, he called Sheriff Brody's number.

"Sheriff Body, here."

"Yes, sheriff, Reverend Anderson, here. I've been wondering if you have any good news from Jeff Locati yet."

"Oh, yes. They freed him as soon as I phoned them the news."

"When was that?" Anderson asked impatiently.

"Last night, after I left the Upshaw place. I figured you would know he'd be let go as soon as the girl told her story. I was all done in after yesterday. It was one exhausting day. And it was all because of that wayward child. I hope you will make her toe the mark. She's had a free rein so long, I'm afraid you folks have a hard row to hoe."

"Don't worry, sheriff. Say a little prayer for us."

"I'm afraid my prayers would go under the bed, preacher."

"No. No, God hears everyone. Try him."

❦   ❦   ❦

Shae's words were hardly audible when she said, "Come in," to Vivian Anderson's knock on the door.

Easing into the room where Shae stood fluffing a pillow, Vivian took a dress from a hanger and laid it on the bed. "You may wear this dress to church today, honey. It'll go best with your tennis shoes. We'll go to town after school Monday and buy you some nice Mary Jane slippers, and a pretty bonnet hat for church."

"Do I have to go to church today?" Shae's eyelids dropped as she thought of Mary Crawford's critical stare and then she buried her head in the pillow.

"You'll love it, once you get used to it, Shae."

Vivian gently pulled the pillow from Shae's face, fluffed it up and laid it on the bed. "All children need to learn about Jesus."

"But I've never been to church. I'm afraid…"

"There's nothing to be afraid of, Shae. I'll be right by your side all the time."

"But, I'm afraid that Mary Crawford and Tracy Allen will be there, and they look at me, and wink at each other, and…"

"If I ever see them do that, I'll ask them to mind their manners," Vivian assured. "I'm sure their mothers would not approve of it."

"If I knew my friend Jenny would be there…." Shae stood thinking for a moment.

"Do you mean Jenny Stevens? She's there every Sunday. Her mama, daddy, and baby brother, too. You can invite Jenny home with you for dinner anytime you want to."

Shae's frown turned to a smile, and she asked, "Could I?"

"Sure, we would love that. And when your papa gets well, maybe he will come with you also."

Shae thought about it, but knew her papa never felt comfortable visiting, not with the crude clothes he and Shae had to wear. Then, too, the shelling season was an everyday job like fishing, and it was her papa's only way of bringing in the sow belly and beans, which they lived on in summertime. Shae knew her papa believed in heaven; because he'd told her many times that her mama was happy there.

But, she pondered, if there is a God and a heaven, why does he let the people at Cache River treat me and my papa so awful? Is it 'cause we're Indians?

It was Tuesday afternoon before the Andersons had time to take Shae shopping for more clothes. She allowed that she had lots of dresses, and her papa had bought her new underclothes, stockings and a Mexican hat when she'd started back to school.

"I know," Vivian agreed, "but I want you to have different dresses for church. All the girls have pretty gloves and hats to wear on Sunday."

Shae couldn't help wondering what anyone would need with gloves in August, but she kept quiet.

Ignoring the expression on Miss Bickles' face when she and Shae entered the store, Vivian went straight to the rack of dresses and the hat rack nearby. When Miss Bickles offered help, Vivian said, "I would like to look around before I decide on Shae's clothes."

"Help yourself," Miss Bickles offered as she cut her eyes to Shae, who stood eying the overall counter. Pretending to be preoccupied, Shae listened closely as Miss Bickles sidled over to Vivian and made conversation.

"I hope you don't think you'll be able to mold that child into a lady," Miss Bickles mumbled. "I'm afraid she's run wild too long."

"It's never too late to try," Mrs. Anderson assured. "We feel that the Lord has laid this on our shoulders. In the right environment, any child can be taught. We promised her father we would take care of her until he gets back on his feet, which we are praying for."

Within thirty minutes, Vivian had a lot of finery laid on the counter. She knew the price tag was far more than a minister's salary could afford, but this had been her dream to dress a girl up like a princess. Her husband had asked for this, and he would just have to suffer the consequences. Then she thought of the hat. Picking up the blue organdy dress, she went to the hat rack and matched the lace on the ruffles to a white hat.

"Aren't you going to look pretty?" Vivian laid the hat next to the patent leather slippers for Miss Bickles to add up. Shae stood mute as Miss Bickles wrapped the packages and handed Mrs. Anderson the bill. All Shae wanted to do was run. Run back to the swamp, skin into her chopped-off overalls, and go to the dock to see Scar.

CHAPTER 25

❀

"I can't wait to see you in these pretty clothes." Vivian tried to excite Shae as they carried the packages to the car. "We'll roll your hair in rags and make long, round curls. You will be the most beautiful girl in church next Sunday."

Without a word, Shae hurried to the car and tossed her bundles into the back seat. The only thing she wanted to go to church for was to see her friend Jenny and her little brother. He was probably walking by now. When she'd spent the night with them, he was already standing up to things. Shae loved Jenny's mama, too, and was hoping to see her as well.

Reverend Anderson had brought Sandy from the swamp that morning, and Shae couldn't wait to ride her. By the time the car stopped rolling, she was out the door with an armload of finery, and headed for the house.

By the time Vivian got to Shae's bedroom, she was skinning into her chopped-off overalls. With one gallus buckled, she was working with the other one, making ready to go for a race.

"Just a minute, Shae. There'll be time to ride your pony, but first we must have a talk, and make a schedule. School comes first. We'll have to find time to do your homework."

Shae stopped in her tracks as she buckled the other gallus, wondering what she'd done wrong. Bewildered, she eased back into the room, where Vivian started unwrapping packages and hanging dresses on hangers. She stood looking at the woman who she was supposed to answer to until her papa come back home, if he ever did. Finally, she ventured. "Did I do somethin' wrong Mrs.—er, Vivian?" She stood wondering what she should call the woman with the angel hair, marcelled to perfection, and blue eyes which stared at her without knowing just what to say. Vivian looked almost untouchable; nothing like Shae had pictured her mama.

Re-adjusting her thoughts, Vivian said softly, "No-no, Shae, you did nothing wrong. And you may call me Mrs. Anderson, or Vivian if you wish. I'm not your mother, but I'd love to be your friend." She went on as she measured a dress to Shae, "We must try your clothes for fit, so I can stitch them in here and there. You may try this one on while I go for a needle to stay the tucks."

Oh no! Shae groaned to herself as she unbuckled her overalls, and let them fall to the floor. What a garb!

Pulling the ruffled petticoat over her head, Shae stood wrestling with the organdy dress, as Vivian came back into the room with her mouth full of pins. "Shae—" She talked around the pins. "—we want you to be happy in our home, but we live by a very busy schedule. We will make time for your ride on your pony, and you will be expected to care for her, though it will have to be early in the morning. There will have to be time for schoolwork, bible study, and I want you to have an hour for piano lessons each day." She did not mention the speech lessons she planned to add onto the other lessons. There would be time to talk about that later.

As soon as Vivian sat back after checking the fit, Shae pulled the dress over her head and tossed it on the bed.

"Could I go look about Jock?" Shae laid the dress on the bed. "He must be starved for water."

"Sure, but slip back into your school dress. Our brush-arbor revival will start on Friday night, and the associate pastor will be dining with us, anytime now. We will have to be bathed and dressed by six every night.

Shae picked up the overalls, folded them away, slipped into the other dress, and went outside. Jock lay on the porch, whimpering. He had food and water nearby. The minister had thought of everything, but Jock was too stiff to move. The gash on his nose had festered, and he felt feverish to her touch. She could see his ribs move as he breathed.

"If Papa was here," she said, combing his bristles with her long, skinny fingers, "he would put a fatback poultice on your nose to draw the poison out. I doubt if the Andersons know about things like that."

Shae bathed his nose in cool water. "Come on, Jock." She tried to lift the dog upon his haunches. "You will die of thirst without water."

Jock only thanked her with sad eyes. As she sat watching his laborious breathing, Vivian called, "Shae, if you will wash your hands, I'll show you how to set the table."

Rushing into the dining room, Shae took the plates and glasses Vivian handed her, and stood waiting for instructions.

❧   ❧   ❧

Jeff Locati relaxed on Sunday, and foundered on his mama's chicken and dumplings. On Sunday morning, he went back to Forest Park to talk to Ralph Boyd about his old job. Boyd was more than happy to have him back. So much so, he gave him a promotion. He happened to need help keeping records on the breeding and birthing of the animals, and moving them from one location to another. Boyd knew that he could depend on Jeff to do the job right. He was more than happy to have him back.

It was Tuesday night before Jeff finally sat down and wrote his girlfriend, Sara, a letter that he knew would be the shocker of her life.

It had been a busy two weeks for Sara, in her aunt's home, with a premee baby to care for on top of all the other work. She was looking forward to going home. She had only had two letters from Jeff, but she had hardly had one moment to call her own, much less write a letter, and she was anxious to get back to her job at the hospital.

She had been more than busy all day, trying to get the laundry caught up, some food cooked ahead, and spelling her aunt a few more days. When she finally got time to go to the mailbox, she was surprised to find another letter from Jeff, along with the weekly newspaper.

Handing the newspaper to her aunt, who sat holding the baby, Sara opened Jeff's letter, anxious to hear if he was going to be home on the weekend. The first line took all the wind from her sails. It read:

Dear Sara,

I am so sorry to have to write you this letter, but I have put it off as long as I can. In case you have not seen a newspaper, I got myself into some bad trouble down in Cache River. I honestly did not do a thing, but will people believe me, including you? It was one of those unavoidable mistakes. I was locked up in jail for twenty-four hours. The most horrific night and day of my life! All I can say is that I'm so sorry it had to happen. If you ever want to speak to me again, I will try to explain what happened. Please don't judge me before you hear me out. I-I, oh well.

Always your friend, Jeff

After Sara read Jeff's letter, she noticed her aunt had dozed off to sleep. She went into her bedroom to try to get herself under control.

This just couldn't be true! Had she known Jeff all these years without finding out who he really was? After reading the letter over a second time, she went back to where her aunt had dropped the paper over the sleeping baby. When she stooped over to take the baby from her aunt's arms, Jeff's picture stared up at her from the front page.

For a moment, she stood staring at his picture. The three day growth of black beard and his dirty clothes made him look like what she imagined a convict would look like. Finally, she picked up the paper and read the bold headline:

Forest Park Scout Charged With Kidnapping a Twelve Year Old Cache River Girl

"Oh, no," Sara groaned. "This can't be true!"

Dropping the paper, Sara rushed back to her room and started throwing her clothes into a suitcase. She had to catch the next bus for home. The new baby wasn't out of the woods yet, but her aunt Mary would have to handle it. There was a bus leaving at three o'clock, and she had to catch it.

When Sara got home her parents were ready for a straight jacket. They knew Sara planned to marry Jeff Locati the minute he asked her, but how? Her father asked himself, could he give his beautiful daughter to a man, who would be remembered forever as a jailbird?

"Sara," her father said cautiously, "You can't marry Jeff. I think for the sake of your name and the children you might bear if you did marry him, it would be best for all concerned if you didn't see him anymore."

"But, Father, the paper clearly states that Jeff knew nothing of the girl being in his truck. She said so.... It could happen to anyone, even you!"

"I know, daughter, but people are going to say, where there's smoke, there has to be a little fire."

"Father, I don't care what people say! I know Jeff would never do a thing like he has been accused of."

Her father sat shaking his head. Whirling around, Sara went into her room, slipped out of her sweaty clothes, and stepped under the shower.

When Sara came back into the room, she was dressed in a cool cotton dress, sandals, and her hair was tied back in a ponytail. She walked over to the phone on the wall, and rung Locati's number.

"Hello."

"Mrs. Locati, this is Sara."

"Oh…how are you Sara? When did you get back into town?"

"On the five o'clock bus, I only got the bad news today in the weekly paper. My relatives do not have a radio, and the mail is slow. Is Jeff home?"

"Not yet. He works until late. Maybe you have hot heard, but he went back to the park to work. He has a different job, though. He goes later, and stays until the animals are bedded down for the night."

"Oh, I see. No, I did not know." Sara hesitated, she had never before called Jeff to make a date. She knew it wasn't the proper thing for a girl to do, but she had to talk to him, and get the straight of the situation. Finally, she ventured, "Would you please tell him to call me when he gets home?"

"I sure will, Sara. We've missed you. Thanks for calling."

"Thank you, Mrs. Locati. Good-bye."

Sara hung up the receiver and started biting her fingernails.

What did Jeff's mother think of her? She had never had to handle a situation like this before, and she was ready to fall apart. She had no way of knowing that Jeff's mother was glad to know that Sara wanted to see Jeff, and had thought nothing of the phone call. Jeff and Sara had been best friends since the eighth and ninth grade. With their families living in the same neighborhood, they had been together always, and Sara planned to keep it that way.

It was an hour before Jeff's voice came over the phone, and by his nervousness, Sara figured he hardly knew how to start. After a moment's hesitation, he said, "I got your message, Sara. Is it all right if I come over?"

"Why not meet me at the drugstore for coke? Things are…well, let's just say I…I want to see you alone, okay?"

"Fine, I need forty-five minutes to wash away the grime. I will see you then."

Sara sat at a table, back in a corner, and it was all she could do to keep from jumping up, and throwing her arms around Jeff's neck as he walked toward her, but that would start a rumor for the Globe. She noticed that Jeff did not have his natural swagger, but she soon put him at ease with a smile of confidence.

After Jeff ordered two bottles of coke, he sat next to her, and they knew all eyes were on them. Even a whisper carried all over the drugstore.

A few sips of coke later, Jeff asked, "Have you eaten supper, Sara? I have not had time to eat, and it's been a long day."

"I'm not hungry." Sara turned the coke bottle around in her hand. "But get something if you wish. I had a candy bar on the bus."

The waitress brought a menu and Jeff ordered a hamburger and a large fry. He and Sara carried on a nervous conversation while they waited, knowing some of the neighbors were watching them with a question mark on their lips.

The food arrived and the waitress left.

"You may help me with these." Jeff pushed the French fries toward Sara, and handed her the ketchup.

Sara picked up a potato string, dipped it into the ketchup, and sat nibbling on it, while Jeff polished off the burger and fries in about two minutes.

"How was your vacation?" Jeff finally got around to asking.

"Busy, if you could call it a vacation. With a new baby, and a family of six to cook and do laundry for, I have to say, I will be glad to go back to the hospital."

"I'm glad to be back at my old job." Jeff sighed. "The scouting job wasn't as good as Jake Lang put it up to be, and he failed to tell me that the folks at Cache River would not tolerate any color except white. Black, Indian, or Italian they are all darkies as far as they're concerned. And they made no bones about it."

Sara suggested she and Jeff leave, so they could talk and not risk providing fuel for the newspaper.

Jeff's truck still smelled like a snake pit, and he apologized to Sara as he steered it toward Riverside Park, near the mighty Mississippi. It was suppertime and the park was quiet. Jeff led Sara to a secluded place, where they walked along a gurgling stream. A cool breeze stirred the leaves of a whispering Aspen tree.

"I read the paper, Jeff, but I want to hear the story from you."

Jeff looked straight into Sara's eyes. "Will you believe me?"

"Of course, I will. I know you will tell me the truth."

"I did nothing wrong." Jeff started from the beginning, and told exactly what happened.

Sara listened to every word. Finally, she stopped him, her arms creeping around his neck. "I wish you had never gone to Cache River."

"I know," Jeff said. "It turned out to be a big mistake. I went in hopes of making enough money to buy you a promise ring, that is, if I ever find the courage to ask you to marry me."

Sara's smile told Jeff all he wanted to know, and she said, "I thought you would never ask." Her mouth was so close to his, he could not resist kissing her.

"Is that a promise, without a ring?" Jeff held her close, waiting for an answer.

"Cross my heart." Sara stepped away and made the sign of the cross. "And you have sealed it with a kiss, signed, sealed, and official, Mr. Locati. Who said I have to have a ring to make a promise?"

Arm in arm, Jeff and Sara walked back to the truck, and rattled along home. The truck was just one step from going to the junkyard.

Holy Mary! Jeff chided himself, after he'd left Sara at her door. He'd been putting the question off for years, and there had been nothing to it. Sara had put the words into his mouth. Like they say, all's well that ends well....

Jeff could hardly wait to get home and tell his parents the good news. But when he stepped into the house, his mother was talking on the phone and he knew from the look on her face that it was not a pleasant conversation.

She handed the receiver to him. "It's for you, Sonny."

"Hello," Jeff spoke cautiously into the receiver. "Did you say Sheriff Brody?"

"Yes, Sheriff Brody from Cache River. Am I speaking to Jeff Locati?"

Jeff's legs turned to water. For a moment, he stood speechless, wondering if the Upshaw girl had changed her story. When his voice came back, he said, "Yes, this is Jeff Locati. Is something wrong?"

"Yes." Brody hesitated. "I'm afraid I have more bad news for you, young man. You were exposed to typhoid fever. Dr. Bond has been trying to contact you for three days. I finally got your home number from your boss at Forest Park."

"No!" Jeff groaned over the phone. His face turned paper-white as he thought of how sick Clay Upshaw had been when he'd left Cache River. It had to be him.

"When did you first contact Clay Upshaw? It's very important to know. As you know, typhoid is very contagious. I believe Dr. Bond said the incubation period was two weeks."

Jeff thought for a moment. "I-I can't remember exactly, ten days, or more."

"The doctor gave a mass inoculation here in Cache River, and he advises anyone who had been in contact with the man to go at once for an inoculation. It sounds as if your time is up."

"Thank you, Mr. Brody. I will go at once."

Jeff put the receiver back into its cradle, and stood in shock. The first one he thought of was Sara. As if he had not caused her enough grief, now he might have infected her with typhoid.

"What happened, Sonny?" His mother broke his train of thought. Like him, when she'd heard the word 'sheriff', she was petrified.

"I was exposed to typhoid, Mama."

CHAPTER 26

❧

Murphy's store was abuzz with the usual crowd of men around Cache River on Saturday afternoon. The crops were laid by, and all the timber men took the afternoon off to catch up on the gossip and to buy groceries for the coming week. The black-guarding outhouse jokes were in full swing when Reverend Anderson stopped by the store for a loaf of bread and some lunchmeat to make a sandwich. He'd missed his lunch, and was on his way to work on the brush arbor over in the woods. The revival meeting was to start on Sunday. The seats weren't laid, and there needed to be a load or two of straw scattered around to keep the dust down. There would be a lot of traffic the next two or three weeks, and a lot of shouting.

As Reverend Anderson stood waiting for his purchase, Jim Brody came swaggering into the store, with his gun hanging from one hip, and two pairs of handcuffs dangling from the other.

"Hello, sheriff," the minister greeted him. "You're the fellow I'd like to speak to. I've been wondering if you ever got in touch with Jeff Locati. I'm worried about him. I'm sure he was in contact with Clay Upshaw a week, maybe ten days, before he left here. His incubation period is about up."

"Yes. It wasn't easy. I finally got a phone number from his boss at Forest park. I understand he went back to his old job. It scared the wits out of him when I told him that he was exposed to typhoid. He promised to start his shots at once."

🍁   🍁   🍁

Jake Crawford and three of his cronies sat at a table over in a corner, playing checkers, and listening closely to every word that was being said.

"I hear you've been over to see the Indian, preacher," Crawford said, breaking into the conversation. "How's he doin'?"

"Not well." The minister ignored Crawford, hoping to get out of the store without having to say more.

Knowing that a dozen different rumors would start from what he had already said, he turned toward the door with his sack lunch, but he didn't get away before Crawford asked, "What does his doctor say?"

"I haven't talked to his doctor, Mr. Crawford," the preacher said over his shoulder as he hurried out the door.

Crawford leaned in closer to his partners, and talked in muted tones. "If the old Indian checks out, there couldn't be a better time to get rid of that young squaw. We've got to do somethin'."

He spat a long shot of tobacco juice toward the wash pan under the front of the stove, and moved a king around the checkerboard. "I've got a son about grown, and you fellers have two apiece. I say it's time to act. Ain't that right, Abe?"

"I'll second that," Abe Allen agreed. "If that do-gooder had kept his nose out of it, Brody would've had her in the orphans' home where she belongs. What do you suggest we do, Jake?"

Sam Smith, the ever present lumberjack, sat on a bench, playing solitaire on a table along the wall. Sam was never one for shaving and keeping his hair trimmed, but he kept the wax out of his ears, and he was straining to grasp every word. He sat scratching his fiery-red beard, studying his cards as if he was sure he had old Sol in a tight spot, while all the time his donkey ears listened to the men hash over their plans to take care of preacher Anderson. Jake Crawford moved a king around the board, and scooped up three checkers, breaking up the game, before he said, "Whatever we have to. I ain't havin' my sons marry a Redskin, under no circumstances. We've got to have a meetin'." He thought for a moment and then mumbled, "Meet me at the lodge at ten o'clock."

Jake usually boasted about his meetings before he left the store, but he slipped out the door without a word.

Sam Smith heard what he'd said, and he knew the lodge to be an old abandoned school house. The lodge was called the Order when his father belonged to it, and he knew the Order was the Ku Klux Klan. It was better known as the Hoods.

"Well, now…" Sam stacked his cards in place and bit off a plug of Red Star. He could concentrate better with a cud of tobacco in his jaw. "…just what can one man do about a situation like this? If I go to the preacher, he will call me a trouble maker. If I go to the sheriff, I'll have to prove what I heard." Sam picked up his old worn out hat, stacked it on his head, and moseyed toward home.

When bedtime came, Sam gathered up some fishing gear. "Dovie," he said to his wife, "I think I'll sleep out on the screen porch. I want to go bass fishin' early tomorrow. That way, I won't wake up the kids. I'll be back in time for breakfast."

When the family settled into bed, Sam slipped from his cot, dressed carefully, and went to the barn to bridle old Paint.

Disturbed, old Paint looked Sam over with suspicious eyes, which asked, "What goes on here? I've worked in the logwoods all week skinning logs, and I need my rest on Saturday night." He refused the bridle by slinging his head first this way then that. When Sam threw a gunnysack over his back, he started bucking.

"Yep, old boy," Sam calmed him. "We're goin' fer a ride. We got some unfinished business to take care of."

Sam knew it was going to be a miserable trip. The mosquitoes were so thick; he could hardly keep them out of his ears and mouth.

But once he got Paint headed toward the lodge, he forged on without protest.

It was no more than five minutes after Sam got Paint tethered to a sapling a quarter of a mile out in the woods, and stationed himself behind the dilapidated brick schoolhouse, before he heard footsteps. He moved and peeped around a corner of the building, and saw a man carrying a lantern. One side was shaded, and the other was smoked so black, it only made a flicker of light. But he recognized Jake Crawford, Abe Alien, Bob Nelson and Bill McCoy, the three men who were playing checkers with Crawford at Murphy's store.

The four of them kept silent until they got inside the building. Sam moved back to a window with a board nailed over it. The weather had warped it, and he could see what was going on inside.

It was dark outside. A wolf howled nearby. A whippoorwill called. Sam stood like a statue, knowing that if he moved, he could stick his foot into the mouth of a copperhead moccasin. What was he doing on this one-man thwart, anyhow? But he couldn't stand by and let a thing like this happen to a good man like Reverend Anderson, who was just trying to help a sick man.

When the four men got situated, Jake Crawford took over the stage. "Well, fellers," he said, "I never attended more than three sessions of this clan, but since the rest of you have no knowledge of it at a'tal, I guess it's up to me to do the preliminaries. This group was outlawed when I was about twenty-two. I never got in on a flogging, but I heard about a few. I'd hoped we didn't have to do this to the preacher, but I've talked to him, and he turns a deaf ear."

After the other three took oath, Crawford said, "The first thing we'll do is put a note on his door, meaning Anderson. If that don't work, we will have to carry out our threat. We cain't let the young squaw grow up here among us white people. It's against our way of life. The old Indian is sure to pass on. We've got to act. Agreed?"

"All agreed," the others said in unison.

"Now," Crawford went on, "who will volunteer to hang the note on Anderson's doorknob?"

None spoke up. The others looked at the door as if they wanted to run through it, but they'd taken the oath, and there was little they could do.

"Well…" Crawford waited for a response. "…I hadn't counted on doin' all the dirty work. Who will hang it on?"

"I'll do it," Bill McCoy muttered, "if Bob Nelson will go with me."

Bob nodded and asked, "When do we do it?"

"After church, tomorrow night," Jake said. "We will all be seen at church. The two of you can slip out early. We will give him till Tuesday. If he refuses to turn the girl over to the Red Cross, we will do what we have to do."

Sam Smith kept his ear to the crack, and he could hear every word, but he had no idea when and where this would take place, until Crawford said, "We will have to gather up some hoods. I know of two, and a sheet will do fer a robe. We all know where the big black snag that stands with the grove of trees around it. If nothin' happens before Tuesday night, meet me there after church. I'd say…twelve o'clock, and we will talk. Understood?"

"Yes, sir." Bill McCoy almost saluted Crawford, but decided he was already into enough trouble.

When the four men left the building, Sam waited until they were out of hearing before he moved a muscle, then he went back to old Paint and rode slowly home, thinking, where do I go from here?

🍁 🍁 🍁

Vivian waited an hour overtime for her husband to come home. When he didn't show, she said, "We will dine, now, Shae."

Unsure about the word 'dine', Shae sat, bowed her head, and folded her hands in her lap while Vivian asked a lengthy blessing.

Too tired and nervous to eat, Shae picked at her food until Mrs. Anderson finished eating.

"Can I feed my milk to the animals?" Shae asked. "I'm afraid Hobo has gone back home."

"May I," Vivian corrected and then said, "Yes, you may."

Rushing out the door, Shae looked anxiously toward the swamp, wanting to run and run until she reached the cabin.

"I brought you some milk, Misty. You look starved." When the feeble cat made no move toward the milk, but gave a weak meow, Shae dipped her fingers into the pan and put them to Misty's mouth.

"C'mon, Misty." She stroked the ailing cat. "Your ribs are stickin' out. I know what's wrong with you, Misty. You need a baby to love." She looked into the cat's blank eyes, and stroked her belly. "Shadow, my mother cat, has four. She suckles them, and washes their little faces for hours. I'll bring you one when she weans them, but you can't have it till she does. Your nipples are as dry and puckered as a 'possum grape in October."

Shae sat for a long time, coaxing Misty to eat. Suddenly, Hobo leapt from the bushes, scaring Shae out of her wits. He landed with his front paws in the pan, and lapped greedily at the milk.

"Hobo!" Shae scolded. "Where have you been? I was sure you'd gone back home." Placing Misty back on her gunnysack bed, she turned to Jock, where he lay whimpering under the edge of the house. "Are you thirsty, Jock?"

Shae filled his pan with fresh water and watched as the wolf dog tried to get to his feet. His legs buckled under him, but he drank the whole pan of water.

"I'll bring you some food, Jock. You'll soon be all better, and you can catch cottontails. The young ones are as thick as flies, now."

As Shae talked to Jock, she heard Vivian's call. "It's time for your bath, Shae. We have to be up early tomorrow. Sunday school starts at ten."

Shae went to the door and talked through the screen. "Ca...may I feed Jock before I take my bath? He tells me with his eyes that he's hungry."

"Sure, you may." Vivian gathered scraps from the table. "What would he like?"

"He will eat anythin'. He loves rabbit, but it will be a while before he can catch one."

Jock ate heartily of the pan of bread and milk Shae carried to him, and thanked her with grateful eyes.

When Shae was scrubbed and cologned to Vivian's satisfaction, they went to her room to lay out her finery for church on Sunday. Shae could feel the lace around the neck of the blue organdy dress scratching her chin already, and she was sure the Mary Jane slippers would cramp her feet, but she decided there was no way out of it.

It was long, long after dark when Shae finally stretched out on her bed, and longer still before she thought of sleep.

I don't know what to do at church, she laid thinking, but I can't wait to see Jenny.

She thought about all the things Jenny had told her about the birds-and-bees, and she still wondered how it could be. But when she remembered Jenny's mama with her big amber eyes and friendly smile, she knew that she would never tell Jenny anything that wasn't true.

A light breeze stirred the curtains at her window. Tangled in innocence, she laid half in and half out of sleep, like a butterfly cracking its cocoon until sleep claimed her.

It was after midnight when Reverend Anderson got home, but he was up by daybreak, caring for the animals. Shae was anxious about Jock. As soon as she dressed, she went outside, where the minister cuddled Misty.

Reverend Anderson acknowledged Shae as she walked outside. "I think Jock is much better than he was yesterday."

Jock's attempt to stand was much stronger, and he looked up at Shae with a question in his eyes.

"He's askin' about Papa. He knows there's somethin' going on."

"I got word from your father, yesterday. His fever is breaking, and he's getting better each day. But he will have to stay in the hospital for two more weeks."

"Sure enough, will I get to go home when he gets well?"

"When he gets able to care for you, and keep you in school. We don't want to wear him down too soon."

With Reverend Anderson being the minister, the three of them were the first ones to gather at the brush arbor that morning. There must have been seating for a hundred people, and Shae had never seen that many people at one time. She stayed close to Vivian while people visited, then they took a front seat. The temperature was over a hundred degrees in the shade, and the pasteboard fans were swinging full speed.

Shae kept an eye out for Jenny, but instead, Mary Crawford and Tracy Alien marched up front to sing in the choir. She hoped they would not recognize her under her poke bonnet hat, but they had heard that the Andersons had taken her in. She saw them look at her, then at each other. She lowered her eyes and thought of all the taunting names she had endured from them, and others.

Reverend Anderson's sermon occupied a torturous hour of her life. The organdy dress stuck to her skin, and her white, starched petticoat itched her so bad, she squirmed around until Vivian laid a hand on her knee. She had not the slightest idea what the minister was talking about. Yawning, she started swinging her feet. Finally, Vivian said, "It will be over soon."

By the time the "Amen" was out of the minister's mouth, Vivian had Shae by the hand, leading her toward Mary and Tracy.

"I want to invite some of your friends home with us for dinner." Vivian leaned close to Shae. "You will get to know them better that way."

Swallowing the lump in her throat, Shae hesitated. But seeing that she was trapped, she followed Vivian to where Mary and Tracy stood giggling.

"Pardon me, girls," Vivian interrupted. "Shae would love to have you girls come home with her for dinner."

"Oh, thank you, Mrs. Anderson." Mary put on her Sunday face. "But Tracy is going home with me. We have plans. Maybe some other time."

Another lady broke into the conversation. Tracy inched closer to Shae, and whispered, "You are all dressed up like an Indian princess, aren't you. Where are your boots?" She looked at Shae's Mary Jane slippers.

Humiliated to tears, Shae threaded her way through the crowd and ran toward the door.

Looking around in time to see Shae go outside, Vivian rushed after her. By the time she caught up with her, Shae was in the back seat with her hands over her face, and her head in her lap.

"What is it, Shae?" Vivian brushed a strand of hair from her forehead. "What happened?"

"Nothin'. It wasn't nothin'."

"But it must have been something." Vivian patted her shoulder. "Did the girls say something?"

"It wasn't nothin'." Shae wiped her tears away and straightened her face before Reverend Anderson got to the car.

An expert on sad situations, he knew Shae had been insulted, but he suspected Vivian had been cross with her too. The English can wait, he thought as he drove around the crooked curves in the road.

Shae went through the motion of eating dinner. She had been promised she could take Sandy for a ride in the afternoon for a whole hour. She gloated over the time. A whole hour! She could ride to the swamp and back in an hour. She'd hardly gotten to straddle the pony since leaving the swamp.

As soon as she was excused from the table, Shae gathered the dishes and scraped the scraps into a pan for Jock and the cats. Vivian washed, and Shae dried dishes. Shae did not mention the incident at church, and Vivian thought it best to let her share it when she was ready.

Shae hung the dishtowel in its proper place, and made sure she didn't flub her English. "May I ride Sandy now?"

"For one hour." Vivian made her word good. "Then you will have to study your bible verses for youth meeting tonight at six." Vivian talked to Shae's back as she raced to the back porch for her overalls.

Loping to Shae's wolf-whistle, Sandy could hardly wait for Shae to ride her. She pranced around as Shae bridled her. When she straddled her from the pump bench, one goose in the flank sent Sandy around the pasture in a hard run. Her hoof beats brought Vivian screeching into the yard.

"Oh, my gracious! My gracious! Go stop the child, Fred! She'll be thrown off and crippled for life!"

"No, she won't," her husband grinned. "She's been riding the colt since it could carry her. It's a way of dealing with her frustrations. We're strange to her, and she misses her father. She's never been away from him."

"But…" Vivian stood wringing her hands. "…you didn't tell me she was such a wild tomboy."

Reverend Anderson stood grinning. "Tomboy, that's a new one. Don't think I ever heard the word before, but it fits well."

"How," Vivian muttered to herself, "how will I ever cope? Maybe Miss Trisha was right."

Chapter 27

❀

"It's no laughing matter." Vivian propped her dainty hands on her hips and dressed her husband down to size. "How am I going to teach the child anything, when you let her run wild?"

"I'm sorry, Vivian." Reverend Anderson wilted under her siege. "We'll have to handle her carefully, until we win her confidence. She didn't get this way in a day, and we can't change her in one."

Loosening his tie, Reverend Anderson walked toward the pasture gate. "I'll see what I can do."

🍁   🍁   🍁

Shae pulled the reins and slowed the filly to a walk as she rode to the gate and waited for the reverend to speak.

"Did I do somethin' wrong?" She sat waiting.

"Could we slow the filly down a bit?" Anderson spoke kindly. "She's already in a lather."

Nodding, Shae tried to hold the filly down, but she was rearing to go. When Shae pulled on her reins, she slung her head, and went tearing around the pasture in a hard run. When she finally got the horse slowed to a trot, she agreed that this was no fun.

"Just wait till Papa gets home, Sandy. We'll burn that river road up."

The hour was over all too soon. By the time the piano lesson was over and the bible verses memorized, Shae was ready for a straight jacket. She had never been able to memorize, and the chicken tracks in the song book were beyond her. But Mrs. Anderson was persistent.

"I'm afraid to get up before a crowd." Shae tried to edge out of reciting the scripture verses.

"Pray for courage. God answers all prayers, Shae."

"That's what Miss Trisha said, but I don't know how to pray."

"Psalm Chapter 130. Verses 1 and 2 are a prayer." Vivian opened her bible and read the two verses aloud from the New Testament.

"Out of the depths have I cried unto thee, Oh Lord. Lord, hear my voice. Let thine ears be attentive to the voice of my supplications."

"See, Shae, you are asking the Lord for help. Let's see if you can recite them."

Vivian was not surprised when Shae recited them without one mistake.

"Wasn't that easy? You did wonderful. It will get easier each time you recite."

Shae was dressed in her prettiest pink dress and Mary Jane slippers when they went to church, and she promised herself that she would show Mary Crawford and Tracy Allen that she wasn't the dummy they made her out to be. And she would make the Andersons proud of her.

Weak in the knees when Youth meeting opened, Shae doubted herself. But when her name was called, she marched up front and quoted chapters and verses. When she recited them without a mistake, the crowd rose to their feet for a standing ovation.

Thanking them politely, Shae walked back to her seat next to Vivian.

"You did perfect, Shae." Vivian gave her a hug. "I knew you could do it."

❦   ❦   ❦

All four of the would-be hoods were in the crowd at church. Jake Crawford sat near the front, amening every word the minister said. Bill McCoy and Bob Nelson sat in the back row, where slipping out would not be noticed if they eased out during prayer. Bill McCoy carried the note which Crawford had brought snugly in his pocket. In the middle of the first prayer, McCoy eased out first. Nelson followed soon after. McCoy had left his car out of hearing of the arbor, and the two of them walked hastily toward it.

By the time they stepped from the car at Anderson's house, Jock let out a savage growl and barked a feeble bark.

"Does the preacher have a dog?" Bob Nelson inquired.

"Not that I know of." Bill McCoy stopped in his tracks. "I'll bet it's that wolf dog of Upshaws. I've heard he will tear your leg off at the least provocation, but he must be tied up, or he would go back to the swamp."

"Maybe," Nelson said, "but I ain't crowding him." He picked up a stick. "Go on. I'll stand by. If he comes after you, I'll club him down."

Jock went crazy when McCoy went to the Anderson's door, but there was nothing he could do. His legs would not hold him up, and the men soon found that out.

McCoy hung the note on the doorknob, and they were back in church when the meeting broke.

When the Andersons arrived home, Vivian found the note. She didn't think it unusual. It was probably a sick call. She laid it on the table and went about pouring lemonade. They were choking for something cold.

Vivian noticed the shock on her husband's face as he stood staring at the bold black letters scrawled on the note.

"What is it? What happened?"

Without a word, Reverend Anderson handed her the note, and sat down in a chair.

Vivian read the note out loud. "Get rid of the half-breed. This is a warning." She handed the note back to him and poured herself a glass of lemonade, grateful that Shae had gone outside to check on Jock's water. "Who would do a thing like this?"

"Don't say anything before the child," the reverend prompted his wife. "We will discuss it, later."

Shae came inside and told them Jock looked like he was getting better. Then, after saying it'd been a long day, she went to her room.

Reverend Anderson wasn't a man for quick decisions. He sat thinking, but didn't have to think twice to know who the instigator of this plot was. But that man had been sitting in the second row at church. He could not have delivered the note. It was put there after they had left for church, but who could his followers be?

"Just what do you think the warning meant?" Vivian filled their glasses with water. They had almost died of thirst in that dusty brush arbor.

"I could guess, but I can't think anyone would be foolish enough to try to take the law into their own hands these days."

"You don't think they would…?"

"I really don't know what to make of it. The only thing I can think of is to hand the note to Sheriff Brody."

※　　　※　　　※

On Monday morning, before breakfast, Reverend Anderson knocked on Sheriff Brody's door. He had not much felt like eating.

"Well, hello, preacher. What brings you here so early in the day?"

"I wanted to catch you before you left. I think I have a problem. I found this note on my doorknob when I got home from church last night. I'd like for you to take a look at it."

Brody unfolded the note and read it. Taken aback, he read it again. He brushed his unruly, red hair from his brow, and finally asked, "Do you have any idea who could be at the back of this plan?"

"Well...I wouldn't have to make two guesses, but that man was in the second row at church last night, and he was there when church broke up. The note had to be delivered while we were gone."

"Keep your eyes open." Brody folded the note and stuck it into his pocket. "We will keep it quiet. I will be working on it."

❦   ❦   ❦

Brody spent a lot of time around Murphy's store Monday and Tuesday, but he found no clue. About dark on Tuesday, he finally got the break he was looking for. Sam Smith knocked on his door. He had seen Smith around Murphy's store, and if he remembered right, Sam had called Crawford a hog thief one day. Sam stood as if he wished he had not come.

"What can I do for you, Mr. Smith?"

Sam stood debating just how to word his message. Then he said, "Sheriff would you like to come with me to a meetin' tomerrer night, 'bout twelve o'clock behind the old black snag?

I'm shore you know where that is."

"Just what's the meeting about, Mr. Smith?"

"Wal, I don't want to say. It's some more men's meetin', but I think you might like to listen in on it."

"Well, sure, if it's of interest to me. Where will I find you?"

"In the cypress trees behind the old black snag. Be there by 'leven o'clock. The meetin' starts at twelve. Just call my name when you get there. I'll be the only one there."

"I'll be there, Sam," Brody edged, "but I would like to know what this is all about?"

"Well, ah cain't prove nothin', sheriff, but ah jest don't want to stand by and let a good man get hurt."

"I appreciate that, Sam. I'll be there."

❦   ❦   ❦

When Sam got home, he said to his wife, "Ah think I'll sleep on the screen porch again tonight, Dovie. It's so much cooler out there."

"All right, Sam, suit yourself." Dovie was beginning to wonder what was going on with Sam. He was in a stupor most of the time. Could he be slipping around on her? She put it from her mind and went sound to sleep.

About eleven o'clock, Sam eased from his cot, dressed in a long sleeved shirt. He knew the mosquitoes would be swarming. He wasn't stationed in the big, hollow cypress long, before he heard his name. It was almost a whisper, but he recognized Brody's voice.

The woods were dark as a dungeon, but Brody followed the sound of Sam's voice when he said, "Present," which he'd answered when he was in the one room school house when the teacher called roll.

The tree was hollowed half away, big enough to hide a cow. Brody squeezed his six-foot frame in beside Sam, and they sat waiting.

It was a long fifteen minutes before they heard a sound, other than a hoot owl, or the frogs croaking for rain. Five minutes past twelve, they heard mumbling. They could not see their hands before them, but they knew there were at least three, probably four men. A flashlight was turned on as the men seated themselves on stumps around the black snag.

"Well, fellers." Jake Crawford opened the meeting as usual. "Y'all know what we're here fer. We have got to decide when, where, and what. Will we take him on the road from church or go to his house?"

"No," Abe Allen spoke up. "We had better wait till after midnight."

"I say go to his house," another piped in.

"What do you say, Sid?" Crawford asked.

"Go to his house at about one in the morning, knock, and take him."

"All agreed?" Crawford waited for an answer.

"What if his wife comes to the door?" Bill McCoy asked.

"She won't," Crawford assured. "Remember the punishment is the same for a shirker."

All Bill McCoy could say was, "Agreed." But then he realized he would be the one to knock on Anderson's door. "Who will follow up in the car?"

"Wal," Crawford hum-hawed. "Ah think I'd better take care of the tar and feathers. I'll be right there when you bring him out. Be shore and tie your sheet down. Understood?"

"Understood," the others said in unison.

"One o'clock, Thursday mornin.'" Crawford held out his hand for a shake all around, and they all left as quietly as they had come.

Brody crawled from the cypress, reached out and pumped Sam's hand. "I don't know how to thank you, Sam. We could have been working on this case for months without proof. I'm going to appoint you my deputy."

"What?" Sam kept pumping Brody's hand. "You mean…?"

"Just what I said, do you have a gun?"

"Yeah." Sam dropped Brody's hand. "But it won't do nothin'. Only makes a big noise. It's a twelve-gauge."

"That's all we need. Is it a double barrel?"

"Yep, but sheriff, ah don't know nothin' about law. Ah might get myself shot." Sam stood wishing that he'd never listened in on the Ku Klux Klan.

"You don't have to, Sam. You have shown me that you are a good detective. We know all the details, thanks to you. All you will have to do is take cover near Anderson's house. I will pick you up at twelve-fifteen. Be waiting out of sight of your house. We will go to Anderson's and I will park my car in the grove of trees about two hundred yards on the road they will come in on."

"What about that dog of Upshaws? If the girl is at the Andersons, the dog will be there, and ah heard he's a bad one."

"Do not worry, Sam. The wolf dog got mixed up with a wolf. About all he can do is bark. Anyhow, he'll be tied up to keep him there."

"Wal…" Sam hesitated. "If you say so, but what if they're there early? Ah wouldn't want to have to shoot somebody."

"You won't, Sam. Trust me."

🍁　　🍁　　🍁

Sam's wife, Dovie, was doing some mental detective work of her own. She lay awake on Wednesday night when Sam informed her that he was going to sleep on the porch again. What in tarnation was going on with that man, anyhow? She lay hashing the situation over and over.

I'll bet a pewter nickel he's mixed up with one of those ornery bootleggers….

I know he's up to no good…slippin' out of bed every night and comin' back home in the wee hours of mornin'….

Brody let Sam out of the car and drove on past Anderson's house. Nobody thought anything about his car prowling around at night. That was when he did his detective work around Cache River. But the Andersons did not live in Cache River; they lived in the next little town.

By the time Brody got his car hidden among the trees, Sam had circled away out around Anderson's house and come in from the back. When Jock growled deep in his throat and barked viciously, Sam darted into the outhouse. Then he heard the preacher yell for Jock to be quiet.

Thinking about it, the outhouse was the most secure place Sam could find, anyhow. And like everything Vivian Anderson touched, it was lye-soap sanitized. Standing his gun into the corner, he made himself comfortable, until he heard a soft knock on Anderson's door.

Jock barked, but nobody answered the door. The next knock was louder. When nobody answered, a voice boomed, "If you don't come out, preacher, we're comin' in after you!"

The door crashed open, and a woman screamed, "Please, please, don't do this to us!"

CHAPTER 28

❧

"Shut up!" A ghostlike figure slapped its hand over Vivian Anderson's mouth. "Or we will take you along for some of the same medicine."

Shoving her back, the nightriders wrestled the reverend from the house, and pinned his arms to his sides just as Sam Smith darted from the outhouse. The moon was giving just enough light for him to see three robed figures crowded around a man that he knew to be Reverend Anderson.

Pointing his 12 gauge double barrel shotgun into the air, Sam pulled off both barrels at once, which roared like a stick of dynamite.

Dropping their prisoner like a hot potato, the culprits broke into a run, their white robes flapping around their legs like petticoats, while the Andersons stood in shock.

"Are you folks all right?" Sam Smith stood his shotgun against the house and walked toward them. "Sorry to scare you."

"Thank you, Lord." Reverend Anderson looked heavenward. "For an angel unawares."

"Oh, mercy, mercy." Vivian looked down at her nightgown and then ran into the house.

"Where did you come from, Mr. Smith?" the minister asked, having recognized Sam's voice.

"Ah guess ah happened to be in the right place at the right time," Sam drawled.

"What have I ever done," the reverend asked Sam, "to deserve this? I thought the Ku Klux Klan was outlawed years ago."

"Ah think these fellers will find out that they was."

As they stood talking, they heard a motor start and the lights of a car come on. Then a big booming voice yelled, "Stick 'em up, boys!"

The three hoods had just made it to Jake Crawford's get-a-way car, and they were ready for the escape.

"Get out of the car, Crawford." Brody held his gun on the others. "I know who you are. I happened to sit in on your meeting around the big black snag on Tuesday night."

Crawford hesitated, as if he thought of taking off, but when Brody shot the air from one of his tires, he crawled from under the wheel and raised his hands into the air.

Brody stood looking the four over. Finally, he said, "Take off your robes, now. I've never seen a Klansman up close."

Nervous, they had problems untying their belts, but Brody stood patiently while they pulled the robes over their heads, and dropped them on the ground.

"Now, since you are doing the honors, Jake…" Brody dangled three sets of handcuffs toward him. "…you can put these bracelets on McCoy, Nelson and Allen. Then I will do yours."

As usual, Crawford stood with a smirk on his face, until Brody said, "Did you understand what I said, Jake?"

After Crawford had placed the cuffs on the other men, Brody said, "Hands, Jake. And give me no lip. If my gun was to bite you, we would have one badly wounded Klansman."

Crawford meekly lifted his hands from his sides. Brody snapped the cuffs on him and then herded the four of them toward his car.

In the shuffle, they'd forgotten to turn the lights off on Jake's car. When Reverend Anderson noticed, he said, "Should we go turn the lights off on that car. The battery will go down."

Sam Smith could not believe what he'd heard. "Do you mean to tell me that you would worry about a man's car battery when he was tryin' to tar and fea…?" Sam caught his tongue. How would he know that unless he'd stuck his nose into someone's business?"

Humbling himself, the minister said, "The Lord says to turn the other cheek."

"Wal…" Sam picked up his shotgun. "…ah guess ah'd better get home. If Dovie catches me slippin' in this time of mornin', ah'll have some questions to answer."

"Thanks, Sam." Reverend Anderson shook his hand. "Sure glad you happened around."

"Always glad to help, preacher. Ah'll see you."

※ ※ ※

The calaboose, a small, concrete job with a tiny window, sat on the outskirts of town, and only accommodated three drunks at a time. So far that had been about all they had used it for, or sometimes a hog thief. This was a different story.

"Well, boys…" Brody clicked the lock on the iron-barred door. "…looks as if two of you will have to bunk together, or one set up while the other sleeps, until I can find another cot. The food is not too bad. The milk's skimmed and the coffee clear. But the oatmeal's fair, only you have to eat it with cornbread for breakfast."

All the men kept mum when Brody said he was going home for some needed rest. "I'll see you in court sometime in the next day or two."

As soon as Brody was out of hearing, they all began to talk about how they could get bonded out, when there was hardly a meal ahead in any of their houses. And they doubted they would have a friend in the county. Everyone wanted the Redskins gone, but not at the expense of the Andersons. The preacher was next to Dr. Bond when it came to helping people.

When the door had crashed and Vivian Anderson screamed, Shae had covered up her head and ears. She heard sketches of Anderson talking to someone in the kitchen, but she asked no questions, until Vivian knocked softly on her door and tiptoed into her room.

"I just wanted to double check to see if you used the body lotion, Shae. I hope you were not too scared about the goings on around here tonight. It will be all right now."

"Yes, I used the lotion." The hand she placed under her chin as she raised up on her elbow, felt like velvet, and she hesitated before asking, "Why did the men in the white clothes try to take Reverend Anderson away? Was it about me and my papa?"

Vivian thought for a moment. Should she tell her, or shun the subject? Then she said, "Don't worry about it. They won't be back. Sheriff Brody took care of them. Try to get some sleep, now. We have a busy day tomorrow."

Shae lay for a long, long time, dreading to wake up to an alien world, whose language she could neither speak, nor understand.

❦   ❦   ❦

Hobo had not shown up for two days, and Shae was sure he had gone home to the swamp. Shadow would take care of him. She would be happy to have him back.

Shae was prim and pretty when she left for school on Monday. She met a bunch of kids running toward the playground as she went into the schoolroom to stash her books and lunch, which Vivian had packed into a paper poke. She wouldn't have to wag the lard bucket home.

To Shae's surprise, her seat was still unoccupied, and Jenny came smiling in to greet her.

"My, my, you look pretty today, Shae." Miss Trisha looked Shae's dress over. "If you will bring your arithmetic up, I will assign your lesson. You have some catching up to do."

Shocked at how far behind she'd gotten, Shae said, "I will never catch up."

"Oh yes, you will. I'm sure Mrs. Anderson will help you."

"She wants me to learn to play piano, and how to be a lady most, so I won't have time to do my school work."

"But, I'm sure she wants you to learn reading, writing and arithmetic, also."

"I'll help you, Shae." Jenny clasped Shae's hand, and they ran toward their secluded place, where Jenny filled her in all she'd learned about the birds-and-bees since she had last seen her.

All ears, Shae sat without interrupting, until the five minute bell rang. Reluctantly, they ran to the pump to stand in line for water.

"I wish I could go home with you to live, Jenny. Your mama lets you play all the time, even if it is with your little brother. And you don't have to be proper all the time."

"I know," Jenny agreed. "My mama is the best mama in the whole wide world."

The next six weeks of summer school was a long gruesome drag for Shae. When she wasn't in school, she had piano practice and bible verses for Youth meeting on Sundays. But worst of all was having to stay primped up for company, or to go somewhere to dine every night.

"Shae," she mimicked Vivian, "you may relax for an hour, then practice your music." She had not had time to ride Sandy for three days. When Papa gets home, she told herself, I'm goin' home. All the animals will be out gatherin' food to store for winter. Hickory nuts will be fallin'. Persimmons will be ripe. I can't wait!

The first of September finally rolled around and school let out for cotton harvest and to make everything perfect, Reverend Anderson announced that her papa would be coming home in three days.

Shae went through the next three days in a tizzy, without hearing half of what Vivian Anderson said. She could think of nothing except her papa's homecoming. She went through the motion of setting the table properly, practicing piano and memorizing her bible verses. She was so happy when Reverend Anderson asked her if she would like to ride with him to pick her papa up from the hospital.

When Reverend Anderson led the way into Clay Upshaw's room at the hospital, Shae looked around for her papa, but she did not recognize the skeleton of a man sitting in a chair, until he held out his arms and said, "My-my-my, how pretty you look, Girly Shae." He sat feasting his eyes on his little girl.

For a moment, Shae stood uncertain. Then dropping her guard, she ran into the old man's arms, laughing and crying at the same time.

"Papa!" She smoothed his clean-shaven face with her velvet-soft hands. "Why did you shave your whiskers off? You don't look like my papa."

"Ah." He chucked her under the chin with his long, skinny fingers. "The nurses thought I should get all gussied up to come home to you, and you don't like me. They'll grow back."

Awed at the reunion, Reverend Anderson wondered why he and his wife ever thought they could give the child more love than her papa.

The Andersons insisted that Clay Upshaw stay in their home for a few days, but he was sure he could do for himself. "But…" He hesitated. "…would it be asking too much if you keep Girly Shae until I get back on my feet? And while we are on the subject, did I sign any papers while I was out on a limb?"

"While you were where?" Anderson, never having heard the expression, looked confused. Then, catching on, he said, "Not to my knowledge."

"I seem to remember someone saying the health department would take charge of my girl. There was a time when I was completely out of it, wasn't there?"

"Well, yes, there was talk. But since you asked, and I agreed to care for her, it's all between you and me"

"I see." Upshaw studied the situation. "You would not take my daughter from me, would you?"

"Of course not, Mr. Upshaw, we're here to help. But since the girl is doing so well and adjusting, we're hoping that you will let her stay through the winter term of school. You need a break from the stress of caring for her, and we will be more than happy to help."

"I will think about it, if I can have her a few days while school is out. Don't think I'm not grateful for all you folks have done for us. I hope I can repay you one day but you understand the girl is all I have." He almost said of Dora, but he hesitated to play on the Anderson's sympathy.

Clay Upshaw watched as tears welled up in Shae's eyes. She looked over at Vivian, and asked, "May I come home soon, Papa?"

"Maybe, Girly, I will have to sell the pearl for some grocery money. You wouldn't want me to hock mama's ring again, would you?"

Without answering, Shae turned to her bedroom, and brought him the snuff box, which held her mama's wedding ring, and the small pearl her papa had found before he came down with the fever.

"That's my girl." He held Shae close for a moment. "Be patient. You can come home as soon as I get back on my feet."

"We understand, Clay. In case you don't sell the pearl, let me know. The good Lord will provide. Trust Him."

"Thank you, preacher, and while we're on the subject, where did the money come from for the new clothes? I have no money to repay you."

"Just come to church some Sunday."

Thinking that it was a small price to ask, Upshaw's eyes brimmed with tears as he turned to leave.

Shae rushed into her bedroom.

"Come, Jock," Upshaw called to the wolf dog as he walked toward Reverend Anderson's car, but Jock hesitated. His master did not look the same in the new shirt and overalls, and no whiskers. But when

Upshaw held out his hand and coaxed, the wolf dog wagged his tail and followed.

"I hope you will take it easy for a while, Clay," Anderson advised. "Stay clear of that river. I will be around everyday to take care of your needs. And Jake Crawford won't be harassing you for a while. He's over in Green County jail."

Upshaw looked over at the preacher in disbelief. "What did he get into now?"

"He and three of his cronies tried to pull a little Ku Klux Klan party, and got caught at it."

"Sure enough? I can't believe he would be that dumb."

"It just goes to show that some people will do anything to prove their point. I pray for the families."

When the minister offered no more information, Upshaw asked, "What did they do?"

"They only roughed a man up a little bit, but Sheriff Brody was tipped off, and sat in on their meeting. Here I am gossiping. I'd best get going, Clay. Remember if you need me, all you have to do is ask, and I'll be there."

The Sunday school collection was set aside every week for Upshaw's care, but when he sold the pearl, he thanked the minister. He could manage on his own.

It was three days before Vivian found time to take Shae to visit her papa, and she was so elated, she could hardly contain herself.

"Can I ride Sandy? She needs to exercise, Papa says." Shae headed for the porch to get her overalls.

"No," Vivian spoke shortly. "I want your father to see how nice you look in your pretty, new dress. And the question is, may I ride Sandy, remember?" Catching herself she added, "Dear."

"I'll try." Shae stood corrected, then turned to her room to get control. *Dear!* She fumed to herself. That's as bad as child. Why can't she call me by my name?

The wheels on Vivian Anderson's Overland had hardly stopped rolling when Shae dashed from the car to where her papa sat sunning on a stump outside the cabin. Jock lay at his feet.

"Papa!" Shae turned on the tears as she ran toward him. "I want to come home with you." Her tears always turned his legs to water.

"Now, now, Girly." He patted her gently as he acknowledged Vivian. "Don't cry."

"Aren't you getting frisky, Mr. Upshaw?" Vivian called to him. "How about a dish of fresh blackberry cobbler? I strained the seeds from them. Dr. Bond said it would be all right."

"Sounds good," Upshaw admitted as Vivian went into the cabin to give the two of them time together.

Adding bleach to water, Vivian washed some saucers before serving the cobbler. One could not be too careful. She had brought fresh milk. Pouring some into two tin cups, she called for Shae and her papa to come inside. The flies would cover their food outside.

Vivian measured out two tablespoons of cobbler for herself, skipping the milk. She watched her waistline to the pinch.

Shae and her papa seated themselves on the long bench at the table as close as they could get to each other. Pulling up a cane bottomed chair, Vivian seated herself, and bowed her head for grace.

While Vivian said a lengthy blessing, Shae sat with her eyes on the cobbler. Vivian did not believe in snacking between meals, and she was famished. This was a special treat.

"Aren't you hungry, Mr. Upshaw?" Vivian asked between bites as the old man picked at his food.

"Not that much." He held a spoon of cobbler halfway to his mouth.

"It looks real good, but there's something I have to get off my mind."

"Let's hear it, Mr. Upshaw."

"Mrs. Anderson, I think you know how hard it is for me to have to say this, but I realize it's the best for my daughter to stay with you folks for the winter term of school. But I want you to understand that I'm not giving her away. It's one of the hardest propositions I have ever had to battle. I hate to be a grudge to anyone, especially to folks who have already been so kind to us. I hope to be able to take care of her by spring. I would be so grateful if she could stay through the winter with you."

"Whatever you wish, Mr. Upshaw. It isn't our wish to hold Shae against your will. We only want to help."

Shae sat staring into her empty saucer, fighting the tears welling up in her big brown eyes. When she looked up, she noticed one creeping down into her papa's new whiskers.

"Don't cry, Papa." She dabbed at the tear with a manicured finger. "It'll be all right."

When her own tears got out of control, she jumped up. Catching Vivian's eye, she stopped, and said, "Excuse me, please," and rushed on into her bedroom. Closing her door, she crashed onto her bed and sobbed silently.

Why did I say it would be all right? It ain't all right.

She beat a clenched fist into her duck-feather pillow.

It never will be all right, but I can't stand to see Papa cry!

CHAPTER 29

Once Shae's tears were spent, she laid thinking of all the nights she'd watched the moon ride by her window. She listened to the wolves howl, the whippoorwills call and the frogs croak for rain. Hobo would be next to her with all four feet pointed up into the air, and she never felt alone. But, she told herself, I guess it's all decided that I will be dressin' in ruffles, goin' to church, and bangin' on that piano for the rest of my life. It's impossible to play a piece perfect, and 'per—fect' is Vivian's favorite word.

While Shae lay raking Vivian over the coals, Vivian wondered how Shae could want to come back to her humble environment and Shae's papa sat picking at his blackberry cobbler.

Shae heard Vivian scraping the saucers. Drying her eyes, she went to the kitchen to help, as she was being taught to do. But never having had a child of her own, Vivian could not understand Shae's tears, and she was upset when Shae went to her papa and asked if she could stay overnight with him.

"You will have to ask Mrs. Anderson about that, Girly Shae. She is the one you have to account to while she is caring for you."

Spilling tears again, Shae turned to Vivian. "Cou…may I spend the night with Papa, Vivian?"

"Not tonight, dear." Vivian wiped the table. "We did not bring your body lotion and manicure set. Maybe one night next week. I would hate for you to break one of your pretty fingernails, after we have worked so hard to perfect them."

For a moment, Clay Upshaw sat wondering what he was doing to Dora's little girl. But he had no choice. He was up against a wall, until he could take care of Shae. He thought of how she used to lace the angle worms on the fishhooks, and open the mussel shells with her nails.

Beat again, Shae stayed her tears, walked over to her papa's bed, and picked up a pair of worn-out shoes.

"Papa, cou…may I have one of these buckskin strings to mend Sandy's saddle? Other twine won't hold."

"Sure, Girly. I can use a string until I can buy a new pair of shoes, if and when we get the money."

"We must be going, Shae." Vivian hung the dishtowel on a nail behind the stove. "We're having guests for supper at six. Picking up her purse, she took out her compact and touched up her powder as she turned toward the door. "We will be back shortly, Mr. Upshaw. If you need us, we will be here."

Shae kept working at the buckskin shoestring as she followed Vivian toward the car.

Her papa stopped her on the porch. "It won't be for long, Girly. I'm feeling better each day, and I promise you can come home in the spring." He held her close for a moment, while she pulled the buckskin string from the shoe. "Be a good girl 'til then."

"I'll try, Papa." She brushed a tear from his cheek. "Don't cry, Papa." Fingering the new stubble on his face, she smiled. "You will look like Papa by the time I come back again." Rushing toward the car where Vivian sat waiting, she left her papa to spend another lonely night.

It was over a week since Shae last visited with her papa. She asked repeatedly if she could ride Sandy to the swamp, but Vivian always put her off with, "Thirteen-year-old girls do not ride all over alone." Shae quit asking.

Vivian cooked extra, and often sent her husband to Clay Upshaw with nutritious meals, but she was too busy trying to make a princess of Shae to visit herself. She believed the more the child was away from the Indian way of life, the less she would miss it.

Each day away from the swamp grew longer for Shae. Summer was turning into fall, the most beautiful time of the year at Cache River.

Some day, Shae vowed to herself. If I ever get Sandy out of that pasture....

One day, she finally got her chance.

The Andersons were having an afternoon business meeting at the church. Since it was of no interest to Shae, she was allowed to stay home to clean her room, practice piano and memorize her bible verses for Sunday night youth meeting.

"May I," Shae began, making sure she used the right word, "ride Sandy when I'm finished? Papa says she will get stiff if I don't ride her often."

"Yes, you may." Vivian was happy not to have to correct her for once. "But be sure to be bathed and dressed by five. We're dining with the Kents tonight."

The Andersons were halfway to the church, and neither of them had spoken a word. "Why so gloomy?" Reverend Anderson asked as he glanced at Vivian. She took her compact from her purse and dabbed at her nose.

"I'm just wondering if I look presentable." Vivian took a long look into her mirror. "It seems that I never have half enough time to dress anymore."

Knowing what she was insinuating, her husband thought a second and then said. "You know, I was just thinking, Vivian, maybe we are pushing the girl too fast. She needs to spend some time with her father. Her piano lessons can wait until school starts. I'm sure her papa gets very lonely for her."

We! Vivian's tone cut her husband down to size. "When have you ever corrected her English, table manners, or told her that it isn't nice for a girl of thirteen to whistle through her teeth like a cowhand. It's just my opinion, but I think the more she's away from the Cache River environment, the easier she will be to handle."

"Wo-ah," the minister broke into his good natured laugh and slowed the Overland to a creep. "I didn't intend to start a war, but the girl needs time. Imagine yourself going to the swamp to live. It's just as hard for her to adjust to our environment. But can we discuss this later?" He stepped on the gas. "We have a meeting to attend."

Believing her husband had no idea what a change the girl made in her busy life, Vivian snapped her compact shut and apologized.

It was two o'clock before Shae had her bible verses memorized. She had not played one piece of music without a mistake, but so what? She always had to take her lesson over for one reason or another.

I'll worry about it when the time comes.

Racing to the back porch, she pulled on her overalls, ran toward the pasture, and whistled through her teeth for Sandy to come to her. She didn't have to flank Sandy, for when she straddled her and turned her toward the swamp, the filly hit a long lope. She slowed her down when she got close to Murphy's store and cut down the river road. If anyone happened to see her, they would be sure to tell Reverend Anderson. Vivian would have a conniption fit if she found out. Hoping that she would not run into anyone she knew, she rode along the river toward the dock. No one could accuse her of playing hooky, because school was out for harvest.

Holding Sandy to a walk, Shae rode along, enjoying the odor of ripe 'possum grapes.

She passed a persimmon tree loaded with fruit, but they would not be ripe until the first white frost. The leaves were falling early, due to the dry summer, and Shae loved the rustle of Sandy's feet as she waded through them.

The river was only a mud hole, now. Sandy reared upon her hind feet when something swung over their heads.

"It's only a flyin' squirrel, Sandy.

Shae clamped her legs tight around Sandy, just in case she stumbled onto a water moccasin. Sandy hated snakes.

When Shae came to her favorite clump of water willows, she slid over Sandy's rump and looked for a sturdy sapling to tie the filly to. It had been so long since she had time to think things out. She had hardly had time to think at all since she'd gone to the Andersons, but maybe her papa was doing the best he could.

Shae threw Sandy's bridle around a buckeye bush the size of her arm, and tied it with a hitch knot. But Sandy had been known to slip her bridle. "You need to cool off, Sandy. Papa would be upset if he caught me racin' you."

Venturing to the river's edge, she eased herself down on the cool, damp sand, where she'd spent hours and hours when she was five, and her papa was digging shells. The baby ducks were grown, now. Picking up a handful of gumbo sand, she let it sift through her fingers. She would have to be sure and clean her fingernails when she got home. They would be thoroughly inspected before they left to dine with the Kents.

After cooling a while, Shae made her way along the river toward the dock. Passing under a vine of 'possum grapes, she broke off a big cluster and sauntered along eating them. She waded into a patch of pesky begger lice. How would she ever get them off her overalls without Vivian seeing them? Forging on toward the dock, she could see her boat high and dry on the bank. Will it ever hold water again? She lamented.

Within a few feet of the water oak, she stood holding her breath. One rustle of a leaf and Scar would be gone, if he happened to be out of his den. He kept his good eye cocked for Jock every second. Easing along on duck-down feet, she jumped when two baby turtles hit the water at once, making a terrible splash. Dashing to Scar's den, she planted herself in his path. In case he was out, she'd have a chance to grab him.

Losing patience, Shae moved to the edge of the slimy water, and grabbled for mussel shells. Finally, she lifted a big almond shell from the mud and worked at it with her fingernails. When she got it open, her eyes bugged at the size of the nacre hugging close to the side of the shell. Tenderly lifting the lump out, she worked at it with her teeth.

What? She asked herself, would Vivian say if she saw me doin' this?

As usual, it was only gristle. Just as she moved near her boat to push it into the water, a big grennel fish flopped onto the bank. Within seconds, the fish was covered with cats of every description. Shadow's last litter of kittens was almost grown, and Shadow was fat again. Shae knew why. Shadow was going to have more babies.

Shae pulled her knees up under her chin and closed her eyes tight as the cats tore flesh from bone, until the fish was devoured. Full and content, Shadow retreated to her stump, and Shae followed. Sure enough, a new bed was ready for her new babies. As Shadow lay washing her face, Shae wondered what a mother would be thinking at a time like this. She thought of all the stories Jenny had told her about the birds and the bees, but she still couldn't understand how Shadow was going to bring it all about. The cat had weaned her other kittens. That meant she was making room for new ones.

"By the time I get back out here again," she said, rubbing Shadow's round belly, "you will have another bed full of blind babies. I wish you would have a solid gray one. I would take it to Reverend Anderson to replace Misty."

As Shae sat soothing Shadow, she caught a glimpse of Scar slithering toward his den. He was moving cautiously, his bad eye toward her. With the speed of a bullet, she was upon him; with her long fingers wrapped around his neck in the choke-hold her papa had taught her when she was no more than nine. Scar whipped her with his tail until she cuddled him to her. Relaxing when his good eye recognized her, he lay passive in her arms.

"Poor, Scar. Have you missed me like I've missed you? Your eye looks better, and the gash on your back is all healed up. I would take you home with me, but Vivian Anderson is scared to death of a snake. She's even scared of a horse. If she had any notion that I'm out here…"

A low gut-growl brought Shae up with a start. Jock was no more than a hundred yards from them. Scar made one quick dash and was in his den.

"Jock!" Shae screeched. "Why do you always have to ruin everything?"

Realizing she had screamed loud enough to be heard to the cabin, she slapped her hand over her mouth. If her papa heard her, he might come looking, and she'd be in real trouble.

Jock tucked his tail between his legs and hightailed it toward the cabin. Shae ducked behind the river bank and ran toward where Sandy was hitched to the sapling.

"Sandy…" She untied the filly and led her down the river. "…if someone catches us here, especially Sheriff Brody, he'd be sure to put me in the orphan's home."

The filly was in a lather when they got back to the Andersons. Knowing she had to keep Sandy from water for fifteen minutes, Shae combed her down and rode her slowly around the pasture. Sandy pawed at the watering trough until Shae got the pump primed, then gulped the water faster than Shae could pump it. After drinking her fill, she walked away to graze, and Shae rushed to the house, hid her overalls, and took her bath. She could pick the begger lice from the overalls later.

When the Andersons returned from the meeting, Shae was sitting at the piano in her Sunday dress, Mary Jane slippers and hair-bows, playing her favorite song as if she loved every minute of it. The Andersons stood outside listening as Shae played Silent Night.

"Shae," said the Reverend, "you are doing so well."

Vivian glowed like a firefly. "You must have worked very hard this afternoon."

Thanking them for the compliments, Shae rose from the piano for the inspection, which she knew she would have to pass. "Do I look all right?" She primped at the pink ribbon holding her long, black hair back from her face, and brushed the wrinkles from the back of her dress. Then her eyes followed Vivian's to her hands, and Shae groaned under her breath.

"You look beautiful, Shae, but I believe you forgot to manicure your nails. You may do that while I dress."

Happy to get from under Vivian's scrutiny, Shae rushed to her room for her manicure set. She hated the hour Vivian spent in front of the mirror, doing her hair, retouching her face, and all the other things it took to get her ready to go to church, or wherever she was going.

❦   ❦   ❦

September was fast turning into October. The best time of the year, when the bright blue Indian summer days made Shae's blood run wild. The confinement of Vivian's restrictions was almost unbearable. She often asked to ride Sandy, hoping that she would get a chance to go back to the swamp, but there were always excuses, excuses. They were having company for supper. Or she had to be close for fitting clothes, which Vivian was forever stitching. So the days turned into weeks. Soon school would start and she'd miss the best of everything.

One day her papa came to visit. Shae begged to go home with him, but he thought it best that she stay with the Andersons through the winter. Shae felt he was just giving her away. That night as she laid thinking of hot biscuits and simple syrup, the fall rains started. For three days it came down in torrents, and Vivian sewed a red velvet dress for Shae to wear to church on Sunday. Shae tried to keep the chores up, but they were never ending. Every track was to be mopped the minute after they were made. The dishes were forever dirty. And the silver had to be polished everyday, in case they should have unexpected company.

Friday afternoon, the rain stopped and the sun came out. Shae worked like a trooper, hoping to have time to ride Sandy on Saturday. Maybe there would be another meeting and she'd have time to go to the swamp. The Cache would be everywhere after all this rain. She would not get near the river again until spring.

"Gracious." Vivian looked out the window. "I hope this storm calms down before church time. I'll wash the dishes, Shae. You may clean your room and then dry the dishes while I take my bath.

Shae rushed into her room, knowing that nothing would keep the Andersons from church on Sunday. Reverend Anderson had gone on a sick call. Being one for punctuality, he would expect them to be ready when he returned.

"Shae," Vivian called from the parlor as she destroyed the last cobweb on the ceiling, "your dress is on the hanger. And be sure you wear the slip with the lace on the bottom."

After wrestling into the Sunday clothes, which Vivian had chosen for her, Shae crammed her feet into the Mary Jane slippers. Her feet had grown and the shoes pinched her toes.

"Oh, Shae…" Vivian rushed in with a hairbrush to help with Shae's hair. "…you look beautiful. Do you like the dress?"

"Huh?" Shae was looking out the window. The bright October weather had turned gray, and she was sure the geese would be flying to the Cache any day now. It was hard to keep her mind on pretty clothes, when she could be out with her papa watching the geese vee in by the hundreds.

"You didn't answer me, Shae." Vivian spoke short. "I asked you if you liked the dress."

"Yeah." Shae's mind was on the river. "Er…yes," she corrected herself, making another mistake.

❦   ❦   ❦

During the next two weeks, the sky turned a muddy gray, and the wind howled, which meant November was just around the corner. The frost was white every morning, and school was in full swing again. Shae hated every minute of it. Each day as she walked to school, the geese flew over her head, and each night she lay listening to their honking as they flew over the house. Somehow, she had to get to the river. But each Sunday they went to church, then had a houseful of high-falutin' company for dinner.

One Sunday when Shae got up, she noticed flakes of snow fluttering through the sky, and she knew the woods would be alive with geese and ducks of every description. But Shae had already been informed that she and the Andersons would be dining with friends for lunch and supper.

As usual, Vivian chose the red velvet dress, and the poke bonnet hat for Shae to wear. They would be staying for youth meeting that night, and she wanted Shae to look her prettiest to recite her bible verses.

After Vivian went back to her bedroom to finish dressing, Shae sauntered onto the back porch, sure that she'd heard a flock of geese somewhere. She knew they would be flying in ahead of the storm. When she looked up, there must have been a hundred in a vee right over the house.

Unable to stay any longer, Shae untied her sash, ripped the dress, and slipped it over her head in one swipe. Kicking her Mary Jane slippers in the opposite directions, she ran for her riding clothes which were hanging on a nail, and socked her feet into her gum boots.

Swift as a fireman, she was into her shirt, overalls and jumper when she looked up and saw Vivian standing in the door, with her mouth hanging open.

"Shae…?" Vivian held her powder puff half-mast. "Where on earth are you going in this storm?"

CHAPTER 30

❀

Without a word, Shae jumped off the porch and hit the ground running like a hound-chased rabbit toward the pasture. She whistled through her teeth as she ran, but the wind blew it back into her face. The snow was coming down in big, wet flakes by the time she got to the pasture. The filly stood contented under the makeshift shed, which Reverend Anderson had thrown together for her, and she was not anxious to go out into the swirling snow.

"C'mon, Sandy!" Shae grabbed the bridle from a nail on the wall. "We're goin' to the swamp to see the honkers and quackers come home."

Bracing her front feet, Sandy snorted and slung her head when Shae tried to lead her from the shelter to the watering trough to mount her. Shae jerked the bridle. "Don't be so stubborn!"

For five minutes, Shae pulled and hauled on the filly's bridle, while keeping an eye out for Reverend Anderson. She knew Vivian would not go out into the storm in her new clothes and pretty spike-heeled pumps, not even if the house was on fire. But if Reverend Anderson caught Shae there, she'd wind up in church in that red velvet dress and poke bonnet hat.

What a life!

Unable to coax Sandy from the shed, Shae managed to get on her back by climbing from the feeding trough. One goose in the flank sent the filly tearing down the wrong road in a runaway gallop. She had run a mile before Shae could get her turned around and then she balked under a willow tree, refusing to budge. Breaking off a keen willow switch, Shae laid it across the filly's rump. The sting sent her off in another runaway.

It took all the strength Shae could muster to hold on. Snow sifted down her jumper collar and she was freezing into a human icicle.

Remembering her papa's warning not to race Sandy, Shae tried to slow her down. Sandy turned down the river path, but two men ran out onto Murphy's porch when they heard hoof beats. Shae knew they would blab it all over that the Upshaw kid was back home with her papa.

🍁 🍁 🍁

Reverend Anderson rushed into the house from his sick visit and noticed Vivian sitting in a chair, dabbing her eyes. "What's this all about?" He asked.

His wife didn't answer, but he began to suspect something was wrong when he saw the red velvet dress sprawled over one of the chairs. "Vivian, where's the girl?"

"She's gone." Vivian tried to control her quivering voice. "What have I done wrong? I tried. Honest I did!"

For a moment, the minister stood mute. Finally, he said, "I know, Vivian, but maybe we expected too much too soon. Did she ride the filly?"

"Yes. She rode past the house in a hard run, without a hood or gloves. She's sure to catch pneumonia."

"No, she won't. She's followed her papa up and down the river since she was five, in all kinds of weather. She didn't catch typhoid, I've noticed. And she's wallowed in the river with the filly all summer."

Reverend Anderson straightened his tie and went to the chiffarobe for his Sunday-go-to-meeting coat. Speaking shorter than he intended, he snapped, "Get dressed! We're late for church already."

❧   ❧   ❧

Clay Upshaw slept little on Saturday night. The wind howled all night and he laid thinking of Girly Shae.

If she was here, he thought, we'd be bundled up in long drawers, mackinaw and gumboots, settin' in a goose-blind by daylight tomorrow.

I wonder if she misses me as much as I do her. I feel like I can't wait another day to see her, but the Andersons will have a houseful of company today and my chambray shirt and overalls don't fit in very well for Sunday visits.

Waking up to a cold, blustery morning on Sunday, Upshaw shivered as he fired the King heater, thinking that this was harsh weather for this time of year. It was a good morning for biscuits and gravy, but it wouldn't be the same without Girly.

"Mornin', Jock." Upshaw patted the wolf dog's head as he came to lick his hand, and stretched himself into shape for the day. Jock was wise to the weather. He knew it would soon be time to go coon hunting. After Upshaw had eaten half of the skillet of biscuits and fed the other half to Jock, he moved over to his rocker to nurse his third cup of coffee. It seemed like he'd spent a lot of lonely hours there since Girly was gone, but at least his appetite was back and he was feeling good.

Jock stood with his head in the old man's lap. Somehow, Jock had a way of knowing when his master was down in the dumps.

"You miss the girl as much as I do, don't you, boy?

Wagging his tail, Jock looked up with sympathy in his eyes.

For a long time, Upshaw sat brooding. After he finished his coffee, he reached for his corncob pipe and filled it with tobacco. Glancing out the window, he noticed snowflakes fluttering down.

Unbelievable!

He got up and moseyed over to the window, thinking it wasn't even Thanksgiving yet. He would have to hustle out his hip boots, mackinaw, and stocking-leg cap to sit in a goose-blind today, but a big, fat goose sure would taste good. He was grateful for the food Reverend Anderson delivered every week from the collection cup at Sunday school, but it afforded no extras.

Each time the minister came; Upshaw assured him that he was able to take care of Shae. He could take her to school if necessary. But each time, the minister reasoned that it would be best for all concerned for the girl to stay with them through the winter, which made the old man wonder again if he'd signed any papers while he was unconscious.

He could shoot a wild pig any day, now, and he had heard the geese and ducks honking over the cabin for several nights.

🍁   🍁   🍁

There was little time for conversation as the Andersons drove to church, but the Reverend had time to change his sermon to 'Pruning Too Short', which he was pretty sure Vivian had been guilty of.

Knowing that her husband's sermon was for her alone, Vivian sat twisting her gloves in her lap. It was the longest sermon she had ever heard him preach. Feeling every eye on her, she could hear them saying, 'I told you so'. But she told herself she'd done the best she could, until the minister closed his sermon with, "Pruning the prong too short will cause the rose to go back to the wild."

After pausing long enough for the impact to hit home, he bowed his head. "Let us pray."

Understanding that the situation was not pleasant with the Andersons, their dinner hosts accepted their rain check graciously. Another time would be just fine.

The Andersons spoke little on the way home. Finally, unable to stand the suspense any longer, Vivian asked, "What are we going to do about the child?"

"Nothing." Anderson opened the car door and helped her out, and walked her to the house like the gentleman he was, saying, "She might come back after she visits her father. I'm sure she is very lonely for him."

"And if she doesn't?" Vivian swung the door open and looked back in time to see her husband shrug, telling her that the subject was closed. Sighing, she hurried into her bedroom to change her clothes.

❦   ❦   ❦

When Clay Upshaw heard a flock of geese honking over the cabin, he hustled into he warmest clothes he could find, stoked the King heater, and locked Jock in the cabin. He couldn't sit around with hundreds of geese going to waste, never once dreaming that Girly would be coming home.

No sooner had he gotten situated in the goose-blind, Shae rode up to the cabin, loaded herself off Sandy and yelled, "Papa! Papa, I'm home!"

When Jock answered her, trying to claw down the door, Shae knew her papa was already goose hunting. She tied the filly to a fencepost, wondering how she would ever get into the cabin without letting Jock out. She knew her papa had left him home to keep him from scattering the geese, but she had to get inside.

"Jock," She knuckled the door. "Go 'way. I want in! I'm freezin'."

But Jock kept scratching and barking for five minutes. Shae couldn't get in. Finally, she thought of her bedroom window. If the door was shut between it and the kitchen, she could climb in that way.

Swollen tight from the damp weather, it was almost impossible for her to raise it. After a while of struggling, she managed it up enough to squeeze through. By that time, Jock was at her bedroom door. No way could she push it open with his hundred pound body against it.

Getting smart, she walked across the room and knocked on the opposite wall. Confused, Jock ran to the front door. Dashing across the room, Shae pulled the latchstring on her door and was into the kitchen in one stride.

Meeting Shae with a big bear hug, Jock almost knocked her to the floor. He stood with his bear paws on her shoulders, licking her icy face with his warm tongue.

"Fooled you, didn't I, Jock? Did you miss me?"

Pushing the wolf dog away, Shae moved to the heater and unscrewed the damper. Pretty soon the King heater was red hot. She rubbed her hands over the heat and pulled off her boots to warm her feet. Her lacy socks weren't much for boot warmers.

After she had thawed out and dried her clothes, Shae looked in the cupboard for a biscuit, but Jock had taken care of that.

"Oh, well. I'm not hungry anyhow, Jock. Vivian Anderson cooks three meals a day and serves them with silver and napkins. But I'd rather live with my papa. I'm not goin' back to the Andersons. I won't. I won't! And Jim Brody is not big 'nough to make me."

Picking up a big chunk of wood, she stoked the stove and screwed the damper tight, then went looking for her stocking-leg cap. She talked to Jock, watching for a chance to get away from him, but he had an eye on her as well.

Finding her cap right where she'd left it after the winter term of school was out, she stuffed in under her jumper and slipped into her boots. She hoped Jock would tire out and curl up behind the stove for a nap. But Jock had no such intentions. He knew Shae was going out and he planned to go with her. He kept on her heels and she knew if he got out there would be no goose for supper, and Jock would get a whack across his nose.

It seemed forever, but Sandy finally nickered for Shae. Confused, Jock went to the front door. Shae darted into her room and shut the door. Pulling on her cap, she wrapped the leg twice around her neck, opened the stubborn window and squeezed outside.

Jock went berserk when he heard Shae talking to Sandy. She had pulled the wool over his eyes, for once. She was all warmed up and ready to find her papa.

"Let's go to the boat dock, Sandy."

Shae mounted the filly from her favorite stump. "I'll bet Papa won't be far from there, but we have to take it slow. If Papa finds out we've been racin', I'll be in for a tongue lashin'. We don't have to watch out for Jake Crawford. I heard Reverend Anderson tell Vivian that he's down on the chain gang for a whole year. They prayed for him and the others that went with him, but I don't care if he stays there til I'm grown an' married."

It was hard to go slow with the swirling snow peppering her face. Shae held Sandy's reins with one hand and poked the other into her jumper pocket. Once warmed, she changed hands.

The gumbo was beginning to get boggy and Sandy pulled one foot free, only to mar down with another. When they finally got to the dock, Shae sat watching their boat dance in the river as it overflowed its banks. The woods were very still. Where could all the animals be? Shae heard nothing. Not even the honk of a goose. She knew where the cats had gone. They always went to Crawford's barn for the winter. He had a loft full of hay and the mice were thick around there. They had no way of knowing Crawford hated them.

After securing Sandy, Shae stood for a minute watching the snowflakes cover the filly's back.

Where could everything be hiding?

She gave a wolf-whistle, hoping it would not bring Sheriff Brody instead of her papa. Her papa would know her whistle, and he had to be out here somewhere. He never loafed at Murphy's store.

After several attempts at whistling, she tired of the wind blowing it back in her face and stood hugging herself for warmth.

Why did I come here, anyhow? Why didn't I stay in the cabin where it's warm?

"Sandy, be still. You're goin' to be stuck in the mud if you keep prancin' round."

Shae decided she could hear as well inside the black snag. The snow wouldn't sting her face there. If only her papa would shoot a gun, she could decide which way to go.

Finding the snag damp and cold, she hunkered near the wall, wrapped her stocking-leg cap around her face, and thought of all the secrets she'd overheard here. It was here she'd heard Jake Crawford tell Jeff Locati his life story, and saying that he'd like to get rid of her papa.

As Shae sat hashing it all over, she thought she heard goose language. Peeping from the snag, she saw two beautiful geese sauntering up the river bank. She could tell by their markings that they were a goose and a gander. The gander walked proudly ahead of the goose, while she limped along, nursing a broken wing.

Shae couldn't resist making a goose call, but it didn't come out like her papa's. The gander took flight, leaving the goose hip-hopping along the edge of the river.

"You poor thing." Shae crawled from the snag and called, "Come, goosie. Come goosie." The goose limped as fast as she could and stayed far enough ahead to keep Shae playing the game. Each time Shae got close enough to touch, the prize slipped from her hands. The goose was getting closer to the river with every step.

"Come, goosie," Shae coaxed as she followed along in the sticky gumbo. "Papa can fix your wing and then you can fly away."

The last time she reached for the goose, she marred ankle-deep into the gumbo and the goose swam out into the river.

"Oh!"

Shae pulled her boots from the gumbo mud "If I could only touch somethin', I would…I would…. What would I do?"

CHAPTER 31

❀

Shae watched a vee of geese bearing toward the river. When the leader spied her standing in the mud, he gave a warning honk, turning the flock into a circle and away from the river.

Where could her papa be? If he was in a goose-blind, he could not hear her.

Shae gave one wolf whistle after another. When there was no answer, she untied the filly and led her up the boggy river path. The only goose-blind down the river was a mile away, and she would freeze stiff by the time she got there. Besides, the river was sure to be all over the swamp down there.

After examining three blinds, without a sign of her papa, Shae decided to go back to the cabin. She was leading the filly along the soggy path when she heard gunfire. As she stood listening, Sandy pranced around and worked herself knee-deep into the gumbo mud.

"Papa! Papa!" Shae screamed. "Help! Sandy's stuck in the mud!"

Sandy worked her way into a loblolly. Finally exhausted, she stood nickering for help, but Shae was helpless. Her hands were frozen stiff. She pulled and hauled at the filly's bridle, until she was worn out. Hovering close to a tree, she got her breath back and gave two cowboy whistles. They carried to her papa in a blind a quarter of a mile on up the river.

Clay Upshaw cupped his hand around an ear and listened.

If I didn't know better, he told himself, I'd swear that was Girly Shae's whistle. What in tarnation is she doin' out in this storm?

Crawling from the shelter, Upshaw gave a long, sharp whistle, but the wind was against him and he got no answer.

"Girly Shae!" he called as loud as he could, but still Shae did not hear.

Trying once more to free Sandy, Shae decided that the filly was working herself deeper. Giving up in tears, she held on to her boots, pulled her feet from the gumbo, and walked as fast as she could up the river, calling her papa, then stopping to whistle. The woods had changed from a quiet place to a roaring blizzard.

Why did I ever do this?

Shae ran as fast as she could in her boots.

"The Andersons won't have me back and Papa has already decided I will have to stay through the winter. Sandy will be stuck so deep, I'll never get her out. Everybody will be mad at me. What will I do?"

About the time Shae went up the river, her papa rolled down his hip boots and walked away from the river. He was not strong enough to pull through the ankle-deep gumbo. He thought Shae's whistle came from near the road by Murphy's store. Finding no sign of her, he ambled back toward the river. When his shotgun began to wear him down, he stood it beside a tree and called, "Gir-ly Shae! Why don't you answer me?"

Once he caught his breath, Upshaw shouldered his gun and walked on toward the dock. Then he heard something, which he thought was a horse snorting. Stopping, he listened. It came again, loud and clear. Sandy. But where was she? He was sure it was the filly. She had probably tired of being cooped up in a pasture without any exercise, and decided to come home. But why would she come to the river?

Forging on, Upshaw turned from the river when it started lapping at his heels. If he got stuck in that bog, he'd never get out. He was within a hundred yards of Sandy when she nickered, but she was behind some cypress trees, and the snow was coming down fast and furious. When she nickered again, he was almost upon her.

Shocked at what he saw, the old man stood for a moment, wondering what to do. The filly was bogged down to her knees, and in a lather of sweat.

What in tarnation was she doing out here? She was in the same shape she'd been when he pulled her from the quicksand when she'd been only a baby.

"Easy, Sandy. Easy."

He looked around for something solid for her to step up on, if and when she ever got a foot out of the mud. Walking around in circles, he found where someone had been cutting cross-ties. Picking up two long slabs, he eased toward the filly, but he was marring in the mud to his ankles. She needed help in a hurry. Placing a slab on the ground, he stepped on it and laid the other one in front of the struggling filly.

Excited, Sandy pulled one foot from the mud, stepped over the slab, but now it was stuck between her legs.

"Now what, Upshaw wondered."

Upshaw stood on the other slab. It was sinking under his feet. The next slab he found was wide enough to hold him up out of the gumbo. Tossing the short slab closer, he again placed the other slab in front of Sandy. Close enough now to touch her, he raked a handful of lather from her trembling body. She could catch pneumonia from this, but what about the girl?

He caught himself up. She could get frostbite to her feet in a pair of gum-boots. He was sure the Andersons hadn't consented to her coming out in this storm.

The wet, heavy snow was falling like popcorn, and the clouds were as black as night. It would be dark by four o'clock.

"Take it easy, girl." Upshaw calmed the filly as she fought the sticky gumbo. Winded, Sandy rested on the slab under her belly, blowing steam from her nostrils.

While the filly rested, Upshaw stood against the wind, calling, "Gir-ly Shae! Curving his hand around his ear, he listened. When there was no answer, he went back to work with Sandy.

"Come on, filly." He pulled on her bridle. "You can do it. Atta girl." He patted her cheek when she managed to get both of her front feet on the slab. "Now rest," he coaxed.

For ten minutes, it was nip and tuck, one step forward and two steps backward. But each time she moved forward, the ground grew firmer. Finally, Sandy pulled all four feet free of the gumbo and stood, shaking with a chill.

"It's all right, girl." Upshaw peeled off his mackinaw and draped it over her back. "Whew!" He stood shivering in his chambray shirt and overalls, thinking it wouldn't take long for that wind to cut a fellow off at the pockets. His girl ought to have her bloomers busted for this, but he thought of how she was changing. He couldn't do that.

Unable to stand still in the raging snow storm, Upshaw stamped around to keep from freezing while the filly caught her breath. Staring into the dense timber, he wondered how he'd ever picked his way. The cypress stood stark and black against the swirling snow and he could hardly see his hands before him. But he could not follow the river path. The Cache was boiling out over the swamp by leaps and bounds. It would only last a day or so, but he wouldn't want to get the filly mired down again, and decided to take her to shelter and come back for his Girly.

Jumpy as a scared cottontail, Sandy followed Upshaw as he made his way through the cypress knees. The roots gave her footing and they edged on toward the cabin. Every few steps, the filly wiggled the mackinaw off. Once when Upshaw stooped to pick it up, his good ear picked up the last two letters of papa. Listening closer, he heard nothing. Finally, a gun blasted off back down the river. He hoped she wouldn't get too close in. The Cache was a tricky river.

After placing the mackinaw back over the filly's back, the old man called out her name loud and clear. But the huge cypresses closed him in as if he were calling from inside the cabin.

Meanwhile, realizing she'd gone much too far, Shae turned back down the river. When she heard the gun blast, she was sure it was her papa. A blister on her heel slowed her down to a limp. She had to get back to Sandy, or she'd be mired in gumbo mud to her belly and Shae would never get her out. She hoped the water hadn't caught up to her horse before she got back.

If I lose Sandy....

On and on, Upshaw stumbled through the timber up stream while Shae limped down stream. She was closer to the river. Though neither of them knew it, Shae and her papa were getting closer together by the minute. Struggling through the mud was keeping Shae warm, but Upshaw's blood was thin from his long bout of sickness and he was shaking with a chill. The next time Sandy twitched the mackinaw off, he picked it up and hastily pulled it onto his cold quivering body. He wouldn't want to catch pneumonia, himself. He couldn't accept more charity from the Andersons. They had already done more than enough for them.

As Upshaw stood buttoning the coat up to his chin, the wind died for a minute and he was sure he heard someone talking. But it sounded as though it was down the river. Pretty soon, he saw a big vee of geese flying overhead, making their way to the Cache. But he couldn't shoot. The filly would run away, and could hurt herself among these slick cypress knees.

Staggering on another hundred yards, he heard it again. Then he saw Shae standing behind a big blade cypress tree with her hands rolled up in the leg of her stocking cap, watching the geese fly in. He distinguished the words, "I wish...I wish...." Then she wrapped the cap around her head and stood still and numb against the tree.

"Girly!" He called to her. "What are you doing out here in this storm?"

He hurried as fast as he could toward her.

Shocked at the sound of his voice, Shae stood for a moment and then she said, "Lookin' for you, Papa. I wanted to watch the geese fly in, but Sandy got stuck in the mud. I couldn't get her out."

Gathering her to him as she ran into his arms, he brushed the snow from her cap and squeezed her cold, blue hands into his own. "Girly Shae, what in tarnation are you doing out here on a day like this?"

Pulling his gloves off, he worked them onto Shae's hands. "You are frozen stiff. Did the Andersons consent to this?"

"No." Shae's big brown eyes gazed into her papa's troubled ones. "Mrs. Anderson had me all dressed up in a red velvet dress and Mary Jane slippers to go to church. While she was dressin', I went out on the porch and I saw a flock of geese flyin' over the house. I just had to come to be with you when they came home, so I stripped my clothes off and left 'em on the porch. I hate dressin' up like a princess!"

"Did they know you left?" Her papa asked, shaking his head in disbelief.

"Yeah, Mrs. Anderson saw me when I jumped off the porch. She yelled for me to come back, but I couldn't, Papa. I don't want to go back, ever. She can't make flapjacks like you do, and she said that she had never learned to make sugar syrup, or biscuits."

"But Girly Shae, you should never have done this…"

"I know, Papa. They will hate me after this. Please, can I stay home with you? I'll go to school every day. I can paddle my boat to high ground. I'm thirteen, now. Please, Papa?"

"Of course you can, Girly Shae." The tears in Shae's eyes were more than the old man could handle. "There's not enough law in the state to take you away from me."

Picking up Sandy's reins, he laid a protective arm around her shoulder. "We've got to get you and Sandy out of this weather, before you both catch pneumonia."

THE END

978-0-595-41912-8
0-595-41912-7

Printed in the United States
72762LV00004B/277-324